Never Lose ...

Head. Heart. Spirit.

T. M. Nagarajan

Strategic Book Publishing and Rights Co.

Strategic Book Publishing and Rights Co.
12620 FM 1960, Suite A4-507
Houston, TX 77065
www.sbpra.com

ISBN: 978-1-61897-477-8

- This is fiction.

To
my
wife
Mallika

Preface

Unbundled leisure after retirement and persistent persuasion of my friends induced me to write this fiction. My laptop became an obliging companion for months on end to absorb my thought flow as a document of words. Set in an Indian backdrop, the story is about a boy, Arvin, born in a remote village, virtually given up as a dying child, who is then nurtured and brought up by his compassionate grandma and grows into a multitalented man. Hopping from the university corridor to a renowned bank's cabin as an officer, Arvin is determined to rise to the top through dedicated work and honest means. Life and career are invariably interlinked. He encounters varied characters in his life, as kith or kin, colleagues or bosses, friends or foes. Warding off all obstacles, he climbs up and up, without losing his head, heart, or spirit. Arvin's character is such that if the immortal poet Rudyard Kipling met him, he might have exclaimed, "You are a man, my son!" Arvin seeks to share his experiential knowledge with others. Meant to be more than a mere work of fiction, this book presents a peep into human behavior, spiritual experience, musings on banking business, leadership styles, and life values—all with a literary touch.

Constructive suggestions and praising comments posted by the author community at Harper Collins Authonomy website, where the manuscript had been substantially uploaded for a preview, and the warm responses evoked by a water-testing POD publication in India at pothi.com propelled me to create this global edition through Strategic Book Publishing & Rights Agency of USA.

T. M. Nagarajan

Acknowledgements

The author gratefully acknowledges the encouragements and cooperation extended by his friends, wife, and children; suggestions and compliments posted by the author community at Harper Collins Authonomy Website; the user-friendly facility at pothi.com; and most importantly, the efficient project execution by Strategic Book Publishing & Rights Agency, but for whose professionalism this endeavor would not have succeeded into fruition. The author's gratitude and thanks are due, in no small measure, to each one of them.

I

• On the Stage

The sun on its diurnal journey is due to retire for the day. It will soon plunge, with no snorkel, into the Arabian Sea. For the whole night, perhaps, it will search for the idols of Ganesh immersed beneath the waves.

The sky is entirely exposed. The cloud cover has been blown away by the impish westerly winds. Proud of its pristine beauty, the sky is nonchalant about its nudity. The blushing sun, however, shy of diving naked into the water, hides behind a skyscraper.

At 4:30 p.m., people are hurrying out of that high-rise building. Cascading down the steps, like a waterfall, they rush toward the road. It is a rather unusual spectacle. Normally, such an outpouring occurs at around 6:00 p.m., when the office closes. This magnificent tower stands in a residential locality, adjoining a multistoried apartment complex. Many watch the tower anxiously from their balconies chatting aloud.

"Any fire inside?"

"No, I don't think so. No billowing smoke, no fire engines, no helmeted brigades, no turntable ladders . . ."

"A safety drill?"

"Certainly not. People are not gushing out and gathering outside. They are fleeing away from the building."

"Tremor?"

"No. The earth is still."

"Why then this mass exodus, like rats from a sinking ship?"

"Hmm. Oh, yeah. I know—bomb scare! Do you remember the media reports about threatening e-mails?"

"Maybe the latest threat is real. Maybe they have to search."

"Possible, but there are no curious onlookers, no controlling cops, no sniffing dogs, no chaos…"

The debating balcony watchers are unnecessarily speculative. Nothing serious has happened. Today, the floodgates opened much earlier than the usual time. The office is being closed for the day, almost an hour and a half before the normal time, to enable all staff to attend a farewell function. The hurrying workers will shortly join with a sea of humankind surging into the Mumbai suburban electric locomotives at Churchgate or Victoria Terminus.

The stage is set. The last scene of a long drama is slated to begin. It is more of a ritual dictated by custom and courtesy, sponsored and directed by the management. The locale is not an artificial setting, nor is it an ivory tower. A real, concrete edifice embellished by powdered marble and polished granite, it stands majestically against the backdrop of the back bay of the Arabian Sea. Its hard, mainframe facade harbors multitudinous "mice" click-playing with the software inside. The hall in that tall building—over a score of floors—is filling up fast, while a number of staff is fleeing to the bus stop.

"Bosses may come, and bosses may go. Let's go home early today. There will not be enough chairs for all. We can stand for two hours—no problem. But, we can't stand the s-p-e-e-c-h-e-s! Let's miss the vocal, not an early local."

Urban compulsions jokingly brush aside any vestige of courteous sentiments. Catching a less-crowded, pre-rush-hour, local train is by far the preferred option.

A few fragments of sentiment and courtesy, enough to fill a heart, still linger. The hall is full. The cacophony echoes the positive personality of the guest. Suddenly, the babble turns into silence. The guest of the evening, a retiring executive for whom the stage is set, comes down, warmly escorted, and arrives at the stage, amidst the audience's clapping. Time has been kind to his appearance. He has effectively managed to tone down any outward manifestations of wear and tear from the job.

Upwards, it takes years to climb,
Step by step,
With no lift!
Exit, as a contrast, is as swift
As a falling leaf.

As the guest walks up to the stage, his rumination keeps him company.

The function begins with welcome remarks by a master of ceremony. The guest of honor is offered a series of bouquets of varied sizes but all of fragrant flowers of vibrant colors. The bouquets are from different quarters. Some are from those more accustomed to handing, as a bounden duty, only brickbats. Soon a verbal shower begins. The guest is drenched with elation and embarrassment. Even his well-preserved, protective umbrella of equanimity quivers; the ego- and joy-boosting shower-cum-breeze of the evening is indeed strong.

Arvin falls into a reverie. As if Ctrl + Home were pressed, the home page of his memory file opens . . .

1

• "This Is *Satyam.*"

"Oh, God."

The old woman who had gone to look at her daughter-in-law in an adjoining room was shocked to see the scary scene. *Oh God, I have been dreaming, praying, and waiting for five years. Will my sweet dream be shattered?*

A cobra was crawling toward the peacefully sleeping young woman. Sliding up, the visiting reptile perched itself comfortably on her ballooned belly, with its flattened neck and raised hood fanned in the typical serpentine style. The U mark on the back of its hood reminded the scared onlooker of the sacred mark on the forehead of Lord Vishnu. Involuntarily, the old woman raised her palms together to pray. The bespectacled snake, ignoring the old woman, peered and hissed at the face of the sleeper as if trying to wake her up. At this sight, the mother-in-law stood transfixed, frozen with fear.

"No. No. I should not shout and distract the snake. It may get annoyed and bite her. No. She should not be harmed; she is my boon bearer," she murmured to herself.

A child is always a delight. Doubly delightful is a grandchild. The would-be granny was excited to know that her daughter-in-law had conceived. She started conjuring up the images of cradling, fondling, and dressing up her grandchild, yet to be born. She was doting on the carrier of her grandson. She had no doubt in her mind that her daughter-in-law would deliver a baby boy. There was no rational basis for that belief. She had not heard of scanning. The precedents in the family and her strong, biased wish were more than enough.

In a patriarchal system of society, a male child used to be preferred. If the first issue happened to be a boy, the joy in a family would defy description. If the first son got his first son, it was deemed a virtual boon. The potential grandma was looking forward to being blessed with such a boon. She was particularly glad that she would have a grandson to perform the last rites when she left the Earth. How could she be so sure? She might outlive her grandson. It was only a belief, a trust. Life depends and runs on such trust. The human fatality factor is often ignored or wishfully forgotten. The generally observed human longevity lends credence to this trust.

Will my sweet dream turn into sour reality? She shuddered to think of such a possibility. Her unassailable faith in divine powers compelled her to silent prayer. So as not to bypass the immediate, threatening authority, she also implored the snake directly.

"O, *nalla paambu*, I know you will not harm anyone unless provoked. No one—my son, my daughter-in-law, nor I—none, none in our family have ever done anything to annoy you. Have we? Tell me. Why do you want to harm our family? I pray to you now: Please, please spare her. Please leave her. I beg of you. I promise to keep your name for the child, boy or girl. This is *satyam*."

2

• "Let the Dying Child Die."

Is a snake more formidable than a mountain, immovable even by faith? The passionate entreaty of the pious woman led to a prompt retreat of the righteous reptile. As if pleased with the pleading and the promise, the cobra crawled away.

With a jerk, the old woman woke up, profusely sweating. She looked as if she had just cried, with her tears yet to be dried. *Thank God. It was only a dream.* The dream was during her rapid eye movement sleep, and her vision was not a replay of something she had actually witnessed in her life. Immediately, she got out of the bed and ran to the other room.

The distressed mother-in-law heaved a sigh of relief. Kayalvizhi, or, Kayal, as she was called, was sleeping safely with no alien being whatsoever on her body. No snake was found around. The old woman hurried to the Puja room, prayed for a moment, took a pinch of *vibhuthi*, rushed back, and applied it on the forehead of her daughter-in-law. Kayal was still blissfully sleeping.

The next morning, the old woman described the dream to her son and daughter-in-law.

"Ma, don't take the dream seriously. Everything will be all right."

"Subbu, I can't take it so lightly. The way in which the cobra withdrew the moment I made the promise . . . See these goose pimples on my arms? It is still vivid in my mind!"

"I am scared, Mami. Is this an ill omen?" Kayal was afraid of a reptilian reprisal.

'No. No. Don't you worry, Kayal. Forget it. I do not want you to brood over it and spoil your health. I have talked to the cobra. It will do no harm. I shall keep my word. All you have to do is," she smilingly added, 'deliver—safely—a grandson for me." The old woman affectionately touched her daughter-in-law's tummy and kissed on her forehead. *In-law* was an irrelevant suffix in the description of their emotional relationship. In fact, the bond between them was even more than that of a mom and a daughter. Kayal's eyes were wet with the dew of emotion. She was happy to become a mom and happier to present a grandson to her mother-in-law.

Soon, the dream faded from the memories of the family members.

Kayal was in her seventh month of pregnancy. Whatever the comforts in her husband's home, a pregnant woman used to long for her mother's tender care and tasty food. Today, expectant daughters living abroad expect their mothers to cross oceans, risking venous thromboembolism, mostly for cost-effective domestic help. Kayal, however, was more traditional. Her mom's home was only some four kilometers from her village, less than an hour by oxcart.

It was Pillaiyar Chadurthi Day, an auspicious day of birth of the Lord Ganesh *(Pillaiyar)*, the eldest son of Lord Shiva. An elephant-headed god with a proboscis, pendulous ears, and protruding belly, a god of knowledge and wisdom, Ganesh is believed to be an obliterator of all obstacles in life. A devout Hindu will break coconuts as an offering and invoke his blessings before initiating anything new or important. And, Pillaiyar is specially worshipped on his birthday. Kayal, a religious-minded housewife, had performed the traditional puja that evening, offering a broken coconut and *modhaham* (unbroken, coconut-shaped sweet dumplings) to Pillaiyar.

A decade later, Pillaiyar idols themselves were broken by some sporadically as a symbolic protest, for a social cause, and with a political aim. Kayal would have been brokenhearted to witness this outbreak of agnosticism. Rational or irrational, the faith, however, remained unbroken. As if every splintered particle formed an image, Pillaiyar idols became omnipresent in every nook, center, and corner. Invariably, now all street-facing-houses have Ganesh idols on the compound walls to ward off evil. Traditionally a household affair, Pillaiyar Chadurthi has emerged as a popular, community festival. Kayal would have been ecstatic, if she were alive to see it.

"Kayal, have you taken *Prasad*?"

"Yes, Mami, I have tasted. I am going to bed."

"Okay. May God bless you! Kayal, look, while in the bed, don't turn suddenly. Be careful. Don't jerk. Understand? Take care of my grandson."

The entire house was asleep, except the child. The child grew impatient to get out of its amniotic abode. *Why wait for two more weeks until the due date?* It started kicking. The sleep was slowly kicked out of Kayal too. Soon, she started having labor pains.

The day was yet to be born. The pair of hands of the clock on the wall had just parted from their midnight union. Monday was delivering Tuesday. Enduring the pain, with no epidural anesthesia or water buoyancy, Kayal delivered a bundle of joy. Happiness was unbundled. Mother was happy. Father was happy. Grandma? She was simply ecstatic! She got a grandson. There was nameless splendor everywhere at home.

Was the transiting star Swathi or Visakam? Some said Swathi.

Others contended that it was Visakam. At the time, all agreed that the zodiac sign is Thula (the balance and scale). Everyone around logically predicted that the child would grow into a balanced-minded person. None, however, could even remotely foresee the child's fate hanging in balance—except one.

There was no compulsive need to name the child immediately on birth, and no craze to choose something esoteric or a totally unfamiliar or utterly meaningless bonsai name. Only a few names used to be recycled, with some variations, permutations, or combinations, in a family to perpetuate the memory of ancestors. On an auspicious day, the child was named. It was not too difficult for the relations around to suggest a suitable name. The spontaneous choice was impeccable.

"This child is surely going to die. It is only a matter of days or months," an elderly woman declared confidently and crudely.

The child was, in fact, growing into a sick baby. The baby suffered from a congenital liver problem. He was fed with more liver cure medicine than baby milk powder. By the time the child was two, he had almost lost his fair complexion and looked emaciated with a ballooned belly. The child's distended abdomen and recurring digestive disorders were causing concern. Was the cause genetic, a metabolic defect, some simple infection? There was no competent doctor around to rightly diagnose. Medicines were tested, but the child was still suffering. The maternal grandma had no hope left. She urged the paternal grandma, too, to give up. "Why do you waste your money, time, and energy?"

Give up? For the paternal grandma, it simply meant a merciless withdrawal of all medical and maternal care. In fact, it would mean utter disregard for sanctity of life or even parent-assisted infanticide. The child's parents and paternal grandma were not so heartless. They would not abandon their hope, faith, or the child.

"Don't be so cruel. For Heaven's sake, my grandson will live for a long time. Mark my words: he will surely live and grow into prominence." Paternal grandma was compassionate, hopeful, and determined. "I will save my grandson at any cost."

Today's biological anthropologists would wonder, "How is it that a paternal grandma is so attached to her grandson?" For now they know that her genetic contribution (X chromosomes) to her grandson would be zero.

The child was looking innocently at the two grannies of opposing beliefs. He did not know his fate was, in fact, hanging in *thula*—with rising and falling sides of hope and despair, determination and indifference, life and death.

Paternal grandma was morose. Right from the beginning, she had been unhappy. It was not that she did not appreciate the appropriateness of the spontaneously suggested name, but she had not forgotten her word.

"Subbu, I am not happy about the choice of name for the child."

"Why, Amma? Ganesan is an apt choice, a divine name."

"I have not forgotten my dream. I want to keep my word. I told you that I promised the cobra to keep its name for the child."

"Amma, these days, people do not bother to honor even written and signed promissory notes. Your promise was, after all, unwritten, unreal."

"Don't talk like that. A promise is a promise, Subbu. I shall keep my word."

A breach of promise was anathema to Grandma. Had she not promised, in her dream, to name the child after the cobra, it would have harmed, in reality, Kayal and also the child in her womb. She believed that firmly, even if she were dubbed as irrational.

"The cobra obliged me based on my promise. In turn, I must redeem my promise."

"What, Ma, are you really serious?"

"Yes, of course. I don't want to commit a breach of trust. I do not want to incur the wrath of the snake. Maybe the child has been sick because we have not yet honored my word. I can't lose my grandson."

The old woman had a passion to be honest. She stood firm. The elders then were respected and listened to. They were not ignored or brushed aside. When the child was formally named Aravendan, meaning king of snakes. Grandma was happy. She was now sure of the boy's survival. She did not know that Aravendan would be minimized before long. Grandma and the child's mom, Kayalvizhi, devoted their full time to attend to the child. Grandma constantly prayed, "Oh God, if you want, take my life; let the child live!" She believed in complete faith and constant prayer. Her penance-like devotion and indefatigable nursing continued for two years. The child was yet tottering on the brink of death. *Will the life of the child prove to be a brief candle?* Many were dead sure of the candle being blown out any time. "The god whom I worship will not let me down. My grandson will be all right soon," Grandma said. The others pooh-poohed Grandma's grand faith.

3

Tongue Untied

Thank Cobra! The tiny candle was not blown out. The cobra was pleased to be benign. Protected by a loving mom, paternal grandma, and divine grace, the candle grew into a torch. But, would it be splendid? "Why not?" Grandma challenged.

"Subbu, Aravendan is nearing five. He is healthy and active. God has been kind. Still, he is not able to speak clearly."

"Amma, his pronunciation has improved a lot."

"I think there's some structural defect in his tongue. Better bring him to a doctor."

"Maybe, once he goes to school and starts conversing with other children, his speech will improve."

"I don't think so. We should consult a specialist. The sooner, the better."

The school was within shouting distance from the boy's home. On an auspicious day, he was admitted.

Sophisticated preschool institutions patterned on kindergarten or Montessori, though in vogue for decades elsewhere, were unheard of in villages. They had sprung up in some cities and big towns, along with the growing Western influences on parents in higher echelons. All that the village could boast of was a municipal elementary school. It was meant to cater to the needs of children of all strata of society. There was no uniform for the students. Almost all were wore soiled, rumpled clothes. There was no garden or house atmosphere, no toys to play with, no creative or sophisticated teaching or learning aids, and no more than one or two teachers for hundreds of children. Individual attention was impossible. The teacher or a boy would read aloud a letter or a word or a multiplication table, and all students would repeat it in chorus.

This school did believe in the curative effects of punishment. There were no rewards but plenty of punishments. The medium of instruction was indeed the cane. The parents, far from complaining, were rather happy that their children were duly disciplined.

When the cane-wielding teacher was tired, he would ask the erring student to stand up on the bench or do, until further notice, *thoppukkarnams* (sit-ups, done while cross holding ears). This was what the teacher had to do to control the students decades back. Certainly, he was not aware of the beneficial aspects of his unpatented brain-yogic exercise.

A boy of five, Aravendan could not speak as clearly as the other children of his age. He would watch, with open-mouthed wonder, the long-range movement of their tongues. *Do they have longer tongues?* They could stick their tongues out between their lips. Some could even lick the tips of their noses. They would challenge Aravendan to do so. But, like a shy village girl, his tongue would not cross the threshold of its home. The students started to tease the tongue-tied boy.

Everyone in the family thought that the lisping, common for a small child, would vanish when he grew. To their utter surprise and utmost concern, the boy's lisping lasted longer, even after he starting school. A closer look into the problem revealed that Aravendan was tongue-tied, literally. Anatomically, the mucous membrane, which links the midline of the tongue to the floor of the mouth, was attached very close to the tip of the tongue. Normally, the tie stretches or breaks as the child grows, permitting free range of movement for the tongue.

Aravendan grew, but his tongue remained slavishly tied. Through nonviolent means, it could not break free. The doctor who was consulted was not a Gandhian. His suggestion was carried out. The tissue was cut, and Aravendan's tongue achieved its liberation. The freedom was almost total. Still, a tiny part of the tissue, too loyal, refused to sever its connection with the base. In fact, it was operational negligence. As it did not matter much, it was ignored. The tongue celebrated its newfound freedom. No longer shy, it was now a celebrity. All his fellow students were now keen to have a glimpse of it.

Teasing ceased.

4

• Unseen Power

It was no more than a hamlet. Besides its bucolic splendor, the village had elementary facilities—wide, clean, sandy streets squaring a Shiva temple; a bathing pond adjacent to a Ganesh shrine; and an elementary school.

The village accommodated people of all castes. People of certain castes exclusively inhabited some streets. It had been so historically. Why such sequestered settlement? Even burial and cremation grounds were all segregated. Dead bodies were carried along with caste suffixes, but the suffixes were never buried or burned. Is casteism immortal like the soul? None could enlighten Aravendan, who was considered too young to comprehend the "unquestionable" wisdom of the ancestors. Fish vendors would, as a rule, avoid peddling in upper-caste areas. No rules, however, exist without exceptions. Fish vendors occasionally liked to demonstrate their defiance. The bathing pond was public property. The water was cool to the touch of any and, yet, could turn too hot for some to touch. By any standards, however, it was a peaceful village.

The village recently got the luxury of electricity. At first, there were not enough people willing to connect. Even affluent people were analyzing the costs of kerosene lanterns versus electric bulb options. Frugality apart, they were too contented to adopt any modernity or luxury. They were also seized with some fears about the unknown. It required a lot of persuasion by the *Panchayat* to convince the thrifty to go in for the utility. As feared, a shocking incident took place within a month.

A teenage cowherd wanted to exhibit his valiance to his entourage. Waving away all their "foolish" fears, and without listening to the cautioning advice of some sensible persons around, he climbed a transmission tower to touch the overhead wire. He held no belief in any unseen power. Ignorance is not always bliss. At times, it may spell misery. While ignorance is understandable, ignoring sensible advice is regrettable. He knew not.

"When a feathered bird can sit comfortably on the overhead wire, why should a muscled lad be afraid of simply touching it?" he asked. The logic electrified the enthusiasm of his friends—all much older and no wiser. They cheered their hero; after all, their lives were not at risk. They were worse than some investment advisors of today. The hero possessed the worst part of valor. He could not grasp the fact that, by gripping the high-tension wires, he could be electrocuted, or in other words, his body and soul could be segregated and dispatched to two different destinations—one down to Earth and the other up into the ethereal world.

Anxiously, the friends craned their necks and watched the adventurous climb of their hero. The boy touched a wire by a hand. The crowd gave him a big hand. The brave boy planned to t-o-u-c-h another, parallel wire with his other hand; he wanted to swing. He did not realize that his fate was hanging in that wire. With two hands reaching, the electric current and gravitational force yanked the power tester down to dusty Earth. The boy fell with a thud, utterly powerless. And, all this happened in a fraction of a second.

"Is he dead?" an anxious voice disturbed the deadly silence. He was lying deathly still on the ground. His friends were shell-shocked.

A crowd gathered, and wailing rent the air. The inert body was rushed to the town hospital as fast as a pair of bullocks could run.

A day died; none could save it.

"Aravenda, what happened to Sambirani? Any news?"

"Don't you know?"

"No, I don't know. Has he died?"

"No, no. He is OK."

"Really?"

"Yes, he was in hospital only for one day. He is lucky, maybe destined, to be alive."

Sambirani—that was the name of the foolishly brave boy—was discharged from the hospital the next day with his body and soul together. Yes, he survived, with scorched palms and shaken confidence. His fingers were burned so badly that he would never ever touch even a lamppost. He'd experienced enough of the unseen power.

5

A Distinguished Name

Aravendan was weaned away from the village school and admitted into fifth form at a high school. Of the high schools in the town, MHS was the best. Established by a philanthropic-minded landlord, reasonably well managed, and located at the center of town, this vernacular school, with good teachers, was preferred by parents. A competent disciplinarian, Mr. Jacob had been specifically brought in as headmaster to reinforce discipline following one or two isolated incidents of externally assisted student misbehavior.

The town was only three or four miles away, depending on which route one took—the asphalt-paved bus route or the shorter, sparsely graveled road.

The thinking was that a good walk twice a day would keep the doctor far away. It would not be a lonely walk; there would be other boys and girls of the same age group.

No research reports were then available to claim that even one forty-five minute walk a day, three days a week, would considerably improve one's episodic memory and executive control functions. Umpteen justifications were, however, used to persuade Aravendan to walk six miles a day for school. The road snuck through the lines of municipality-owned and consecutively numbered tamarind trees. The right to pluck the half-ripe tamarind was claimed and, with impunity, exercised by the school-going children. A number of boys would try to prove Darwin's theory of evolution. Aravendan never joined them in their simian activities. It was not the fear of falling that restrained him from aping his friends. His nature was different.

As per the custom in the part of the world where he was born, a man used to carry a given name preceded by an initial representing his father and followed by the name of his caste. By the time Aravendan was born, the practice of adding a discriminatory caste suffix was discretely waning. At the high school, enrolled in the same class, was another boy by the same name, S. Aravendan, who had different proclivities, creating confusion and at times awkward situations. The simple solution found by the schoolteachers was to prefix the village name to one of the boys as a factor of differentiation. Aravendan's name was thus elongated—his given name, together with the village name, as the first and his father's in the middle—and came to contain a record number of letters—as many as thirty-five. He was happy to have the longest name in his school. How could he foresee what kind of problem his long-winding, distinguished name would spell and when?

6

• "Let This Year Pass."

The school was closed at 1:00 p.m. one day. There was some function in the school that morning. After the usual prayer parade, the correspondent, one from the founder's family, gave a brief, spasmodic speech. What his coughs could not accomplish, the persistent clapping of the students did. He ended his speech quickly. On account of a marriage function in the founder's family the next day, the students were set free at noon. Duty-bound teachers were required to serve as errant boys—oh, no—as event managers. On the day of marriage, some would not miss the chance to exhibit their literary skills, or rather, personal loyalty, by reading out their eulogistic poetry. A twenty- or thirty-line poem would extol the correspondent, his ancestors, his community, his nobility, his ability, his charity. Of course, a couple of lines would be dedicated to wish cheer upon and bless the newly wedded.

Four of the fourth form students set off for their homes. They would have to cycle three kilometers. *Biking every day will keep the doctor farther away.* Aravendan had humored his father and secured an external means of transportation. Thanks to peer pressure and Dad's pleasure, he was now a proud rider of a brand-new Raleigh, made in England, bought from a Singapore-returned sahib.

It was a different era. Unlike children of today who throw tantrums to get whatever they like and find their parents ever ready to pamper them, Aravendan was a patient, reasonable, and undemanding boy. "If a child is accustomed to get whatever he likes, he will not grow into an adult with the mental strength to bear any disappointment later. A false notion of love and affection does not nurture but corrupts children." So believed Subbiah.

"Aravenda, it's very hot. I have a suggestion. Let us go to the temple, have our lunch, and play for some time. In the evening, we can go home."

The suggestion was unanimously endorsed as a good idea. The temple was not far from the school. They whiled away some time in the famous "one anaa and two anaa shop" (sixteen anaa equals one rupee), situated almost opposite to the school. There, you pick up almost anything and pay only one or two anaa. The boys, however, did not pick up anything. From the shop, they went to a nearby *Brahmanal* hotel. A fading notice board, meant to bar the entry of anyone suffering from any "major" diseases, remained tucked in a corner, like someone sickly, old, and uncared for. The hotel was unimpressive in looks but popular for its menu of many special delicacies. The boys had their lunches packed in banana leaves and wrapped in old newspaper as takeaways then proceeded, riding their bikes, to the temple in the heart of town.

When they turned from the bazaar to the street leading to the temple, the clock tower showed 2:15. On the way, they passed the houses of considerably rich and locally famous landlords. They were living off largely inherited wealth. Generally known to be more abstemious than assiduous, they believed in consanguineous marriages to confine their accumulated wealth within close circles of their relations. They were more concerned about capital protection than multiplier growth. The unwise misers were blissfully nonchalant about changing paradigms. Complacency had seized them. Years later, their egos would remain intact but not their wealth. Hit by the land-ceiling and cheated by the cultivators, they would be left with little land to lord over. And, they would simply keep wondering, "Who moved my land?"

"Aravenda, you are getting very good marks on exams. You must be working very hard, hitting the books for hours," one friend observed.

"You are lucky. Your relations here are all rich landlords. If I were in your place, I would not bother to study; I would rather marry a daughter of a rich relative and live comfortably," another said. Aravendan did not respond. He did not like these kinds of remarks.

They parked their bikes at a shop outside the temple and went in. Leaving their schoolbags behind a pillar of a *mandapam*, they took their lunches from the banana-leaf parcels. Thereafter, they played around the *mandapam*.

At 5:00 p.m., it was time to leave. Each one picked up his bag. Aravendan did not find his. He ran from pillar to pillar in frantic search of his bag, but there were only pillars. His friends, too, searched for the bag more vigorously. Aravendan turned panicky. He shuddered to think of facing his father. Though kind, his father was quick-tempered. When angry, he would not speak; his cane would.

Aravendan was agitated and aggrieved. Tears welled up in his eyes. All four had kept their bags behind the same pillar; they had eaten their lunches together, squatting beside the pillar; they had played together around the pillar. How could only his bag disappear? It was a mystery. The pillar was only a mute witness.

Were his friends playing childish pranks? Aravendan pleaded with each one to return the bag, if one was teasing him. Each one denied any such mischief and, in fact, looked offended by this suspicion.

His friends looked sadder than Aravendan. They sought to

console him on the loss of his schoolbag. "Don't worry. You are so intelligent that you don't need books to pass the exams," said one. *Was he sarcastic or supportive?* Another observed, "Why worry? Let this year pass." *Was he trying to lighten the moment? Or was he really looking forward to such a prospect?* The third boy was silent. *Or, was he eloquent?*

As his ill luck would have it, that day, his bag was full of almost all his books and notes. At this point in time, when his final exams were hardly two months away, new textbooks would not be available at shops; no one would have extra books to spare; nor would anyone lend a book either. What would he do now? In one moment, he thought he could manage the situation; in the next, he shuddered to think of failing his examinations for the first time. He closed his eyes and prayed to God—with no effect.

7

• A Mixed Bag

Aravendan reached home without his bag; no one noticed. A month passed peacefully. Every day, he went to school without his usual bulging bag but only with one or two thick notebooks on the carrier of his Reliegh; no one noticed. One morning, when he was about to leave for school, his father found him going out without the schoolbag. He casually asked him about the bag.

He was caught empty handed. *I should not hide it anymore*, thought Aravendan. For a month, he had not told his father or even grandma about the loss of his schoolbag and books. Now, he did not fumble. He let the cat out of the bag. He told his father the entire story. Subbiah was furious. This time, both he and his cane were eloquent. But for Grandma's judicious intervention, Aravendan would have been subjected to even more undue cane-speak.

Tearfully, Aravendan assured his father that he would surely pass; he had already copied significant portions of the relevant textbooks and class notes in his notebook. This he had done by borrowing books from his teacher and other classmates by turn, fully utilizing free time and games periods at school while also working at home in the night till the wee hours. Subbiah was not satisfied. The next day, he accompanied his son to the school and met the class teacher. The teacher took Subbiah aside, out of Aravendan's sight, obviously to tell him something confidential.

Weeks passed, exams were over, and the result was out. Two boys were very anxious to know: Did Aravendan fail or not?

Aravendan started to reflect on his experience. He felt he should not have hidden the fact he lost the books from father. He did not make a voluntary disclosure, because he did not want to make his father worry. He was also scared of his punishment. But, he did not simply keep brooding over the loss of the books. Nor did he remain irresponsibly casual. With determination, he took all possible steps to manage the crisis. He put in a tremendous effort to copy the gist of the lessons and the class notes, borrowing the books from his friends and teachers. He was confident of passing the exams. His plan was to astonish his father, disclosing everything after passing the exams. His plan failed; the cat escaped the bag too soon.

The very next day after the result was out, the boy who remained tongue-tied on the day of the bag's disappearance came to Aravendan's house.

"Aravenda, please pardon me."

"Why, Mani, what for? What did you do?"

Mani's voice was shaking. Tears spilled.

"Mani, Mani, don't cry. Tell me. What is the matter?"

"I didn't do it. But . . ."

"You didn't do what?"

"Kalian and Singan did it."

"Did what? Say it clearly."

"Yes, Aravenda, those two tossed your schoolbag into the temple tank."

"When? Why?"

"When you went outside the temple for a few minutes."

"Why did they do it?"

"Because . . . because . . . they were jealous of you. They wanted you to fail. In fact, they were planning to push you from behind into the pool and run away."

"Oh my God. Then what?"

"But, they gave up the plan once they found out you know how to swim."

"Why didn't you tell me earlier?"

"I am sorry. I was scared of them. They warned me of dire consequences. Honestly, I admire you. You have not merely passed; you are second rank in the class. Really, God is by your side."

Now, Aravendan recalled the sequence of events on that day. The twosome's suggestion of the temple visit; their mischievous comments, glances, and smiles; their exaggerated expressions of sympathy for the missing bag; their being offended by his pleading for the return of the bag; and their sarcastic remarks about letting a year pass. Strung together now, these clues revealed their scheme. It dawned on him that he had been fooled. He should have been more alert and not so naïve. He learned a lesson: Always be alert.

Ultimately, the miscreants did not succeed. Aravendan passed creditably. To the contrary, both the boys failed miserably. That they failed and dropped out of school did not make Aravendan happy. But, he realized this bizarre incident was educational. As he had to copy a lot, all in longhand, cracking his aching fingers countless times, whatever he copied in his notebook was automatically pasted in his brain. What an effective way of committing something to memory! It was a great discovery. His handwriting, already good, got even better. But for this episode, his teacher, father, friends, foes, and why, he himself would not have recognized his own tenacity and capability. As he realized later, negative is but one side of things. Never lose sight of the other side.

8

• Embedded Softness

Aravendan had performed admirably despite the loss of books. Subbiah now disclosed to his son what the teacher told him. "Sir, I know he has lost his books; don't worry about your smart son. He's intelligent, studious, sincere, and hardworking. He will surely pass; I guarantee. Do not chide him too harshly. Go back. Relax. Cheer your son."

That night, Aravendan never forgot, Subbiah sobbed silently for having given his studious son unwarranted corporeal punishment. It was the third occasion of revelation of this softer side of his strict dad.

The earlier occasion that Aravendan could recall was when, as a seven-year-old boy, he had a spider bite on his leg just above the ankle. Eight-legged spiders, though distant relatives of scorpions, seldom bite unless disturbed. Aravendan did not remember disturbing any spider or any of its distant or close relations. A spider injects so little poison through its poison fangs that the bite appears to be no worse than a mosquito's. But, if neglected, the bite could, as Aravendan learned to his horror, prove to be much worse.

Instead of taking him to the only hospital—municipal—then available at the nearby town, the boy was treated by a local *vaidhiyar*, a traditional medical practitioner. He first applied the essence of a bunch of herbal leaves, and when the sore deepened, he started stuffing it with a ball of mashed herbal leaves. In fact, he seemed to be boring into the youngster's leg for weeks on end rather than curing it. A stage was reached when the wound was so deep that a rupee coin could easily be lost there. Aravendan used to scream with excruciating pain during each session of treatment. Unable to witness this searing sight, Subbiah, too, sobbed like a child, revealing the softness within.

Ultimately, when Aravendan was taken to the town hospital, the doctor said that, if the boy had been brought after another two weeks' time, he would have had no option but to amputate the boy's leg at the ankle. After a month, he was cured but not without leaving a permanent, rupee coin-sized, shining, memento-like scar on his leg.

9

A Boomerang

The book toss incident was indelibly ingrained in Aravendan's impressionable mind. When he grew up, he used to reflect on this at times.

Where did I go wrong? I could not judge the two classmates properly. Is judging a person an art? If so, should I not learn that art to become fit for survival?

He was also at a loss to understand why the two boys had behaved so heinously. These boys, as he knew, used to catch dragonflies, pluck their wings, tie strings on, and play with them as yo-yos. They would pour a handful of jewel beetles into an unsuspecting buffalo's ears and giggle. In short, they would indulge in all sorts of childish pranks of the cruelest nature. But, he had not expected them to do this kind of mischief to a schoolmate, to a close friend. By throwing Aravendan's schoolbag away, they might have caused his failure in his exams, and they would not have gotten any extra marks for themselves. Why were they so bad, so jealous, so cruel? Was it congenital traits or improper upbringing? Human behavior baffled him. He did not know then that he would encounter even more grown-up embodiments of envy later in his life.

Aravendan recalled a story someone once told him:

Vembu and Sambu lived in opposite houses. Both were friends. They had one son each: Vengi and Shankar. Vembu was a kind father but a disciplinarian. Hailing from the middle class, he wanted his son to study well and move up in life. He got his son admitted into a good, private management school.

It's somewhat costly, as compared to a municipality school, but it doesn't matter. Vengi must have a good education. This is the least or the best I can give him, so thought Vembu. Vengi grew as a good, obedient, and studious boy, one of the top-ranking students in the school.

Sambu was an ambitious father and an aggressive businessman. He had already crossed into upper middle-class status. He got Shankar enrolled in a luxurious residential school in a hilly station and provided an uninterrupted cash flow for his son.

"Let him not worry about his pocket money. He should concentrate on his studies. At any cost, he should reach greater heights." Sambu was sanguine. Shankar became a popular guy on campus, a chocolate boy! His friends, too many, were too jealous of him. They cursed themselves as their dads were not so generous, so indulgent.

In a year's time, both Vengi and Shankar would complete their schooling and then go to college after graduation.

One evening, Sambu saw Vengi on the riverside and called him. "Vengi, come here. How do you do?"

"Fine, Uncle."

"How are you faring in your studies?"

"Not bad, Uncle."

"What were your marks in last year's final?"

"Ninety-eight percent, Uncle."

"Really? Vembu didn't tell me. Why were you so charitable? You gave up two percent?" Sambu joked, smiled, and left.

In that year's annual exam, Vengi narrowly escaped failure, having managed to secure just passing marks. Vembu was shocked. "What happened to Vengi? He almost failed—such poor marks."

Vembu made inquiries with the teacher. He could not believe what he heard. Vengi had missed many of his classes. His attendance was just adequate. A few days more and he would have been disqualified to sit for exams. Vengi had no health problems. He never stayed at home on any school working day. The family had not been away for any purpose. Why, then, had Vengi skipped the classes? Where did he go during school hours? It was a mystery.

Vembu did not confront his son immediately. He did not scold him. He made further inquiries with his schoolmates discreetly and gently. Vembu came to know where Vengi had been. He now asked Vengi, "What made you change like this?" Vengi broke down and disclosed all that had happened.

That night, as he could not digest the fact that Vengi was such a brilliant student, Sambu could not sleep. "Vembu's son is so brilliant, and I did not know it for so long." A burning sensation nagged him. He hit upon a soothing solution: "Vengi should be taken care of." One day, Sambu called Vengi.

"Vengi, have you seen the movie now running at Raja talkies?"

"No, Uncle."

"What a shame. It's such a nice movie. Shankar says he has seen it at least six times."

"Really, Uncle?"

"Yes. I will get you a free balcony ticket. Go and see."

"No, Uncle, thanks."

"Why? Are you afraid of your pa? I will tell him."

"No, no, Uncle."

"Don't be a bookworm. Relax, young man."

"Okay. Thanks, Uncle."

This was how it all started, as the first part of a burgeoning plan.

Vengi thereafter did not miss any film that was released at all the three talkies in the nearby town. Not once or twice, but umpteen times, he would see a film. The tickets were given by Sambu, all gratis. On every show, he got icing on the cake! The theater manager would arrange a cone of ice cream during intermission. It was all through Sambu's gratuitous arrangements.

Whenever he was free, Sambu would call Vengi for a long chat.

"Vengi, you should develop reading habits and not merely textbooks. I have a good book collection. I will give you some. Read."

He passed on carefully chosen books to Vengi—initially a few classics and, later on, all filthy novels.

"I should have known this earlier. I did not know Vembu's son was so brilliant. No. No. I will not let Vengi pass in his exams," Sambu vowed. He craftily spotted some soft points to strike.

"Vengi, have you ever been to Pondy?"

"No, Uncle. Why, Uncle?"

"It is a beautiful place, like Paris. This Sunday, my friend is going. If you are interested, tell me, and he will take you in his car. You can return in the evening. Have some diversions, boy. Enjoy."

Sundays turned into Fundays! Sambu's loyal friend was equally kind. At Sambu's behest, he helped Vengi develop a new kind of thirst. There was no prohibition to quench it. Initial inhibitions were soon lost thanks to Sambu's ally. Those days, there was no Internet, no camera phones, no drugs. Otherwise, Sambu would not have left any of these untried to lure and spoil Vengi.

"Vengi, do not cry. Whatever happened has happened, forget it.

You are a grown-up. You should understand this world. Realize this: Uncle is not on your side. His intentions are not honorable. He wants to distract your attention, to spoil you. He wants you to fail in the exams. Obviously, he is jealous and wicked. See the result yourself. Once a high ranker, now you are about to fail. What is your aim in life? To see all the films ad nauseam? To taste all bad things? Or, to study well, get a good job, and rise in life? It is for you to decide. Do not allow yourself to be misled by anyone or by sweet words with sinister motives. Ultimately, you and you alone will suffer. Tell me if you want to see a good film. Go and watch. But, do not be obsessed. Do not get addicted to such things. This year is crucial—school finals, public exams. Only if you secure very good marks can you go to college and get the course of your choice. You are intelligent, capable. Your future is in your hands."

Vengi was intelligent, good-natured. He realized his folly. He was remorseful. He was retrieved from the clutches of Sambu just in time. Thank God, the annual exams had intervened. Poor marks had exposed the adverse change in Vengi. Vembu effectively intervened. Without throwing tantrums, he handled the issue with tact and maturity, with care and concern. He made Vengi realize the disastrous consequences of his own deviant behavior, or else Vengi's life would have been wrecked beyond repair.

Vembu also felt that he should have kept an eye on his son, his activities, his movements, his habits just like an effective coach who lets his trainee play in the field freely but keeps a constant, watchful eye on him to correct and guide him, if and when necessary.

Never lose oversight of your children.

Strange is human behavior! There may be many fellow beings, more intelligent or more beautiful or more successful, scattered in this world. They do not cause pain or generate any jealousy or evoke any ill feelings. But, if a neighbor or a friend or a classmate or a colleague or a near relation or a neighbor's son happens to be a winner, some become envious and even furious, even if it does not adversely affect them in any way. Why is this so? Is it the proximity and familiarity that inflicts some complex and breeds jealousy? Vembu was perplexed.

"Vengi, behave normally with Uncle. Better, deftly avoid him. Don't talk to him much. Politely say no if he offers tickets, storybooks, or pleasure trips. Give some excuse. Do not mention anything about your studies."

Normally, in such circumstances, anyone in Vembu's shoes would have had a nasty verbal duet with Sambu. Too gentle and mature, Vembu chose not to utter even a word to Sambu about the matter. His reasoning was this: *If I raise this issue with Sambu, he may react smartly.*

"I am sorry, Vembu. I did not expect Vengi to become addicted to films. I only suggested to him with all good intentions to have some relaxation. Don't worry. I will advise Vengi."

Or, he may turn openly hostile.

"Why do you blame me, Vembu? Control your son . . . if you can."

In any case, bitterness will be the outcome. Better let correction begin at home. Let me tackle Vengi.

Sambu was not aware of the exposure of his villainy. Immensely happy, he was. "My scheme has worked. Vengi has been sufficiently spoiled. This year, without my intervention, Vengi will fail. I am sure." He had peaceful sleep.

School final public exams were over. The results were out. Vengi had secured—hold your breath—ninety nine percent in the aggregate! A school topper! State first! Congratulations.

There were felicitations, media coverage, prizes, a chief minister's special award, even offers of admission from reputed colleges. Why not? Vembu was proud of his son. Now, Vembu was confident, Vengi could never ever be spoiled by anybody under any circumstances.

Sambu, however, had the shock of his life. Shankar had gone to

Goa on a pleasure trip along with his pals. The results were out in the newspaper, but Sambu did not know Shankar's number. He had been too busy to keep in touch with his own son's affairs. He ransacked Shankar's messy room. He could not lay his hands on his ticket or anything that had his number. Instead, Sambu stumbled upon a letter from the school principal. Was it a letter bomb? He exploded. "Idiot. Rascal!" Sambu had never been so enraged. The letter was old, dated some months back. It had not reached Sambu's hands at all. Shankar had made sure of that. The letter, addressed to Sambu, read as follows:

"We regret to inform you that, as per the consensus at the meeting of our disciplinary committee, it has been decided to expel Shankar from the school due to his gross indiscipline and misbehavior. You are requested to meet the principal for further information in this regard."

Shankar could not even appear for his school final exams. He had been expelled. Sambu was totally in dark. All along, Sambu's focused attention had been only on Vengi. Shankar had gone to Goa a few days ago. Along with his chums, Shankar was having a gala time at the balmy beach.

Two days later, his friends brought Shankar home. His friends left him and slipped away. Shankar appeared disoriented. He started blabbering. *Is he drunk?* Everyone at home wondered.

The next day, his speech turned filthy. Four-letter words were freely falling from his foul mouth. Folks at home were greatly embarrassed. A doctor was called in. He found Shankar mentally ill. Had he gone psychotic? The teenage boy's prattling betrayed his orgies with whores. Was it premature aging, over obsession, overindulgence, addiction, poison? What caused his pathetic illness? There were no definite answers. Unregulated freedom, easy money, and bad company were a formidable combination key to unlock a *keen-ager's* proclivities for abominable activities. Whatever happened had happened. What was there to do now? All were confused. Shankar seemed to have grown randy. Some suggested early marriage as a possible cure. But, it caused a conscience clash between parental affinity and human morality. Who would venture to give his daughter in marriage knowingly to a mad fellow? Hiding the fact would be heinous. The idea was given up. It took almost six months of psychiatric treatment to bring him back to any semblance of normalcy.

Sambu was familiar with a saying: If you nurture someone's child, your own will grow on its own. Now, he discovered, the opposite was also equally true. The discovery was too late, too costly. All his dreams about his son's great future lay splintered. Sambu experienced hell on Earth for six months because of his son—or sin? He was swarmed with seemingly sympathetic—actually derisive—inquiries about Shankar.

Sambu's conscience whispered, *A penalty for parental negligence or a divine punishment for his deplorable sin?* Sambu again could not sleep. A burning sensation bothered him. It was all now because his plan backfired.

10

• Mistaken Identity

Aravendan was in Form V. One day, Subbiah asked him, "Do you know the girl, so-and-so, studying in your school?"

"Yes, Pa."

"Yes means what?"

"I have seen her in our school; she is one year senior. She comes to school in a single-bullock cart; that is all. Why are you asking me?"

"Yesterday, her father, Arun, my friend, told me, you are teasing her. I could not believe it. I told him that you are not that kind of boy, but Arun was insistent."

Subbiah recollected the conversation:

"Subbu, how badly you have brought up your son?"

"Tell me, Arun. What happened? My son is a good boy."

"That is what every father thinks about his sons."

"What is the issue? Tell me straight."

"I tell you; you better control your son."

"First, tell me what wrong he did."

"My daughter says that Aravendan of Form V has been following and teasing her with lewd remarks almost every day. She cries. I remembered your son's name; I understand he is in fifth form. You better warn him."

"I can't believe it."

"Believe it or not. Control him. Or, I will do it in my own way."

"This is what happened. I assured Arun that I would check up. Tell me now if it is true."

He did not complete his sentence, but the implication was predictable. Normally, by his nature, Subbiah would have believed his friend and taken immediate action against his son. After the lost bag incident, he had realized that the rod spared need not necessarily mean a child spoiled. Unjustified use of the rod might itself spoil a child. While a justified punishment may not reform a recalcitrant, a series of unjustified punishment may harden even a gentle boy into headstrong problem.

Aravendan immediately understood what had happened. It was his namesake who had caused this confusion. The addition of an initial to his name as a mark of differentiation had proved ineffective in such issues. Who bothers about a full name in situations like this? He told his doubting father all about the other boy, S. Aravendan, of the same class but of a different class of habits. As he would not like the jewel of his soul to be stained under any circumstances, he insisted on Subbiah meeting Arun on the next day to clarify his position.

The next day, when Subbiah met him, Arun was the first to speak. He was profusely apologetic; by then, he also had come to know of the real identity of the teaser.

11

• Name or Shame?

At school, he stood apart among thousands as the school pupil leader! He was a versatile student and enthusiastic participant in all competitions. Though a tongue-tied boy not long ago, Aravendan was a regular prize winner, be it studies, elocution, declamation, essay writing either in English or in Tamil. He would venture out to prove his mettle in school competitions and fetch prizes for himself and honor for his school. Aravendan penned the script of a drama to be played at an annual function, and forced by Mr. Jacob, he acted a part in it. To his utter surprise, he even secured a prize each for script writing and acting.

In studies and other extracurricular activities, Aravendan had a formidable competitor, Ram. The first and second positions in the class alternated between these two. Ram, a town boy, hailing from a well-educated family, had three elder brothers, all either graduates or postgraduates.

"My father and elder brother coach me for studies and also for competitions," Ram was candid. "My brother writes speeches for me; I mug it up. Aravenda, who is your guide?" Ram was curious to know about his competitor's mentor.

"None, Ram."

Ram was wonder struck.

Aravendan had no ghost writer. He was a voracious reader and an eclectic. It provided him an edge over others. He himself would gather material on the subject matter, assimilate its essence, organize his thoughts, and structure his speech in his own words with apt quotes. This rendered memorizing unnecessary, infused self-confidence, and drove away stage fear. He would not, therefore, run the risk of forgetting the memorized lines midway and repeating from the beginning all over again to the amusement of the audience. He realized when his thoughts flowed through his hands into writing that his brain, through some remote sensing capability, saved it in backup memory.

But, a sense of deprivation flooded his mind. Unlike Ram, he did not have his own mother, Kayal, alive to wake him up in the early morning and teach him *slokas* and keep awake along with him, giving him encouragement to prepare well for competitions or exams. His paternal grandma, though, filled the bill grandly.

A normally shy boy, Aravendan had developed his own oratorical skill and style. It was strange. While flamboyant, garrulous boys, who would be boisterous in a circle of friends, felt nervous to ascend a podium and utter a few words, this quiet, laconic lad delivered impressive performances with modulations and gestures that would fetch him praise and prizes.

Aravendan also used to write and speak in flowery Tamil, with strings of alliterations and rhymes. His Tamil pundit admired his skill but, worried about the student being identified with a fast-rising political party, advised Aravendan to tone down his language at least while writing public exams. Aravendan, who dutifully obeyed his Tamil pundit, never forgot his first verbal encounter with him.

It was his first day in Form IV. Every student was introducing himself or herself. When his turn came, Aravendan started with his name and where he came from. The Tamil pundit meaningfully smiled and, tying his unruly long hair into a rear tuft, started teasing Aravendan:

"Are you Aravindan or Aravendan?"

"Aravendan."

"So, you are poisonous!"

"No, sir." Aravendan, who understood that the pundit was referring to his name meaning king of snakes (cobra), responded, "Sir, as you know, a cobra, by nature, is righteous, truth bound. Unless provoked, a cobra will not harm anyone. Even if disturbed, it will not strike without a warning hiss. That is why it is hailed as *nalla paambu* (good snake). So–"

"Good snake!" Suppressing his smile, the pundit persisted in teasing, "Okay, do you know what that name of your place means?" Without expecting the young lad to know or reply, the pundit went on, "It means *a place where the goddess of wealth, Laxmi, will never enter.* What a shame."

The entire class laughed. All the boys and girls looked at Aravendan as if he were personally responsible for the shameful name of the village. The Tamil pundit's intention was not to humiliate his student. He was merely exhibiting his proficiency in the language. For spirited Aravendan, however, it was insult to the village. Sitting in the class, he could not stand the insult.

He stood up. "I beg to differ, sir. Our village got its name not today or yesterday; it was named long, long ago. It's a sacred place. Seventh century *Saiva Nayanmars,* who have sung in praise of Lord Siva residing here, have described the natural beauty of this village. A place like this would not have been so inauspiciously named as you have interpreted." Aravendan then paraphrased the name and explained how it could be interpreted, rightly, to mean *a beautiful place full of swans and cows.* A place, full of swans and cows," Aravendan amplified, "must be a place with natural endowments—fertile land and flowing water—a prosperous place, Laxmi's dwelling domain."

Hugging him, the Tamil pundit said, "Excellent, Aravendan, I agree it must be a dwelling place not only for Laxmi but for Saraswati, the Goddess of Learning, too. May God bless you!"

12

• Directional Guidance

Aravendan was a believer. Maybe it was because of his family environment or prior birth linkages or accumulated karma.

One night, he had a dream: He was walking in a lonely locality; he had lost his way. Spotting a Vedic Brahmin by the side of a well, he approached the Brahmin for guidance and the Brahmin pointed and said, “Go in this direction; you will reach Thiruchitrambalam.”

He woke up. The meaning of the dream was not clear. This he told his father and grandma. They, too, could not interpret the dream. But, Grandma was extremely worried: *Will my grandson renounce his worldly bindings? Will he go in search of a bodhi?* She sought to dispel any such inclinations or illusions from his mind. She told him how anxious she was to see their family banyan grow for generations, with multiple branches taking roots. Aravendan was amused. *How has a simple dream rattled my grandma to worry about the progression of progeny? Is a dream a CD of the soul?*

Once, Aravendan had gone on a school-arranged excursion to a neighboring town. The learned teacher who led the students highlighted the significance of the place. "This is a holy place of the Transcendent Supreme Being's ecstatic, cosmic dance. It's known for two great temples—a temple of devotion for dancing Siva and a temple of education for learning students."

The group was taken to the first temple.

"This is Siva temple. The shrine of Siva in the temple is supposed to be in ethereal (*akash* or *ambaram*) form, embodying the *chit*, the secret of divine knowledge permeating the universe. God is believed to be an omnipresent "formless form", a supreme force. Today, even science says seemingly empty space is anything but empty. Maybe, one day, science will stumble upon the unseen energy." Did he mean what scientists now call a God particle? Most of the students could not grasp what the teacher explained. The guide continued: "This thousand-pillar hall was the place where Sekizhar released his magnum opus, *Peria Puranam*, in twelfth century. *Peria Puranam*, you know, is a sacred compendium of versified stories of sixty-three *Saiva nayanmars*, composed at the insistence of King Anabayan. The opening line of the invocative verse was prompted by Lord Siva himself."

Next, the students were led to the other temple in the adjoining space.

"This institution has served as a nursery for a number of engineers, managers, leaders, and scholars—and even politicians." He mentioned the renowned names of golden-hearted founders, silver-tongued vice-chancellors, and scholarly professors of the great institution. Listing many of its celebrity products, he hoped, "Some of you may be lucky to graduate from this university."

After leaving secondary school, Aravendan should have logically chosen, for his graduation, this university at Chidambaram just fifteen miles from his native town, connected by road and rail. Due to misplaced expectations of sustained logistics support, however, he bypassed this proximate institution and went all the way to a college in Madras. The college had relatively more disciplined students, but on that score, Aravendan felt, it did not deserve its derisive description: *Samiar college.* Its students were by no means *Samiars* (hermits), far from being capable of renouncing their juvenile behavior, let alone worldly bondage.

While doing pre-university work, Aravendan joined a short-term competitive course on *Saiva Siddhantha* adding an extra hour every day to his schedule. This caused anxiety and apprehensions on all fronts. His joining the Saiva Siddhantha course drew ire from the family, but not out of fear of Aravendan turning into a *Samiar* or a genuine concern about the possible diversion of his attention from the regular curriculum. Even when he successfully completed the course and secured a publicized prize—without impacting his regular studies—he did not get or, in fact, expect any approbation. It was as anticipated—brushed aside as inconsequential. His own young friends wondered why he had chosen such an "uninteresting" subject. "Because I am interested," Aravendan stressed. "It is really a mistaken notion that subjects like Saiva Siddhantham should be read only in old age. Age is no bar to the study of any subject. If the subject relates to life and beyond, one should read it at an early stage and not at the end. If you have interest, you can read, learn, or do anything. Never lose interest."

His teenage friends gazed at Aravendan: "Is he an extraterrestrial being?"

To pursue his studies further, Aravendan returned to his native place, following hints—big enough for a sensitive person to detect—not to depend on the arrangements to stay in Madras any longer. His year-long stint in the city gave Aravendan exposure to urban life; it was enough. He would no longer mistake urban for urbane. Having creditably finished his pre-university work, Aravendan desired to study engineering. But, he could not secure admission. Admittedly, he was a forward-class student. However, backed by his father, Aravendan was intent on scaling the hill of academic pursuits to its highest heights. There were many who were ready—and, in fact, keen—to sprinkle cold water on his plans and to quench the fire of his ambition. One such water dispenser was his own less-avuncular relation, who counseled Subbiah in all seriousness: "Subbiah, why are you so madly keen that Aravendan should become a graduate? Just because others' sons are in college? Better let him search for a job or admit him in a polytechnic."

Subbiah was internally simmering at the sardonic suggestion. *Am I desperate for my son's earnings? Is my son a below-average student? Why do they want a brilliant boy to be suppressed?*

"Jealousy, nothing else! Uncle himself has not completed his graduation. He is sure of his children never becoming graduates. Please ignore his advice, whatever his motives," Aravendan pacified his dad.

Aravendan entered B. Com. Later in his life, he would not regret his choice of the university or the course. The word *Thiruchitrambalam* also signifies *Saiva Siddhantham* and *Chidambaram.* None including Aravendan related his interest in *Saiva Siddhantham* and his choice of university to the Vedic Brahmin's direction in his childhood dream. But, Grandma did and hoped this would be the end of that direction.

13

A Suspense Entry

"Sir, may I . . ." a voice came from the class.

Accounting class was in progress. A tall, young, brilliant lecturer was trying to solve a complicated problem on the blackboard. The balance sheet did not tally. He tried all permutations and combinations of pluses and minuses of figures but to no avail; the balance sheet remained adamantly unbalanced. Bharadan was nonplussed. He was not at his best that day; he could not figure out what mistake he had committed. The stumped lecturer turned and beckoned the volunteering student to come forward and use the board. The student tallied the balance sheet. Bharadan was immensely pleased; his student solved his problem. From that moment, the relationship between Bharadan and Aravendan transcended that of lecturer and student; they became good friends.

Arvin, that was Aravendan's nickname on the university campus and thereafter in his life, outperformed others in the class. On occasion, he also displayed his oratorical talents. At a function organized to felicitate fresh commerce graduates and postgraduates of the year immediately after convocation, Arvin spoke:

"With great pride and immense pleasure, we welcome the fresh bachelors and masters of commerce of this year. Young graduates, your earnest endeavors in these years, with God's grace, have come into fruition. Proud and glad, and clad with gown and hood, you have received your degrees today. The degree conferred on you denotes the degree of your scholastic success, a record of your performance, a reward for your efforts, recognition of your merit, and a passport to your life. Our hearty congratulations! Your success constitutes as a source of inspiration to us. We shall endeavor to emulate your example.

"While it would be inappropriate on my part to give you any advice, I take the liberty of remembering to you the wise words of Sir T. Muthusamy Iyer, which are most appropriate at this juncture:

"Your value to this university consists not merely in any official position or professional eminence you may attain to, not merely in the fortune or name you may make for yourself, but in the extent to which you disseminate the principle influences awakened in you by culture and convert them well, in the case of others as in your own, from mere general opinion into impulses of action and rules of conduct . . ."

Everyone was impressed. Arvin became a popular guy. He caught the attention of all lecturers, including HOD. He was showered by encouragements to break the trend and secure first class in B. Com. The hopes were not belied; he topped the university with first class. Arvin was now a bachelor, a bachelor of commerce, the first graduate in his family and in his village.

Once they became close, Bharadan started acquainting himself with the family background of Arvin.

"Arvin, are you a hostel student?"

"No, sir, I am a day scholar."

"Are you coming from the town?"

"No. I am a train student coming from Sirkazhi."

"Which street?"

"Not Sirkazhi proper; it's a village four kilometers farther away."

"My goodness! You are commuting daily all the way from the village? How do you reach the railway station at Sirkazhi?"

"By bicycle!"

"At what time do you leave your home daily?"

"At six."

"When do you return home?"

"It depends on the train coming from Madras; sometimes, I reach home as late as eight."

"Don't you find it strenuous?"

"Yes, I do. But, the other option is staying in a hostel, which is more strenuous financially."

"Your relations are rich *jamindars*; will they not help you?"

The reply was laughter, which conveyed a lot. He did not, however, tell Bharadan that, but for some relations, his family would have remained fairly rich. Though not rich, he was not poor either. But, he would not like stretching of his father's hard-earned resources to have the comfort or discomfort of hostel life.

Bharadan's astonishment was visible in his face. "Hats off to you. Keep it up. You should not stop with a mere degree; you should become a postgraduate and also aim at a doctorate. There are very few PhDs in commerce." This was the pep-up tonic he got from a lecturer of a mere three-year acquaintance. Arvin could not help contrasting this with his own relation's unwarranted dose of advice to become a diploma holder or a job seeker rather than a graduate. The motive-free morale boosting outbalanced the motivated discouragements. Arvin stood steady with his unflinching determination to become at least a postgraduate, particularly when he was recipient of National Merit Scholarship.

The academic atmosphere in the commerce division of the university was highly conducive to the studious. The catholic HOD, the immaculate visiting professor, and lovable lecturers were all men of pedagogical proficiency and, more importantly, of the finest human qualities. In any environment, aberrations are inevitable, though not quickly recognizable. One such aberration was one Sriram, whose face did not reflect his mind.

The two-year period of postgraduate course work in commerce proved to be momentous. Arvin had the privilege to deputize his indisposed HOD and deliver a speech in the immediate presence of the vice chancellor. His first-prize-winning article on "Managers—Are They Born?" and his speech came in for high appreciation of the VC, who was an erudite scholar and excellent orator and had been conferred knighthood by the British. Arvin was chosen as chairman of the mock company of the department. He maintained his performance in his studies as well. He was confidently endeavoring toward a repeat performance in M. Com. His lecturers were more confident of Arvin emerging first class first.

Throughout, he had been maintaining his lead. He never confined himself to textbooks and class notes. He made fairly extensive use of the library. With single-minded devotion, he focused on his studies. Having done very well in the finals, Arvin was cocksure of achieving his cherished aim. When the final result was out, he could not believe it. His friends, too, could not. "How did it happen?" everyone wondered.

A surprise entry was baffling, suspenseful.

Arvin did secure first class. He was still disappointed; his well-wishers, too, were upset. Bharadan was utterly sad, as if he himself had lost his rank. Arvin lost his first rank by a thread of difference in marks.

A marginal difference can occur, inevitably, like an accident. In evaluation, marks cannot be so finely measured and granted. Maybe the other chap, though not under reckoning even for a second division, might have labored hard at the eleventh hour and done a grain better in the final, Arvin consoled himself.

Gradually, others, too, cheered him: "The rank is not as material as is the first division. The academic credentials are only a key to secure a job opening. Thereafter, it's only your work and luck that will take you to higher positions. Forget the rank. Be cheerful. Already, you have appeared for job interviews. You will surely succeed. Never lose heart."

14

To Go or Not to Go?

The senescent grandma was terminally sick. Medicines and she disagreed with each other. The doctor threw up his hands. Her end was expected any day. One day, when she was between spells of unconsciousness, Arvin got his appointment letter. He was required to join duty at Madras in the forenoon of the next day. It was his eagerly awaited first job, a coveted one. He would have to travel by train overnight to Madras. When told about this happy news, Grandma's face lit up. Subbiah informed her that Arvin would need to leave for Madras that night and wanted her opinion: should he go or stay? Grandma's vision was blurred and her speech slurred, but she was clear in her mind: Arvin must go.

An emotional war was raging within Arvin's mind. Would it be proper for him to leave his grandma in that condition and go to Madras for his job? She was not merely a grandma for him; she was much more. He was motherless; Kayal had expired when he was hardly eight. It was Grandma who had rescued him as a child from the jaws of infantile death and brought him up. She was a sweet storyteller too. How many stories she had told him about her younger days; about his late grandpa whom he had never seen; about her marriage at the age of thirteen with him; about the sudden demise of his grandfather when Subbiah was entering his teenage years; about how the family was tricked by relations into losing their landed properties; how, uprooted from their native soil and dispossessed of their hearth and stability, she and her two sons had to leave their sprawling, eight-unit house and go, like foraging birds, to their present place for resettlement; about how Subbiah had to forego his formal education and start his life as a village *karnam,* then essentially a part time job; about how, by dint of hard work in supplementary avocations, Subbiah could build from nothing and sustain the respectability of the family; about how he fulfilled her wish to have, again, a house of their own in the new locale so that she could die peacefully in her own house. These stories, embedded in his subconscious mind, forged his determination to succeed in life in honest way on his own with God's grace.

That grand, fond, inspiring lady, who so shaped his personality, was gradually losing her grip on life. Was she not yearning for a grandson to do last rites on her demise? Would it not be an ungrateful act on his part to leave her on her deathbed and go for his livelihood? Could he ask for more time? Would the organization oblige? Even assuming humane accommodation from the employer, how much time he could ask for? One week? Two weeks? She might even survive, as she did during the last bout of illness a month back, or she might continue in the same condition a few more weeks or months. Who could predict? Securing a job was not that easy—and that, too, a job like this! This job was indeed Arvin's pride and his friends' envy! What should he do? To go or not to go—that was the question. Arvin did not have the benefit of any kind of metaphysical advice on the delicate issue of dilemma. Whom could Arvin now turn to? After considerable internal debate and consultations with elders, Arvin decided to go. He prostrated at the feet of his grandma and sought her blessings. Grandma bid him farewell, applying holy ash, *vibuthi,* on his forehead and uttering words of blessing: "With God's grace, prosper."

15

• A Weighty Issue

It was a question of choice. Thank the heavens; it was not one elusive mistress. He looked up at the two beautiful ladies extending their beckoning hands. His elation defied description. He pinched himself. It was not a dream. When many bachelors faced rejections and waited longingly for an acceptance, this chap was lucky. He was overwhelmed. "I wish I could clasp both pairs of hands!" But, bigamy was barred. It was a difficult choice between the two equally tempting offers. If one was a majestic grace, the other was an imperial charm.

Yes. Close on the heels of completing his postgraduate work, Arvin was offered a job, straight in officer cadre, by two banks of respectable standing almost at the same time. He was virtually hopping out of the university corridors into a bank cabin. It wasn't through campus recruitment. Such tapping at source would emerge decades later. It was through a tediously long process of open recruitment. His friend, professor, and guide, a catholic Christian, proffered directional guidance. That first gospel-like message settled the choice. He accepted the offer from that reputed banking institution and was awaiting a formal appointment letter. Almost a year and a half had elapsed since he had applied. Now, he got a telegram urging him come now. Normally, in a village, a telegram, generally associated with bad news, used to terrify the receiver. This wire electrified everyone in the family.

It was the first day on the job—a day looked forward to by any young man, a day to be cherished, a day to be remembered for life. This turned out be a memorable day for more than one reason. He had been appointed as a probationary officer and advised to report at the training college of the organization on a given date.

On the appointed day at 10:15 a.m. with his heart full of joy and his mind full of dreams, Arvin reported to the chief of the college.

"Young man, what's the time now? You're reporting thirty minutes late," the chief's harangue in a harsh tone lasting for another fifteen minutes, unnerving the young man.

"I am sorry, sir." Arvin thought it appropriate to apologize rather than trying to justify the so-called delay. The innocent-looking boy's countenance probably aggravated the angry mood of the interrogator.

"Today is your first day on the job. You were expected to report at 9:45 a.m.; I have never seen such an irresponsible fellow. I can very well turn you back, you know."

What a warm welcome! For a moment, he was frozen. "No, sir." Picking up the courage hidden within and gathering all politeness, he said, "Sir, as per the message I received, I am required to report in the forenoon of today—any time before twelve noon is forenoon, I thought. In any case, I am sorry."

The fair face of the principal, not yet tanned by the Southern sun, instantaneously turned purple. He seemed to realize the unsustainability of his charge of late reporting against the new recruit, but his ego stood in his way of its graceful admission. Maintaining a stern look, the chief condescendingly let the budding officer start his job.

"Okay. That's all right. You may complete the formalities and go to your allotted room."

A formal inaugural program was scheduled for the next day.

Would it not have been nice had the principal, personifying the employer organization, been considerate and cordial while welcoming a new entrant and made him feel at home? Arvin mused.

It was then an employers' market. And, perhaps, it was too much to expect any human relation niceties from such a statutory creature.

This was not the first occasion of discomfiture Arvin experienced as he began his first job. The medical fitness clearance process a month earlier was another. The doctor of the organization found that Arvin was slightly short of normal weight for a man of his age. The low body weight of the would-be officer, who might have to deal with weighty matters, seemed to heavily weigh on the doctor's mind. While flipping through the papers containing vital data of his weight, height, and so on and physically examining him lying semi naked on the clinic bed, the doctor looked down upon him and abruptly shot a question: "Who selected you?" The question floored Arvin. He looked up at the doctor for elaboration. The doctor declared, "You are underweight." The declarative statement was followed by another devastating poser: "How did they select you?"

A university rank-holder with many academic accomplishments to his credit, Arvin could not take it lying down. What a drilling interview this was, even as he was about to heave a sigh of triumphant relief after deftly managing a volley of questions on subjects ranging from the quantity theory of money to instruments of credit control, from Boyle's Law to law of contracts, from accounting to auditing. A panel member also asked his opinion on the ongoing anti-Hindi agitation.

Hindi was a smoldering issue then. It was only a few weeks back that Republic Day had turned into a public protest day in Tamilnadu. The turmoil took the form of protest marches, police charges, arrests, shootings, and self-immolations. A measure proclaimed for national integration was threatening to have the diametrically opposite effect.

The institution was an all-India one, headquartered in Bombay. All panel members were from the north of Vindhyas. The candidate had to be truthful and yet tactful in his response. How could one expect all the interview panel members to be totally free from lingual bias?

"Sir, it is an emotional and perceptional issue. It's not that people in the South despise Hindi. Hindi film songs are popular among the youngsters. Many opt for Hindi as an additional subject. I myself studied Hindi in B. Com. Economic compulsions for people to move to North will render Hindi a necessity. But, human nature being what it is, imposition by a fiat or any other means evokes resistance. The students feel insecure; it is feared that Hindi replacing English as the official language will place the people from Tamil Nadu at a disadvantage. It is also deemed to be a reneging from Nehru's assurance not to impose Hindi on non-Hindi-speaking people so long as they do not want it. It has, therefore, ignited the students' agitation and fomented the political protests."

The stony faces of the panel did not disclose if they were satisfied with the response. His selection, however, did. He leapt in joy to find his name very high in the first batch of scores in the selection list filtered from thousands of applicants through screening by academic merit, written test, and oral interview. Now, this doctor was provoking him. Why? He could not understand.

The doctor's job is to ascertain whether a selected candidate is medically fit and furnish a report to the management. That is all. Why should he go out of his role to insult me? Is the doctor suffering from a virus of sadism or prejudice? Arvin was perplexed, but calmly responded, "They weighed my knowledge, Doctor. I am not starting a weightlifting job."

Will the riposte recoil? A disquieting doubt disturbed his sleep. The doctor, if vicious, could prevent Arvin's career entry by giving a negative report. Thank the doctor—he gave medical fitness clearance but with a provision. Within six months, he should gain six kilograms. Fair enough! But, it meant that the appointment would be provisional. The probationary officer was thus made a provisional officer.

Arvin turned almost frugivorous for a few months. It proved to be fruitful. He gained the required weight and unconditional medical clearance within the stipulated time. It was a different matter that, gradually over the years, Arvin started gaining more weight than he could throw around.

16

• An Undying Pain

Two days passed in his job. Arvin got a message: someone is waiting at the reception to meet you.

Arvin went down to the reception lobby of the training college. His nephew was waiting. The visitor was visibly gloomy. *What could be the matter?* After a few annoying minutes of silence, the visitor broke the news. With a knot of pain at heart, Arvin managed not to break down himself.

His grandma had gone. The night he left for Madras was her last night. It appeared as though she were waiting for her grandson to leave for his job. Even before he reached Madras, she had departed. She had lived an austere and righteous life. Her blessed soul would have surely entered God's world if not merged with the Divinity. Those days were devoid of the convenience and nuisance of mobile phones; even landlines were not long enough to reach villages. Messages of this nature used to be carried by couriers to nearby places and by telegrams to other stations. Family members had decided not to disturb Arvin on the first day of his first job with the news of bereavement.

Even a digital SLR could not have captured and saved the image of the graceful old lady as sharply as Arvin's mind had done. The aged, withering grandma, a typical Hindu widow with tonsured head, with her forehead, nose, ears, and neck all bare, devoid of auspicious symbols of marital status and wearing a pale white sari, was still slim and fair. Though widowed in her thirties, the thought of remarriage did not cross her mind even for a fleeting nanosecond. She devoted, in a spirit of sacrifice, her remaining life—youthful and beyond—to her two sons and their sons. Whenever she described her late husband—a fair, plump figure, with a lock of long, wavy hair knotted into a tuft at the back of his head, covered by a turban, sporting scarlet *kadukkans,* Cornelian ear studs, a pleasing personality, and viewed a respected landlord—she would be lost in the reminiscent image of him on her mental screen and unconsciously blush like a young girl, with eyelashes bent, eyelids cast down, pupils lowered, and cheeks turning faded crimson. The only gesture of girlish bashfulness missing was face covering by palms. Her shyness was inborn and not acquired from any *Bharatnatyam* danseuse. Discretely, she would wipe an exiting tear while exiting from the memory. She would then smilingly change the subject: "Do you know your father too wore a tuft and *kadukkans*? It was only after his marriage that he had his hair cropped and shed his ear studs." Arvin would giggle, conjuring up the image of his dad with a tuft and *kadukkans.*

Arvin used to be cosseted by his grandma. Despite Subbiah's proscription, she would share with her pet grandson freshly brewed filtered coffee, discretely but liberally. No wonder Arvin became a habitual coffee drinker. A champion of graph theory and combinatronics, two branches of mathematical tools essential for computer science, Paul Erdos, an avid coffee drinker who wandered from place to place and proved theorem after theorem, is reported to have quipped, "A mathematician is a machine for turning coffee into theorem." Arvin, however, did not brew himself into a mathematician. Coffee could, at best, stake some claim for Arvin's proficiency in accountancy.

On some moonlit nights, she would tell stories:

"King Akashbhupathi had no issues for a long time. His wife and he intensely prayed to the goddess Kamatchi. Pleased with their devotion, Kamatchi willed her own son, Ganesan, to be born as the prince. The prince named Thundeerar ascended the throne. That domain came to be known as Thondamandalam, famed for intellectuals. Sekizhar belonged to this place. You know, we are his descendants. You were born on Ganesh Chadurthi Day. You must be blessed, I believe. I am sure you will do well in life."

Arvin's memory was in auto-rewind mode. He could not control his rebelling tears. She was truly a grandma. Her lap was indeed an intensive care unit for him in his critical childhood. She nurtured him. She molded him. She petted him. She chided him. She guided him. She motivated him. She raised him. And, she wanted him to rise high in life. All she expected from him in return was to perform last rites on her demise. What a pity! He could not even be present by her side when she left this world. It remained a nagging pain in the heart of Arvin.

17

• Unseen Hand

Arvin did not realize, till he met the gentleman professor, that accidents can also be caused. A deliberate use of an ax or a natural blow of wind can break an overhead branch of a tree and cause it to fall exactly on your head when you happen to pass under it. It was clear now that an unfair hand had discreetly intervened and, like unseen wind, smashed his rank ambition. Whom should Arvin blame? The unfair hand? The unseen God? After all, ax or wind is only an instrument.

Now he recalled a bit of conversation he once had with Raghu, one of his classmates on the university campus. Then, it appeared innocuous. The talk was about a faculty member whose face masked his mind. Sriram, witty and charming, could be so friendly with his smiling countenance and sparkling wit that you would be thrown off guard. As a gesture of comradeship, he would occasionally throw his hand around your shoulder or slide it across your back. The import of the forgotten conversation now dawned. Arvin recalled the talk: "Arvin, did Prof. Sriram pat your back?"

"Yes, Raghu, he did it yesterday; why?"

"Why do you think he did it?"

"Why? Obviously, to compliment me on my performance on the test."

Arvin never suspected or tried to trace the real purpose behind the wandering hand.

"That is what you think," said Raghu.

"Then?"

"Okay. Leave it," Raghu smiled and left. Arvin, too, left the matter unconcerned. What was left unsaid was unclear—then. It was becoming clear now, after a year, in the light of the revelation made by G-P. It was a discreet community-identification strategy adopted by Sriram.

A few months into his job in Bombay, Arvin happened to run into G-P at some meeting. G-P was genuinely happy and proud to find his former student doing well in his job and facing a promising future. He was the gentle professor of immaculate personality who used to advise, "Go as far as you can see, and then, see how far you can go." In the course of chitchat, G-P opened up, "Arvin, I was sorry you missed your first position in M. Com. God is great. I am now extremely glad that you have secured a very good job. I see a bright future for you."

"Thank you, sir. It is all due to your blessings and God's grace."

"Mm. Mm. What is paining me still is that you could have got the rank you deserved but for that fellow."

"What? Which fellow?"

"No. I didn't want to tell you then. My position of responsibility did not permit me. And, even if I had told you about it, you would not have gotten back what you were deprived of."

"Please tell me, sir, what actually happened. You have kindled my curiosity."

"This is between you and me."

"I promise."

"That gentleman, witty and charming, you know . . ." He then disclosed what happened and how. "Anyway, rank injustice has been done. But, as I said, God is great. None can deny what is destined for you. By losing the first rank, I think, you have not lost anything material. Do not brood over it. I just wanted to unburden myself.

Now, forget it. Carry on with your job. There, you will rank as a good officer. I am confident you will. You will shine wherever you go and whatever you do. May God bless you."

"Thanks a lot. Now I know how I lost the first rank. That was unfair. Why? Why should Sriram do it? There was no enmity between us."

"Affinity between them, perhaps!"

"I never imagined my friend would adopt foul means to get his rank. In fact, sir, we used to have a combined study while preparing for final. I had . . . I had obliged him by sharing my notes and my ideas and by clearing his doubts on subjects. If he had honestly beaten me in marks—that is the impression I have been carrying all along—I would not have been unhappy. Now, I can't bear this. I really thought he was as he looks—a simple, good, pious guy."

Arvin was overwhelmed with emotion. There was a lump in his throat, droplets in his eyes, a tremor in his voice, a pain in his heart. G-P could see them all.

"Leave it, Arvin. It is all over. Never lose your cool." The professor patted Arvin and pacified him.

"Okay, sir, I am sorry. If it was God's will, so be it."

"Good. Arvin, I know you will take it in stride. Remember, what is best for you will come to you in time."

"Thank you, sir."

When the rank came out, he did not get wind of what had happened. Now, he knew it was not the unseen wind but an unseemly hand that had caused the trouble. That hand was now exposed.

The loss of first rank did not, however, lead to rancor. Arvin never confronted the first rank snatcher on this perfidy. He never lost his serenity.

18

• A Poetic Slip

The training period over, a regular posting followed. Posted in Bombay, Arvin, a *madarassi*—that is how any South Indian was being generically referred to then, without any subregional discrimination—felt initially like a fish out of water. He had never gone anywhere north of Madras earlier. In fact, his father was very worried but for a different reason: parochial ire against immigrant sons of the southern soil was still smoldering.

The probationary officers, or POs, as a class of direct recruits, were then generally an unwelcome lot in the organization. How could these outside kids expect warm hugs from those within, as old as their fathers and waiting to be promoted as officers? Many of the fatherly superintendents, though short of the requisite qualifications, were experientially knowledgeable. The directly recruited officers would get desk training from the departmental staff, who they would start bossing over a few weeks or months later. This sentiment tormented many who could not bring themselves up to appreciate the inherent merit in the infusion of fresh blood, mind, or talent. When the first batch of these youngsters joined, they were variedly described as *cream of the country* by the top executives, *blue-eyed boys* by the middle management, and *sons-in-law of the management* by the staff. It took months of demonstrated individual performance and, more importantly, interpersonal relations buildup to gain gradual acceptability.

It was the tradition of the department Arvin joined—as he was told—that any new entrant should host a party. He promised to abide by the custom. Two weeks passed; the party became overdue. New to the environment, he did not know how to go about organizing a party. One day, a chit came from a colleague, senior in age and of warrior-like appearance, reminding the newly posted junior of his broken promise with a gentle admonishment, "What happened to the party, my dear? You cannot escape from the tradition here."

Arvin had this reply:

"The party is delayed;
I may be excused
But not denied.
You are assured.
Arrangement is yours—
Please make it.
Payment is mine—
Please take it."

That evening, Arvin was summoned by the head of the department. HOD was a bachelor and a confirmed firebrand. A serious-looking person, seemingly with no proclivity to smile, he was widely believed to condescend to sport a smile only for ladies. Knowing this, the new officer entered the chamber with low spirit and high palpitation. Was it a gas chamber? No. But, his throat was choked up.

The Head lifted his head from a red-flapped file and sternly looked at him. Consistent with his reputation, he didn't smile. To Arvin's utter surprise, however, the Head didn't frown either. From the file on his table, a slip was showing. Either by mistake or mischief, the poetic scrap had traveled along with some prosaic office notes to the HOD. Waving it, the Head asked, "Are you the author of this slip?"

"Yes, sir." Arvin narrated the circumstances leading to penning the poetic piece. Lo and behold, a smile escaped from HOD's face. Usually parsimonious in paying compliments, he appreciated the officer's poetic aspirations. But, unequivocally, he advised him to be as prosaic as possible in his official notings. Till he parted with the institution, he dutifully followed his advice. When he left the organization, the official drafting style followed him. And, Arvin came to be considered as a good draftsman. For his drafting skill, he owed much to the drill he underwent in that renowned banking institution, where a draft, be it a few-line letter or a multipage report, would undergo chiseling by a number of deft hands, yielding ultimately a masterpiece with no ounce of unnecessary flab in any part of the textual body. Every single hand involved would claim the figurine, until a higher quarter found fault with it.

The Head was not heartless. At heart, he was very kind. His sense of humor, normally covered by the foliage of his rather assumed seriousness, would peep out occasionally.

Arvin was transferred to another state. On receipt of the order, Arvin went to take leave of the HOD. After a few pleasantries and good piece of paternal advice, he cautioned him, with a mischievous smile, "Arvin, beware of your boss at the new center! He may get jealous of you!" Arvin could not understand the import of the caution, till he met his new boss.

19

• Fall in Love

Arvin arrived at the new center and reported to his new boss. While he was still a slim snake gourd, his new boss was a burly pumpkin. The apprehended jealousy was understandable. But, no envy ever appeared. On the contrary, the burly man pitied the puny.

As Arvin discovered, it was a land of pristine beauty, still not much ravished by the devilish paws of industrialization. *Nature's own lawn?* His inspection duty involved extensive travel. While traveling, he enjoyed the splendid spectacle of Nature, who seemed to be dancing on the lawn with gay abandon in her ecstasy. His two-year stay, or rather, travel, in the new center was memorable.

Trade union activism was a conspicuous spectacle. More conscious of their rights, employees were vociferous in demanding their dues and nondues alike. To achieve their end, they would go to any extent. Not a day passed without one witnessing a passing procession or a noisy agitation with red flags and rhythmic slogans. None could dismiss their demands as without rhyme or reason. Undeniably, they had ear-pleasing rhymes.

As Arvin traveled by serpentine roads, he could see womenfolk laboring in coconut groves and men folk discussing current politics. While traveling was a pleasing experience, accompanying a senior on an official tour was not always so. It depended on the individual. Some seemed to have misunderstood the concept of leadership. As an underdog, a PO was expected to follow the senior while on foot at a respectable distance, carrying the official portfolio bag containing the senior's papers. To avoid being used as a porter officer, some juniors started carrying their own bags, much to the chagrin of the leaders. "Meet my assistant" would be the normal, authoritative, or contemptuous form of introduction of the accompanying officer; rarely would the introduction be by name or designation.

A funny incident was a perfect example of the relationship. An encounter between two men took place in an odorous enclosure. "What are you doing here?" a middle-aged man inquired of the other man, a boyish-looking young lad. The lad, a colleague of Arvin, hardly six months old in the organization, knew well what he was doing and also knew very well who the questioner was. Instead of telling him what he was doing, which was too obvious, he greeted, "Good morning, sir."

"Don't you know this is meant for officers?"

"I know, sir."

"Then, how dare you come here?"

"Sir, I am an officer—a PO."

The questioner looked peeved.

Both the gents, heaving sighs of relief, came out with an unquestionable understanding of status consciousness.

Once, a senior expected his "assistant" to collect and draw a list of his clothes for handing them over to the visiting launderer at the place of their stay. The "assistant" politely ignored the expectation. It led to some unjustifiable adverse remarks in a confidential report, which remained as discreet as farting underwater. There were a few such seniors. Any refusal to be of such personal assistance to them would invite their wrath. Even if the boss could do no finger-pointing in the area of performance or duty, he could very well dub a man, if not anything else, at least as uncooperative or shy. The purpose was to throw a cryptic pebble of a negative remark into the pool of records so that, even if it didn't create a ripple immediately, it could be fished out at a critical point of time to abuse. The shyness referred to could be, say, the officer's gentility, by no means impacting his official performance. The personalities concerned were incapable of appreciating the gentle attributes they lacked. They were also ignorant of classic instances of really shy people having shined in leadership or authorship.

Luckily, Arvin's encounters with such idiosyncratic individuals were few and far between. As elsewhere, the generally prevalent attitude was that a junior officer could not be—and, in any case should not appear to be—smarter than the higher-grade officer. A popular but exaggerated perception then floating around was that brilliance would be suppressed, idiocy would get itself exposed, and mediocrity would be comfortably encouraged. The implied message was this: It is wiser to be a mediocre. Many were wiser.

Interestingly varied were the personalities of the seniors whom Arvin had the opportunity to follow as an assistant. One senior, a compulsive dozer, would waste not a single chance to fall asleep. Even while reading files, he would doze off. File reading was not known to have soporific effects. Maybe the clock structure in his brain's supra charismatic nucleus was not doing its job of keeping him awake during the daytime. Or, possibly, he was a nocturnal rather than a diurnal bird, busier at night, and the sleep homeostasis was faithfully performing its duty of tracking how long he had been up and making him grow sleepy during the day. Whatever the reason, his sleepy behavior, no doubt, caused embarrassment to his accompanying wakeful colleagues. But for this napping problem, he was a nice, amiable gentleman.

There were some who acted as limiting factors for the junior's contribution or learning. Any observation or finding of the junior, howsoever relevant or important, would not cross the first-draft stage to enter the inspection report if it was beyond the senior's comprehension. For the senior would not be in a position to explain the issue if queried by higher-ups, nor would his ego permit him to let his junior explain and earn credit.

Undeniably, there were a few who were knowledgeable and also affable. Accompanying one as an understudy would indeed be a rewarding experience. Arvin had a reasonable quota of such rewards.

Before leaving Bombay, Arvin had received a scintillating suggestion: You better fall in love. Two years passed. It was ample time for Arvin to fall.

20

• Evaluation

Four years flew by. Arvin was, just as his batch mates were, looking forward to a promotion. More than a career ladder climb or the accompanying pay hike, he was looking for a change in job content. To Arvin, a developmental role was more appealing than a regulatory one. Undeniably, both served societal causes and meant national service. But, in terms of aptitude, he believed, he was cut out more for the former. An opportunity presented itself; two offsprings of the employer organization came out with a common ad for direct recruitment for a higher-grade post. Arvin applied, and he was called for an interview before a high-powered board.

After pleasantries, a member of the interview board, presumably a bean counter, set the ball rolling, "Mr. Arvin, I find you are a master in commerce. I need your advice on a personal investment proposition. I would like to buy the shares of X company; the share is available at Rs. 250. Will you advise me to buy the shares?"

"Sir, I presume you propose to buy equity shares of X company for long-term investment, and you are satisfied with the fundamentals of the company—its line of business, its growth potential, its management, and so on. And, all that you would like to know is whether the price is right; am I right?"

A discreet smile streaked across the member's face. He said, "You are absolutely right; now tell me if I can buy the shares at Rs. 250."

"Sir, it depends on many factors; one fundamental factor is its intrinsic value."

"How will you ascertain its intrinsic value?"

"For that, I require the company's balance sheet."

"Okay. Presume you have been given a copy of the company's balance sheet. Proceed."

"I take it that it is the latest balance sheet, that it is duly audited and the auditors are reputed, that their report is unqualified, and the true and fair view certificate is not subject to any material qualification?"

The interviewer, either impressed or impatient, hurriedly intervened to say, "Okay, okay, all your assumptions are appropriate. You proceed further to find the intrinsic value of the shares. Wait a minute. Before you go to intrinsic value, can you tell us something about true and fair view?"

"Yes, sir. The Companies Act requires the balance sheet and P&L account of a company to give a true and fair view of its state of affairs and its profit or loss. Earlier, the legal requirement was the true and correct view. It stands amended because—"

"All right, all right, enough; explain intrinsic value."

"The intrinsic value of the share can be arrived at by dividing the net worth by number of outstanding equity shares, assuming there are no preference shares."

"What is net worth?"

Arvin explained; in the course of his explanation, he deliberately but not inappropriately continued to use all technical terms like *intangible assets, external liabilities, capital reserves*, and so on, each one leading, as anticipated, to another answerable question.

After exhausting the intrinsic value topic, Arvin branched off to earning per share and price-earning multiple.

Almost an hour of dialog on a number of subjects with each one of the members of the interview board was interesting.

According to the gossip floating in the air, Arvin was topping the selection list for the mutual fund. He didn't trust that. In any case, he was not very enthusiastic about joining that unit. When the result was out, his name did not figure in the selection list meant for the MF.

21

• Singular Difference

Arvin was happy. He had led the interview to success. He got his first career promotion. He had been selected for a higher position in the financial institution. His perception was that an FI would give him wider exposure, a varied experience, and greater job satisfaction. Would his perception tally with reality? Time would tell. Arvin joined the FI and was back in Bombay. Madras-Bombay-Trivandrum-Madras-Bombay—that was Arvin's official circumambulation during the first five years of his career. How long would he now remain in the FI or in Bombay? Would he start rolling again? If so, when? He didn't know. He did not bother to give it any serious thought either. This time, when Arvin returned to Bombay, there was a singular difference.

A six-month-long practical desk-oriented training program had brought him to Madras. Each officer was sought to be made a jack of all departments. This was the period when he lost his singlehood. His sojourn in Madras proved to be an opportune time for his elders to arrange for his marriage. A serious search began for a suitable girl with a matching horoscope. It was not an easy job; his horoscope had such a celestial configuration. It was not rare, though, that matching two horoscopes was deemed all the more necessary to ensure durable wedded bliss. His longevity would depend on planetary positional alignments as per his and his wife's horoscopes, astrologers averred. No parents, believing in horoscopes or not, would risk their children's lives, particularly in the case of a son like Arvin, whose longevity was in grave doubt when he was a child. The search was therefore seemingly endless. A few proposals of prospective alliance were summarily rejected on the grounds of the nonalignment of planetary positions in the zodiac.

A close relation had proffered tempting advice to Arvin to fall in love. His ostensible reasoning was that there did not appear to be a suitable girl in the community in his native state. Whatever the purpose behind it, the suggestion should have been music to the ears of any young lad. Arvin had no ears for this kind of music. He did not want to upset his orthodox father, though his mother and grandmother could no longer protest. But, he didn't realize the power of music to attract a young man. Arvin had fallen, inevitably, in love. The fall occurred in cinema.

One day, Banerji, a colleague of Arvin's, in the course of an informal chat, studied the lines and mounds of Arvin's palm carefully through his bifocals and predicted, with all the authority in his command, that he would never get married. It was the considered opinion of Banerji that, in the absence of a clear-cut marriage line beneath his little finger, Arvin would remain a bachelor for good. To support his palm-based prediction, he cited the instance of Lord Ganesh, whose birthday Arvin shared, remaining a confirmed bachelor. As his wont, Arvin was unperturbed. It was not that he did not believe in the institution of marriage, nor did he have any intention of courting celibacy. He did not believe in Banerji's banter. He had doubts about Banerji's depth of knowledge either in palmistry or in the Hindu Puranams.

Thank God Banerji was not aware of a freak puranic version portraying Lord Ganesh as having as many as twelve wives, all daughters of Lord Vishnu. Otherwise, Banerji would have predicted polygamy for Arvin.

Anyway, Arvin kept the prediction to himself. His predicament was obvious: Had he shared, even casually, the palm-based prediction with the elders in his family, they would have possibly linked it with his childhood dream of Brahmin's direction to Thiruchitrambalam and his subsequent more-than-passing interest in the study of *Saiva Siddhantham* and conjured up a picture of Arvin ending up as a saffron-clad *swamiji*. This would have certainly depressed the elders or, more likely, urged them to hasten the process of bringing him under the yoke of wedlock, by hook or crook, rather sooner than never.

After a prolonged search for a suitable girl, Arvin's father had a chance meeting with a gentleman of the same community who was looking for a suitable boy for his daughter. There were many ominous signs when Subbiah visited that gentleman's home and, incredibly, a number of similarities in the names of relations, the villages, surrounding places, and so on. Subbiah saw the girl. He was impressed with the commonality of many aspects and the personality of the girl. Dispensing with the mandatory horoscope-matching exercise, a parental agreement was struck, though not inked, for their offsprings' matrimony. This was conveyed to Arvin at Madras.

Subbiah was disturbed by Arvin's first response, *Should a well-wisher father not be responsible enough to choose the right bride for his son? Why should he not readily agree? Is it a lack of filial trust or respect? Or, is he in love with someone?* Discreet inquiries dispelled the doubt. It was only the melodious movie songs that he had fallen in love with. Otherwise, he was absolutely love free. All that he wanted was to see the girl he would marry. It took a while for other close relatives to convince Subbiah about the reasonableness of Arvin's desire. Arvin had his demand met and endorsed the choice, much to the relief of Subbiah.

When Arvin returned to Bombay, he was no longer single; he was accompanied by Malar, now Mrs. Aravendan.

22

• Childish Prediction

One evening, the palm-reading colleague of Arvin dropped in at Arvin's flat in Bombay and congratulated the couple while apologetically explaining the circumstances in which he could not attend the wedding at Madras. Arvin's gentility did not allow him to remind Banerji of his invalid prediction. *Banerji would realize his own mistake; there is no need to embarrass him further,* thought Arvin.

When Malar went inside the kitchen to fetch some sweets and a steaming cup of filtered coffee, Banerji, with little embarrassment or emotion evident in his face, took Arvin's palm for reading. Amused, Arvin did not pull his hand back. Perhaps, Arvin thought, Banerji might reread his palm line by line and confess that he had missed a line earlier. It was but Arvin who made a mistake; his line of thinking proved to be totally out of line with Banerji's character.

"Arvin, tell me your date of birth—only the month and the date. I remember the year."

"The 257th day of Gregorian calendar year!"

It took a few minutes for Banerji to do the mental calculations. He got the date. With much more confidence this time, he went on with his predictive utterance, "Arvin, I am sorry to say that you will not have any children."

Arvin, who had done a chance reading of a book on palmistry, did not know whether to pity his colleague for his utter pretense of knowledge on the subject or censure him for his insensibilities. *What is his hobby? Reading palms or breeding misery?*

Anyone in Arvin's place would have been depressed, brooding over the prospect of failing to propagate his lineage, thus offending his grandma's *atma*, or infuriated by his colleague's ignorance and indiscretion. Arvin knew, for certain, that his colleague, a bachelor and a jovial person, was neither jealous nor wicked.

Arvin never had blind faith in predictions of any kind and much less in predictors of all hues. If the so-called predictions were positive, they would please you immediately, no matter whether they materialized or not. Positive forecasts might force you into a false sense of instant happiness and, ultimately, if they turned out to be wrong, your disappointment might be greater. On the other hand, believing in doom sayings could bring it about, or there may not be any room for doom at all. Even if calamity occurred as predicted, could you prevent it? If you did, then the prediction was wrong; if not, there was no use in ruing the potential misfortune, which may or may not befall, and ruining your mental and physical well-being well in advance. More than the calamity, the fear of calamity itself can wrench one's heart badly. If you are a believer in God, why should you blindly believe in men's or even God's men's words, which may be utterly baseless or untruthful? Sambandar rhetorically asked, "If you have divine blessings, what harm can these planets do to you?" *To have Sambandar's audacity, you need not be of divine descent. Have an abiding faith in divinity. Do not get disturbed by diviners. Trust Him, and do what you ought to do. You will surely get what you deserve, for that is reserved for you.*

Having this philosophical and religious bent of mind, Arvin chose to ignore his friend's unfriendly prediction based on his dubious knowledge of the inherent implications of a few lines on his palm. What about Malar? Should he tell her? No. This was not hiding something real. This was, after all, the banter of a blabber.

Certain things were better kept closed than disclosed; while the hiding may not do any harm to any, disclosure may. Discretion was, sometimes, preferable to mindless transparency. He had found Malar very sensitive, very emotional, and very gullible. If told about the barren prediction of the self-styled palmist friend, she would be certainly upset. Arvin took a deliberate decision not to tell Malar anything about the childish prediction of their childless future.

"Thank you, Banerji, for your prediction. Take it from me; these things are not entirely in our hands. In any case, for heaven's sake, please spare Malar of your misfortune-telling"

By the time Malar returned, Banerji's lips were tightly closed. But, he had to open his mouth, inevitably, for relishing the sweets and the coffee.

23

• A Rare Mentor

On his reporting at the HO of the organization, Arvin was posted in a department headed by a manager, Raj. Arvin was expected to report to Raj through an intermediary officer, a lady endowed with vanity. A novice in the institution, though, he was soon entrusted with the task of drafting an important, confidential document containing the organization's comments, clarifications, and explanations in response to a prominent committee's report. It involved reading voluminous back volumes of files in relevant areas, assimilating the factual position and the rationale, and formulating an officially correct response. The first installment of the draft was submitted by Arvin in a fortnight's time and, through "proper channels," reached the table of Raj, gathering practically no additional value en route. As the entire draft reply document was cleared, with practically no changes, at the highest level, Raj was so pleased that he instructed Arvin to report to him directly thereafter. Arvin was extremely happy: *I can now bypass the indifference of the indolent intermediary.* He thus started making his mark in the second institution. Raj was relying more on Arvin for important work. Unfortunately, their association was short-lived.

An orthodox Brahmin, Raj was a staunch vegetarian, unlike some *flexitarians* who are strictly vegetarian at home but ravenously omnivorous outside. Raj had his health spoiled by virtually fasting for days on end, for want of proper vegetarian food, during his rather long tour overseas on an official assignment. When Arvin joined the department, Raj had just returned from abroad. He was suffering from some stomach ailment every now and then. None expected his transfer—an eternal transfer to an ethereal center. One sad day, he suddenly passed at a prime age, plunging everyone in his family and in the department into disbelief and deep grief. In his expiry, the financial institution lost an able, competent, promising executive.

More than a capable officer, Raj was a fine human being—simple, sincere, and unbiased. He had not known Arvin earlier, before the administration placed them together. They hailed from the same region but belonged to different communities. The "time-honored bias" was never honored by him. Raj recognized, encouraged, and groomed Arvin as a good officer. Alas, good things do not seem destined to last long. Arvin lost a confidence-building guide. It was a personal loss. What pained him more, however, was an immediate, insensitive, silly, mundane poser of an aspiring senior colleague. *Who will be promoted into the consequential vacancy?*

24

• "Look Beyond the Boundaries."

"You stay here. Let me go inside; if necessary, I will call you in."
Arvin was disappointed to be left out and to miss the chance of meeting his vice chairman. His boss went inside the chamber. Arvin became an *out-sitting* officer, along with a white-liveried *jamedar* who attended the VC and whose gait and bearing could challenge that of a governor. Arvin found it difficult to avoid the curious stare from the *jamedar.* Arvin entered into rumination.

Arvin never believed in the perfunctory disposal of any file. He knew, of course, the risk involved in being comprehensive. There were always some detractors who would not have any qualms of conscience to dub thoroughness as tardiness and quickness as hastiness. Mostly, the detractors acted out of envy, ambition, or prejudice. You had to either confront and deal or put up with such detractors, literally *leg pullers,* when you went up the career or societal ladder. A firm grip, agility, and some hand-holding luck were essential to maintain the steadiness of your climb up the greasy pole. *Never lose grip.*

Arvin liked to go deep into any matter he had to deal with; he would apply his mind, take an independent view, and stand by it. Once, he had to examine a proposal for expanding the capacity of a mill. In terms of a loan covenant, any expansion project of an assisted corporation required prior written permission or no objection from the lender. A question arose as to whether it needed clearance from the monopolies and restrictive trade practices angles as well. As usual, the matter was referred to the legal department.

The legal language always fascinated Arvin. Whereas the legal opinion was not set out either in Greek or in Latin but in English, albeit with the occasional Latin maxim, the circumlocutory verbiage with ifs and buts and archaic expressions often made it sound Greek or Latin to a layman.

The legal opinion, contained in a multipage note, concluded, "The proposed expansion may need MRTP clearance." No operational official, Arvin had observed, would ever take the trouble or the risk of crossing the boundary into legal grounds. Arvin was always keen to trek beyond his own territory of specialization and peek into other areas as well to broaden his field of knowledge and experience. Arvin examined the issue himself. Marshaling the facts of the case and interpreting the relevant legal provisions, he came to an independent opinion: "The proposal of the corporation will not fall within the mischief of the statutory definition of substantial expansion." His analysis also showed that the expansion would be in the interest of the corporation and its shareholders and would not jeopardize the interest of the lending institution. Sure of his grounds, he submitted his note. The note passed two layers and went to the joint chief manager. The JCM was the operational head, reporting directly to VC. Not inclined to take any chances, he referred the substantial expansion issue back to the legal department, this time directly to the legal advisor. The LA had remarkable professional dignity, undiluted by vanity or affinity. The LA concurred with Arvin. As per the delegation of power, the matter required the VC's approval. The note, therefore, traveled further up. The VC called the JCM for a discussion. The JCM took Arvin along.

That was the first time Arvin was going to meet the VC of the institution; he had been serving for a year now. It was a grandiose chamber with a high ceiling and huge doors.

On the way, the JCM thought aloud on the likely points that might be raised by the VC and got briefed by Arvin. The JCM left Arvin outside the chamber. Even if he had gone along with the JCM inside, he would not have been expected to talk. "I am Sir Oracle, and when I open my lips, let no junior speak" would be the most of the seniors' normal, unwritten, Shakespearian command.

A few minutes passed. Suddenly, a creaking noise brought Arvin out of his rumination. The doors of chamber were nudged open, and the rotund face of the JCM peeped out. He called Arvin in. Momentarily, Arvin recalled his visit to Thirupati. He was among the milling devotees at the doors of the sanctum sanctorum; suddenly, the doors opened ajar. The devotees, including him, were ushered in, and he had the *darshan* of the Lord Balaji. Now, Arvin had the *darshan* of the VC.

The VC studied Arvin and asked him, "Young man, I have seen your note; you have differed from the legal opinion. Can you explain to me your stand?"

Probably, he wanted to test Arvin. Arvin explained in brief but with clarity. The VC listened to him actively, raising a few points for clarification. At the end, he asked Arvin, "Are you a law student?"

"No, sir."

"I do appreciate your initiative and your note. Keep it up."

Arvin did not know what transpired inside the chamber between the VC and JCM before he was called in, nor will it be ever known. Be that as it may, what surprised Arvin was that not a word of appreciation escaped the lips of the JCM. Wait a minute. It was early seventies. The *one-minute manager* was yet to be born.

25

“Who Is the Victim?”

“The insinuation of victimization is exceptionable. I wonder why this unit should be given credit limits.” As if ignited, a bank’s gutsy chairman instantaneously exploded.

In a joint meeting of the bankers organized by Arvin and held to discuss a case of an assisted unit’s dire need for working capital, the JCM who took the chair tried to pin the blame on a particular bank for all the unit’s ills. In his imperious mood, he mentioned that the bank was victimizing the unit through nonprovision of additional credit facilities. He seemed to have totally relied upon the version of the unit’s promoters. The bank’s chairman knew better. To straighten the JCM’s arched brows, the banker reeled off the promoters’ acts of recalcitrance. The JCM was greatly embarrassed, as evident from his blush.

Generally, the approach, attitude, and outlook of a development banker and a commercial banker differ and differ sharply. A development banker supports you to set up a project, and if you face a shower of problems, he lends you an umbrella of protection, too, to save the assets created. Not merely in enlightened institutional interest but in a larger, national interest, he takes a long-range view. In fact, he should, particularly in the case of an honest, sincere, competent entrepreneur. Both development and commercial bankers have their own ethos and constraints. Their organizational objectives, resource mixes, and assets liability maturity patterns dictate their behaviors. It is not that one is pro and the other is anti-developmental. At times, the myopic perspective of some commercial bankers can be frustrating for a distant-visioned development banker. Irrespective of their differing mental models, both must be intent, in their own interests, on seeing their assisted units succeed. The bankers, commercial or developmental, are much more than money lenders. After all, broadly speaking, an FI provides funds to set up a factory and a bank, to run it. And, both shall get their money back with interest. Often, the egocentricity of personalities clouds such relationships. In those days, a developmental banker used to consider himself a banker of superior denomination. The JCM was no exception. In the seventies, who could have dreamed of development banking becoming *epsilons?* Already a quinquagenarian, the JCM would not perhaps live to see the institution reaching its pinnacle of success as a development bank or its subsequent slipping into a nebulous entity. Arvin would sail with the organization on high and low tides, witnessing its rise and slide through quirks of changing circumstances and captaincy, and look forward to a chance of heading and leading it to an exalted state of eminence.

26

• Agony of Leave

Bosses vary in terms of mettle, style, attitude, and habitude. They also play a variety of games. One was punctilious about the spellings of words. In those pre-computer days, the office had no other built-in spell-check facility. No spelling error in any draft letter could slip through his hands. The words used could be wrong but not the spellings. He was also very particular about the submission of a pending list on every Monday morning. The pending list contained the details of fortnight-old references waiting for disposal, with reasons, at the close of business on every Friday. As per the prescribed format, it also indicated the work performed or disposals during the relevant period. This was an excellent executive control system. Computers were unheard of then. The pending lists used to be drawn manually. In some divisions with swarming references, it would take time and occasionally some element of creativity, for the staff to prepare the lists. This particular boss threw tantrums if he did not find the list from any officer on his desk on Monday morning. One must not keep the pending list pending. The pending matters may remain pending; it didn't matter.

There was another boss who would not like anyone going on leave. It was only his prerogative. Even if you availed yourself of casual leave for a day or two, he would become serious. It was best not to talk of a long leave, or his face would become long.

Imagine that you have accumulated leave for six months. You need to go on leave for certain genuine reasons; you apply for a month's leave three months in advance. The boss sits on your leave application for two months. Hardly a month is left. You cannot wait for approval of your leave to book your travel. Because of the summer rush, if you do not reserve your berths in advance, you may not get reservations even on the Bombay-Madras Mail and definitely not on the Dadar Express. Therefore, you have already made your train reservations for you and your family. They are looking forward to visiting your parents at your hometown, some thousand miles away. It takes almost two days to reach there. Your aging father with indifferent health is expecting to see you and your wife and children after a gap of two years. You become anxious. And, you think you will have no problem in getting your leave approved. Hopefully, you inquire your boss about the leave. He turns grim.

"Why do you want to go on leave now?"

You repeat the reason given in the leave application and also elaborate it. He refuses to be reasonable. You further argue.

"I have not gone on leave for two years."

"It is not my fault."

"Last year, you did not recommend my leave on the grounds of exigency of service."

"Leave is not a matter of right, you know." Written rules envisaged as a measure for emergency situations come in very handy for argument's sake.

"Every time I applied for leave, I was asked to defer."

"Okay, defer this time too." This time, queer logic lends a hand.

"Sir, this time I have to go. As I told you, my father is ill."

You expect empathy. Rubbing his nose, as is his wont, the boss advises, "Don't bother about the old man; his time is getting over. Think of your future, your own career."

Now, he rubs your sensibility. Your blood boils. You might start hating your insensitive boss for his outrageous remarks. By dint of self-imposed reticence, you refrain from resorting to verbal violence. You try to reason out your case.

Now, he starts bargaining. "Why don't you take two weeks leave?"

"It takes almost two days to reach my village down south. I haven't been home two years; two weeks will be too short."

"Okay, go for three weeks; if you agree, I will recommend your leave."

Your boss is inconsiderate. And, you are desperate. So, you agree for three weeks' leave. You are asked to modify your leave application accordingly. You do. Your leave is recommended for three weeks as applied for, subject to suitable substitute being provided. The boss is well experienced in well qualifying his recommendation. On paper, he has not approved a leave for a lesser period than asked for, nor has he given any negative recommendation. The proviso, as intended, serves as a potent tool for the administration department to refuse your request of leave on the grounds of nonavailability of suitable substitute. Once again, you get exasperated. You meet your boss and virtually beg him for the leave. This time, he blames the administration department for its unhelpful attitude. You are not amused. You point out his own mischievous condition for the recommendation.

"Oh, I am sorry. These administration guys are . . ."

Now, he takes back the leave letter and modifies his condition by addition of words *if possible*, rings up the in-charge from administration, and tells him to approve your leave without any more fuss. He looks into your eyes to spot a glint of gratitude.

Another two weeks pass. You get edgy. A week before you are scheduled to travel, you get your leave approved. While you had applied for leave three months in advance, the letter reaches your hand three days before your leave starts. Now, you understand the full import of the term *bureaucracy*.

As your leave draws to an end, your father's illness worsens; he suggests that you stay at least for a week more. You seek an extension of leave. Promptly, you get a telegram telling you to report back for duty immediately. Taking the telegraphic advice seriously, you rush back a thousand miles and report for your duty; your boss exclaims, rubbing his nose, "Oh, you have returned! You could have taken one more week. After all, the heavens are not going to fall."

"Why then was I called back?"

"I did not honestly expect you to rush back."

On hearing this, if hell does not break loose, it is because you are not devilish. But, you must be seething inside.

This is what happened to Arvin.

Arvin had to put up with this kind of boss. It was not that this particular boss did not like Arvin. He liked him and had regards for him. Whenever Arvin entered his cabin for any official work, he would set aside whatever work he had on hand and attend to Arvin.

"Arvin, I know you are a busy officer. I do not like to waste your time," he would say with a disarming smile. The best he liked in the boss was his leadership quality, his readiness to assume responsibility. Unlike some, who would read DOP (delegation of powers) line by line and conclude that the required powers rested either up or down and not at his level, this boss would not hesitate to exercise his powers. Once he made a decision, he would stand by it. He used to compliment Arvin openly and generously and, as Arvin was sure, with his tongue in its rightful place, for all his good work.

"If I had the power, I would have promoted Arvin straightaway to general manager," he would openly declare. It would mean skipping a few grades in between. Then, why did he treat Arvin so shabbily in the matter of his leave? Was it purely out of selfishness or arrogance of power or sadistic pleasure? He alone knew. Arvin tried to ignore this eccentricity: He found him a likable personality, a good boss to work with. He did not harass his underlings by playing ping-pong with papers. He was a sharp contrast to one of his peers, who was notorious for tossing the files, passing the buck, shifting the blame, and berating his staff.

27

• "Go to Calcutta . . . Just for Six Months"

After four years in Bombay, Arvin was almost finding his feet in the head office. Malar was getting used to Bombay life; she had picked up conversational Hindi and cultivated a cosmopolitan circle of friends. By this time, the Arvins had two new arrivals—Ram and Pran.

When Ram was born, Arvin told Malar about how Banerji had read his right palm and made the wrong prediction. Both had a hearty laugh, while the child chimed charmingly. Ram started going to a nearby school. Arvin would leave his home at eight in the morning, travel by double-decker for over an hour to reach his office and would return home no earlier than 8:00 p.m. Most working days, which included Saturdays, he would have practically no time to play with his children. The Arvins were steadily fitting into the groove of Bombay life.

Mail from Arvin's brother arrived: Subbiah was not doing well. His peptic ulcer had become acute. All these years, he could not visit his son in Bombay. He found it uncomfortable to stay, for a day, even in a city like Madras, much less in Bombay. Medical treatment could be a good excuse or a point of persuasion to bring him to Bombay. Arvin was trying to convince Subbiah to come while making preparatory arrangements in Bombay for medical treatment.

Arvin did not expect the unexpected. However, the institution's administration wanted his services elsewhere; he got an order of transfer. It was a surprise and not a pleasant one. No doubt, Arvin's was a transferable job, transferable to anywhere in India. He never expected to be transferred to Calcutta. But, if anyone supposed that transfers would not be arbitrary or abrupt, the institution could not be held responsible. HR policy of the government-sponsored organization was akin to divinity—hardly understood but easily felt with no consultations, no articulated policy, and no predictable pattern. There was the least concern for an officer's convenience. The need of administrative exigencies could brush aside any humane consideration for the problems of an officer, howsoever genuine. Any request or representation, reasonable or otherwise, for reconsideration of an impugned order, would be "carefully considered" by the administration, which would invariably regret its inability to accede to such requests without assigning any reasons. It was virtually an automatic response! That was how the administration had been programmed. That was the order of the day and there was no right to information.

The leave-stingy boss was otherwise gentle. When Arvin got the transfer order, he was the one who fought, tooth and nail, against it with the administration—but to no avail. All remained intact—the tooth, the nail, and the transfer order. Having failed in his efforts to get the transfer order canceled, the boss advised Arvin to meet the GM. Too nice a gentleman to intervene in the matter of his own decision, the GM gave Arvin a patient hearing and proclaimed candidly, "Arvin, I won't mind changing the order if you can convince Ramananthan."

If you had ever worked in a government-sponsored organization, you have surely come across a character like Ramananthan. He was a middle-level officer, raised from the ranks, experienced, essentially, in administration. Simple looking but a complicated person and possessor of all-round knowledge of instructions to be selectively quoted to justify whatever decision he made for and on behalf of his seniors, he could harass any of his colleagues. He was a torque, a fulcrum. Remaining fixed, he could rotate people. Ramananthan was, de facto, more powerful than any senior executive. Arvin pleaded with him to reconsider the transfer order.

"Arvin, listen to me; this transfer is for your benefit. As per rules, a casual or leave vacancy in a higher grade for two or more weeks may be filled by temporary promotion of the most senior in the immediate lower grade at the center. In the Calcutta office, your junior has been getting such promotions—frequently—though, of course, without prejudice to your claims. Don't you think this is unfair to you? Now, again, a leave vacancy is arising shortly. The moment you land in the Calcutta office, you will be promoted. That is why we are sending you there—for your benefit."

This kind of temporary promotion, well intended or as union demanded, was at times ridiculous. You'd get promoted to a higher grade in leave vacancy and get reverted on return of the concerned higher-grade officer. A series of such promotions and reversions could make one a laughing stock. An outsider, not familiar with the organization's promotional policy, would wonder what was wrong with the officer. It should be possible, however, to prolong the temporary promotion through an unbroken chain of officers of higher grade going on leave or transfer, either by administration-assisted arrangement or through a path of personal persuasion, for a few months.

"Thank you, Mr. Ramananthan. I do not understand the rationale. The chances of leave vacancy promotion should be more here, in headquarters, than in a smaller office. In any case, I don't mind missing purely leave-vacancy promotions and reversions. You know, I am the senior most. A regular, long-term promotion should come my way soon. Moreover, as I already mentioned to you, I am planning to bring my father here for treatment and need to be in Bombay for some more time. In any case, I have already had four transfers."

"You should get exposure working in a regional office."

"I see. Why don't you, then, transfer me to Madras regional

office; I can arrange for medical treatment for my father in Madras itself more conveniently and at less cost."

"It is not possible."

"Why?"

"There is no vacancy."

"Really? If so, how is it I hear that Mr. Vivek is being sent to Madras?"

"It is a different case. He is being sent on humanitarian grounds."

"What? Are not the same grounds applicable to me?"

Ramananthan then started blandishing, "Arvin, listen. We want an efficient officer in Calcutta. You are the right person. Please go to Calcutta now just for six months. You need not even unpack your luggage. We will accommodate you in Madras at the next available opportunity in a higher grade. Believe me." Ramananthan was shifting and shuffling on the grounds for the transfer. As per the order, Arvin was being transferred to Calcutta on long-term basis.

"Rama, can you please then modify the order so as to say that the transfer is temporary and only for six months?"

A fleeting change in Ramananthan's facial expression was visible.

"No, no. Arvin. The order will remain as it is; if it is modified, you will lose all your long-term transfer facilities."

"That is okay with me."

"No, no. I give you my word. You will be shifted to Madras in six months' time."

Arvin did not believe the doublespeak. His face betrayed his disbelief.

"Arvin, if you don't believe me, meet the GM once again. I am sorry; I am helpless."

Was Ramananthan kind or curt? In any case, Arvin knew the futility of acting on his advice. The GM was a lame duck. Arvin would only become a volleyball. Believing willy-nilly the unbelievable, Arvin reconciled to the reality and agreed to proceed to East India.

Now, Arvin had to convince Malar. He was worried, *Will she be prepared to move to Calcutta, an entirely new city with new surroundings, a new language, and a new culture? Will she argue, resist, quarrel, or understand?* He started mental rehearsing of his lines of convincing explanation:

"Mine is a transferable job. There is no way we can avoid transfers. If not now, we may have to move out after a year or two. It is better to move now. Let us see Calcutta too. This is an opportunity. It is only for six months; six months will fly like six days (he would snap his fingers). But, the only problem is that six months is neither here nor there! It's too short for leased accommodation and too long to stay in a guest house. At the same time, there is no guaranty that the six-month time limit will be strictly adhered to. It may take one or two months more. I cannot leave you and children behind in Bombay. Let us go with bag and baggage and arrange for some temporary-leased accommodations. Hopefully, after six months or at least after a year, we will go to Madras."

There was no need for completing the dialog. Arvin was lucky. Malar was a very reasonable, understanding, and accommodating wife. She understood and stood by him. Arvin knew how some domineering, obstreperous wives could make their husbands' lives miserable in such situations. There was even a reported case of a hysterical wife, opposed to any dislocation, driving her poltroon husband to the brink of suicide. Malar only reminded him of her father's reaction, when Arvin, soon after marriage, got his posting in Bombay. He had then remarked that he would not have agreed to the alliance had he known that his only daughter would be taken as far away as to Bombay. *Now, if he comes to know of the transfer farther away to Calcutta, what will be his reaction?* was Malar's genuine concern. The children were too young to protest.

28

• Patrimony

Tackling the red-clad coolies at Howrah station and piercing through the pell-mell of traffic at the Howrah bridge, the Arvins reached Calcutta city. After a few days at the guest house, they settled, hopefully *pro tempore*, in a leased flat in Alipore. One month went—then two, then three. One needs things like cots, tables, white goods, and so on, to live with reasonable, accustomed comforts. All the wooden crates that came from Bombay had to be unpacked one by one.

"These can be repacked on transfer to Madras."

The Arvins were acclimatizing themselves to Calcutta's environs. Malar was getting familiar with Gariahat market, Rash Bihari Avenue, Komala villas, and Kali temple. She picked up some Bengali words. Ram got admission in the Hindu high school. Cheap transportation—leisurely trams, fast minibuses, rickety private buses, and hand-pulled rickshaws—the low cost of living, respect for women, reverence for Tagore, a fetish of festivities, brahmanic fondness for fish and living faith in an aging ideology, and *Dada-Didi* friendliness were all fascinating. The Arvins gradually grew fond of the City of Joy.

The much-touted leave-vacancy promotion had taken leave of reality. The senior in the higher grade, who was supposed to go on a long leave, yielding the leave vacancy to Arvin, seemed to have had a change of mind or a command or a gentle tug. He cancelled his leave. "If the rules are not made to be broken, they can be rendered inapplicable; or, plainly put, if the preferred beneficiary is denied the chance, none else, including the entitled, shall have the benefit." This appeared to be the local line of thinking. None could be accused of flouting of rules. The question of the promotion, like the vacancy, simply did not arise. The avowed purpose of the transfer was not served at all. It was only after nearly one year that Arvin could get an undeniable chance of promotion.

Six months flew, as expected, quickly. The assurance of the transfer to Madras, too, seemed to have taken wings. *You should not be particular about six months. It may take some time—a month or two more. Wait. Be patient. You are a good officer. You will be encouraged,* Arvin said to himself. Arvin, poor chap, waited and waited. Months passed into a year.

One evening, Arvin got a telegram. It was from his younger brother. "Father serious. Start immediately." The Arvins left for Madras on the next available flight. By the time they reached his native home, Subbiah was semiconscious. He could, however, recognize Arvin. Subbiah was trying to say something; his words were wobbling on the edge of silence. He appeared to be bidding good-bye to all surrounding him. As someone suggested, Arvin lifted his father's head and rested it on his lap. As if he were waiting for this moment, there was cluck, cluck, gurgling noise from his throat. That was the last Arvin heard from his father.

Memories of days with his father, as tears in his eyes, welled up in Arvin's mind.

A touching scene unfolded. As usual, the classes over, Arvin, along with his university student friends, reached the railway station to catch the southbound train from Madras. It was unusually late, running a hundred and twenty minutes behind schedule. A heavy downpour started. The rain continued; there was no sign of the train arriving. Running faithfully, nonstop, was the railway clock! One hundred and twenty was replaced by one hundred and eighty on the notice board. Even one hundred eighty was behind. Suddenly, there was a tintinnabulation—the station assistant struck a hanging rail-piece knell with a small striking iron, announcing the imminent arrival of a train. The train students heaved a boisterous sigh of relief. By the time the fast passenger train slowly reached Sirkazhi, it was 8:30 p.m. The darkened sky was still turbulent, with flashing anger and thundering protestations.

There is no point in waiting indefinitely for the nature's emotion to subside. Arvin started off from the station to his village by bike. Till Semmangudi, there was not much of a problem. It was a tar road with no street lights, but there was some traffic. Beyond Semmangudi, the two-kilometer stretch of partly graveled road was totally deserted. It was dead night. Sepulchral silence rippled by whiffs of wind burst with thunder now and then. There was not even a soul on the road. On the way stood, as a landmark, a sprawling, gnarled banyan tree with drooping branches. Rumor had it that the tree was, of late, a dwelling place for some unknown alien. Normally, a ghost used to be associated with tamarind trees. This particular tenant seemed to have a personal preference for the banyan for reasons best known only to it. The cyclist had to pass this tree without disturbing its tenant. The passersby used to stare at the tree as if a notice board was hanging there with a dire warning: Beware of Ghosts!

In fact, people were scared to pass the place in the night. Arvin remembered the rumor at an inappropriate moment, just when he was nearing the banyan tree. It was densely dark. The dynamo light of the cycle had, with a strange sense of timing, stopped working. It was a new moon day. There was no moon, new or old, in the cloudy sky. During the daytime, he had passed and even rested under the tree with no frightful imagination of any ghastly presence. Now, a chill of trepidation seeped into him. Something appeared in his field of vision. A figure, all white, was waving its outstretched limbs. Could this be the rumored banyan dweller beckoning him? He neither believed nor disbelieved in the existence of ghosts. He believed in God.

If God is near you, the ghost, if any, should flee far away, he surmised. Having come so far, there was no question of flinching. He proceeded, undaunted. His heart went pitter-patter; his lips were chanting divine names.

The ghost should have come down by now if it wanted to meet me or seize me. But, it hasn't. Why? Perhaps it is civil and not evil, Arvin joked inwardly. He had heard that a ghost, a disembodied spirit of an untimely departed person, hovering in transit, might try to right a wrong or take revenge against one who had harmed it in life. To his knowledge, Arvin had not done anything wrong to incur the wrath of anyone, living or dead. Arvin had seen a lifeless body but not bodiless spirit. He had seen the people supposedly possessed by spirits. The villagers were not lacking in superstition; they believed in animism. Invariably, the so-called possessed would be women. He could not understand why. The way in which the possessed women threw unruly, unseemly tantrums was amazing. They called names and abused their husbands and others seemingly revered in normal moments and demanded unimaginable things. Whether it was hysterics or histrionics, none could tell with certitude.

He applied the brake and stood still. *Never lose your nerve.* He stared at the tree. *Better confront the fear face-to-face.* There was no further cognizable action on the part of the ghost, except continual waving of its long limbs. There was a flash in his mind. Arvin remembered having seen, while passing by the tree that morning, that two of its twigs were hanging precariously. Perhaps, the waving limbs were that of the tree. Arvin went ahead. He neared the tree. There was a flash of lightning. Before he heard the following thunder, he could clearly see what amazed him. A fluttering, white rag was draping the two hanging, swinging twigs. A smile of relief broke out on his face. He rode fast past the banyan.

There was yet half a kilometer to reach his home. Suddenly, he saw an orb-like light. As he neared the approaching object, the glowing peck was slowly growing. The seemingly enclosed flickering flame could not be fire. It was coming, dancing, two feet high, legless. A voracious reader, Arvin had read about will-o'-the-wisps, jack-o'-lanterns, fire-spitting phantoms, and the like.

What could this be? Is the banyan dweller returning to its abode? Never lose your grit.

He rode faster. The moving object neared Arvin and stopped. Arvin stopped too. His heartbeat followed suit. A voice emerged from the object. "Arvin!" It was a familiar voice. It was Subbiah with an open umbrella in one hand and a lighted lantern in another. He could not remain at home peacefully. He was worried about Arvin. His fatherly concern, love, and bondage stood there in human form.

The train of nostalgic thoughts continued to roll.

As a school student, Arvin used to assist him in his revenue job. He would accompany his father to the Taluk office during *Jamabandi* time. He had watched Subbiah finalizing accounts and completing various statements and registers, adding, manually, with remarkable speed and accuracy, hundreds of rows and columns of figures of three to eight digits, including two decimals, and after cross tallying, he summarized them into an abstract form—all in blue, pearl-like, beautiful handwriting. He had sheets spread for work and no spreadsheet for aid. Today, if the computers are down, the billing counter of even a grocery shop gets paralyzed. Arvin used to lend his father a helping hand in totaling figures besides attending to him to ease his ulcer pain. The statements were scrutinized—sort of audited—and passed through and carried a series of initials of many hands, the revenue divisional officer, *tahsildar,* upper division clerk of the collectorate, and finally the collector's green signature with the pink rubber stamping of his seal. Almost every year, Subbiah would get a complimentary remark from the collector. Arvin owed his father for his calligraphy and arithmetical skill.

Jamabandi used to be a mela-like affair. A team of officials from the collector's office would camp at the Taluk office. The British legacy of *punga*-pulling arrangements was still in vogue. The awe and authority the revenue officials used to exude impressed and also amused Arvin. He recalled what he read somewhere—Louis XIV's proclamation, "*L'État, c'est moi*," meaning, "I am the state." *Karnams* and *munshifs* of villages tensed up like students appearing for annual exams. Subbiah wanted his son to become a collector. It was a natural, lineal form of expectation. But for the prompt landing on a prime banking job, Arvin would have probably attempted to qualify himself to carry the coveted three-letter acronym at the end of his name. Later in his career, he would have to move and deal with many personified states. He found some of them as administrators par excellence and, surprisingly, the finest of human beings.

Subbiah was a symbol of Spartan simplicity. He was born with a silver spoon, but the spoon was soon pulled out. Thus, he did not inherit much, except for a dilapidated part of a once-sprawling house, which he had to leave in search of a livelihood. "Subbu, never lose your spirit. You will always be successful. See, your ring finger is longer than your index finger," Arvin's grandma used to encourage him. By dint of hard work and frugal living, he rose steadily, earning and saving enough for a decent living, a house of his own, and good educations for his children. "With honest thrift, he held his honor dear." He never wanted to earn just to flaunt nor to flaunt what he earned. He knew the value of each *paisa* he earned and saved. He never believed in spending for nothing. It was from him that Arvin learned that he who saves more, and not he who earns more, could grow more.

Subbiah was a man of courage. Once, Arvin remembered, a knife-wielding drunkard on the road confronted Subbiah in a pitch-dark night with threatening words: “Hey, Subbiah, where are you going? You can’t escape.” None in the village would call him by name. For all, he was *Iyah,* meaning “Sir.” The confronter’s intention was not clear.

Does he want to stab some fear or really a blade into me? wondered Subbiah. *What could be the challenger’s motive? To rob? To kill? There is no enmity between us; probably, he is a dart. The archer may be someone. In any case, never lose your nerve.* He boldly stood, staring into the bloodshot eyes of the hooligan, known for his criminal past.

After a few minutes of deadly silence, the mugger begged pardon with folded hands and went away! Why this dramatic transformation? Subbiah was not a hypnotist. Was it because of his unswerving courage or his unrealized spiritual strength that he could defy the danger? It is not known. But, Arvin always felt, by virtue of his pure thoughts, good nature, and unflinching faith in God, some inexplicable powers had accrued to his father without his realization. Unforgettable were some events.

Subbiah had acquired some wetlands for paddy cultivation on a lease basis. It was a time when the rivers used to flow and rain used to fall, true to the seasons. He used to love to go around the field almost daily to see the growing crop swaying; he used to say that his crops too loved his caring visits. In his view, human presence and caring, like water and fertilizer, nourished the crop. He had no research reports to back up his view, though. The rice paddy crop matured with paddy heads hanging like braided locks. A good harvest was certain.

One foggy morning, when Subbiah went to the field, he was horrified; he could not bear to see the messy condition of the field. Some miscreants had cut the crop. More than being pained at the loss of the yield, Subbiah was anguished at the way in which the field had been plundered and trampled upon; the field looked like an innocent, angelic girl ravished by a bunch of rogues.

“If they wanted some paddy, I would have given it to them. Why should they—whoever they may be—do this atrocious assault on the crop?” Subbiah was seized by anger and anguish.

Days merged into a month. On a sunny day, three chaps rushed to Subbiah and fell at his feet. Subbiah was perplexed. "What is the matter? Get up; tell me."

They confessed. A group of six people, instigated by a person inimical to Subbiah for no reason other than envy, had done the act of vandalism. Three of them had, soon thereafter, been afflicted by a strange ailment of serious nature, one by one. The remaining three were scared. Their apprehension was that Subbiah had cursed them. So illiterate and superstitious were the villagers that they blindly believed in witchery, and there were enough quacks to exploit them. The three culprits had also been misled to think that Subbiah had some such thing done. Subbiah patiently told them that he had not cursed them or done anything to harm anyone.

"It is true. I was pained. But, I have not cursed anybody. I have not done anything to harm you. It is His Will; you reap as you sow. You have now realized your mistake. Do not do such heinous things in the future. Pray to God. Nothing untoward will happen to you."

Hesitatingly, and still plagued by fear, the three musketeers went back. Another three months passed. Nothing untoward happened to them. The other three, too, recovered. This episode had a beneficial impact. Miscreants stopped meddling with Subbiah's affairs. They believed that Subbiah had some mystical powers. In fact, Subbiah had no such power whatsoever. It was only his righteous energy.

Subbiah was sustained by and respected for his lofty values, which constituted the patrimony Arvin relished.

29

• A Jewel Lost

An outline of a distant, hazy figure through fog or mist? A refection in the dust-covered mirror? A painting in jaded color? A vague image in memory? Yes. The recent bereavement of one of the irreplaceable pair kindled the memories of the other lost in childhood—his mom. A rigorous rubbing of memory clears the picture fairly well in the mental frame: She was a short lady, dark but pleasant looking, with silky hair hanging long enough to touch her knees, the hair braided and adorned with jasmine. She had fluttering eyes and an innocent face with a vermilion dot on the forehead. Her nose was neither sharp nor blunt, both sides sparkling with a small diamond stud each. Her ears were adorned with slightly bigger studs, studded with diamonds. Around her neck, dangled a *thaali*—a thick, gold chain with a typical gold pendant designed for Saivites—tied, with three knots, by her husband at the time of the wedding, partly hidden by her sari. Unhidden by the sari, her middle toes exposed silver rings. The vermilion dot, the *thaali*, and the toe rings were all symbols of marital status, warning signals for wandering eyes and talismans for warding off evils.

These symbolic appendages had sentimental value. While her forehead and toes might be freed of the adornments, briefly for inevitable reasons like bathing or changing, the *thaali* would never be removed, even momentarily, in fear of consequent harm to the husband. It always hung from the neck of a married lady, except in the event of the death of the husband or the wearer, whichever happened earlier. Divorce was a rarity. The sentiments were reflective, at once, of superstitious beliefs and the bondage of love.

The lady under description belonged to a different age. For her, *thaali* was sacred. She was not daunted by conflicting cultural demands. She was in her early thirties. There was nothing to show outwardly that she had already mothered four children. She had white teeth, a warm smile. Her sweet voice did not exactly stutter; she had nervous-type rapid speech. She was a nice, simple, tradition-bound lady; a humble, husband-fearing housewife. For her, her mother-in-law was like a mother. She was so emotionally bonded, her mother-in-law was, in fact, more than a mother, rather a protective godmother. She was lucky to have such a loving mother-in-law during a time when mothers-in-law, as a class, used to be considered as monsters-in-fact. Her responsibility would be virtually over with the delivery of a baby; the entire job of raising the child, except for lactation, would be willingly assumed and affectionately performed by the mother-in-law. Grandma's oil massaging and bathing a child, gently cradling it facedown on her stretched or bent, bare knees amidst incessant, lyrical talking or prattling with the crying-in-a-moment and giggling-in-another child, and lullabying the baby into sleep—all with oozing fondness—would be a sight to see. She did not need any orientation classes for rearing a grandchild. This was the self-assumed, devoted role of a mother-in-law in a joint family system in bygone years. It cannot be compared to the haplessly dependent and still-too-useful-to-be-consigned-to-an-old-age-home, widowed mothers-in-law babysitting, more particularly, diaper changing, among other chores as desired, directed, or demanded covertly or overtly, as compensation for accommodation in the selfish nuclear family system of today.

One evening, a few months after delivery of her fourth child—the child was the third alive, its predecessor having predeceased—he was sleeping peacefully in a sling. Kayal was serving dinner. She was placing a vegetable outside the plate on the floor. Was she careless, inattentive, idiotic, indifferent, or insolent? Scolded by Subbiah, she was upset but kept quiet. Her moroseness should have aroused some concern. It aroused anger instead. The incident was attributed to her utter carelessness. The same thing happened the next day. Her quick-tempered husband slapped her.

Mother-in-law spontaneously intervened and admonished her son for his rudeness. Grandma said to her son, "How many times have I told you not to lose your temper?"

In a tender tone of a caring mother, she asked Kayal what the problem was. Then came out, with a torrent of tears, Kayal's genuine problem. Oh, God! Everyone was shocked. Her statement was an eye-opener. She was losing her eyesight or, rather, turning night blind.

Now, they recalled some incidents, one after another, how of late, she was seen to be groping in darkness. Her husband regretted his having been blinded by anger. She was taken to the nearby town for medical checkup. The doctor's diagnosis was this: "Jaundice, neglected, but nothing to worry about. She needs immediate medical attention."

A volley of questions elicited her confession. She had had this ocular problem for quite some time. Her peripheral vision was diminishing. She had noticed a pale yellow tinge in the whites of her eyes. She had frequent indigestion and was losing appetite. First, she ignored these symptoms. Later, she brushed aside the symptoms as probably due to excessive heat. Then, her timidity prevented her telling anyone of her vision problem.

Everyone chided her for her foolishness. Treatment was started immediately. She traveled back and forth between her mother's home at the town and her own home for treatment, with her baby being taken care of by her mother-in-law. A fortnight here and a fortnight there—her health was oscillating like the waxing and waning moon, alternating between recovery and relapse. Her health was deteriorating fast. A doctor is not divine. The doctor, at last, referred the patient to a specialist for further treatment, throwing up his hands. "Now, it is all in the hands of God."

Whatever the root cause or medical treatment, her jaundice worsened. Her liver was badly damaged. With the bile flow to the liver blocked, the bile entered her bloodstream; her cornea was discolored, and her skin started turning yellow. Her abdomen began to swell. She was aware of her failing health. Just like any other typically traditional Indian woman, she would have preferred—and had, in fact, expressed, more than once, her desire—to predecease her husband. But, still in her thirties, she was not prepared now to succumb to her sickness; she had years to go and sons to rear—two of them too young, two years apart and one still crawling. She wanted to see them grow into well-educated, smart men. Already, her relations envied her for her three children, all boys in a row. How long could her mother-in-law, a sexagenarian, be expected to be around? After her, who would take care of her boys? Her husband might marry again. What about her children? Would they get a *loving* mother? *Step* might step in to replace *loving*. She did not want to exit this world so early, leaving her children in the lurch. She longed to live longer.

Given up by the doctor, she was in her deathbed at her mom's place. Her two school-going kids, pulled out from their running classes, were by her side—one eight years and the other six; the crawler, sleeping innocently, peacefully in a cloth swing. She was panting uncomfortably; she realized she was losing her life. The boys were too innocent to realize the visiting misfortune. Her speech was incoherent. She took the hands of her mother-in-law and her children and entrusted to her their future with these parting words, uttered almost into the ears of her mother-in-law: "You please take care of my kids." The stress on the word *you* was significant. As if it were not enough, she added in a tone soaked in pain and disdain, ". . ." What she uttered was almost inaudible. The people sitting or standing around her bed did not properly hear her barely audible, dying declaration. Even if heard, it would not have been fully understood. Even her mother-in-law could not realize the significance of the contemptuous parting remarks. She would learn it soon, of course.

A poor, nay, pure soul left this world forever, having made the last deposit of her remaining worldly trappings, inevitably, at her mom's home and reposing faith in her mother-in-law to take care of her children and husband. Too young to comprehend fully the misfortune that befell them, the boys cried. The first two, vaguely understanding the loss of their mom, and the crawler were blubbering for no obvious reason. The doleful husband Subbiah had been transformed into a crying child. His realization—of the value of what he had just lost, of his own folly of not having recognized it when in possession, of the void created, of the responsibility left on his shoulders, and of the meek suffering of the soft goodness at the hands of his quick temperament—melted into dripping repentant, mournful tears.

The jewel lost was Mrs. Subbiah, now late Kayalvizhi.

30

• "Don't Trust . . ."

The meaning of the parting words of Kayal—don't trust—began to emerge. Subbiah learned of the happenings during Kayal's treatment period. Six months vanished since she started periodical visits to the town for treatment. *Only months?* As any typical south Indian lady, she was fond and in possession of valuable gold jewelry. Every time she went to the town, she wore, heavily, strings of jewelry. She returned, every time, considerably lightened. She would have unburdened most of her gold ornaments at her mom's home. This periodical transfer–deposit was going on unnoticed. Over a period of sickly months, her entire treasure, save the bare minimal, daily wearing pieces—a nose stud, a pair of ear studs, and her *thaali*—had changed location. *Or, hands?*

She had been persuaded, very gently, of course, to bring her jewels in installments so that they could be remade on current patterns. "When you come next time, bring some more ornaments; by then, your first lot will be ready, duly remade, and you can take them back." Gullible as she was, she fell for the prospects of having all her ornaments thus redesigned. The flow of valuables, however, turned out to be unidirectional. She did not doubt the anticipatory action of a person, thought to be a loving mother. Shouldn't *loving mother* be a redundant expression? Yes, of course, it's a rule. But, no rule, alas, is exception free.

She was losing her eyesight but gaining insight into some mortals' immortal behavioral pattern. Is not a mother a mortal too? So simple, so innocent, so ignorant, and so blind, she had not donned even a milligram of doubt in her mind about the trickery being played on her. She failed to see the emerging pattern in what she was being persuaded to do. She knew her health was failing; she knew not that even maternal love could fail. She herself was a mother, and her love for her children was undying. So, would be her own mother's love for her, she supposed. How simple was she? Dying presupposes living.

Her mother and sibling had spotted her approaching end at the very beginning of the treatment itself, hence, the trick and the treat! They had tricked her, thinking that she would never know. The jewels' designs would be visible. But, when the innocent lady understood the invisible design, it was too late.

Months followed for Kayal. Her jewels were not returned, remodeled, or unchanged, to her family. The mourning period was not the reason. In any case, it was too long. A year passed. There was not a word about the jewels. Veiled references were in vain. Polite requests were repelled by impoliteness. Storming questions were raised; some were with thundering logic indeed. "What jewels?" As if realizing the futility of outright denial, the questioner modified the question: "Why do you need them?"

"For her children's future."

"They are too young."

"They have to grow; they need to be given good educations."

"Where is the guarantee that you will use them for that purpose?"

"Those are our assets—both the jewels and the boys. It is my responsibility to protect them."

"Let them become major and then stake a claim."

"Look here, the jewels are ours. Better hand them over to us."

"No. We won't give them to you. What can you do? Do whatever you can."

The import of the parting advice of Kayal was now glaring. The dialog was inconclusive and unyielding. Nature, too, was furious. A cyclonic storm lashed the coastal areas of Tamil Nadu. Many parts were isolated. All means of communication were disrupted. It took a few weeks for normalcy to come to rule again. The dialog resumed. A mediator intervened. Unilaterally chosen by the custodians or, rather, possessors of the jewels, he was too embarrassed to be impartial. The mediation had no effect. The designs were now unmistakably clear. If not recovered now, they would become NAA (nonavailable assets) to the detriment of the interests of the children. Subbiah was driven to think of going to court.

"Okay. We shall meet in the corridors of a court."

None from a respectable family liked to step into a court, even as a witness. The mediator came in again. A compromise was suggested.

"We will pay you the value of jewels."

To cut short the disgusting dispute, Subbiah accepted an arbitrary valuation. Before handing over the amount, he was asked to sign a letter. It was a letter of renunciation of any more claims to properties, or any dues from, or relationship whatsoever with, Kayal's parental family. It was a sad moment of family delinking.

The paternal grandma did not want the relationship to end, despite whatever happened; she wanted it to continue with no rancor and with no materialistic expectations. She did not want the children to develop any kind of animosity or ill feelings. The matter was never discussed in the presence of the boys. Arvin came to know of the jewels of contention, accidentally, much later, from an external source and was corroborated by Grandma, with an unequivocal advice: "Forget it, and concentrate on studies. Never lose your grace."

Frugal and prudent, Subbiah never squandered this money. He was waiting for a good investment opportunity to come by. A peregrine falcon was also waiting to swoop in for a grabbing chance.

One dusty, sunny evening, the neighbor dropped in, casually, with a smiling face.

"How do you do, sir?" The neighbor was much younger than Subbiah. He was a school dropout, chasing eluding employment.

"Not bad. Come in."

Grandma served aromatic filtered coffee. The coffee, it seemed, stimulated the articulation of the serious purpose of the casual visit.

"I need some money; I do not want to borrow from any Kuppan or Suppan."

"Good policy. Keep it up."

"I wonder what you will be doing with the money you have now."

The neighbor, it appeared, was well informed and ill willed. He came to the point directly, without beating about the bush. He was aware of the bird nestling inside the bush. And, he wanted to catch it quietly.

"I need it for my children's educations."

"Come on; you are not going to spend it all now for education. I will return it in installments or whenever you need it."

"Mmm," Gentility choked Subbiah's throat.

"If you want, I will pay some interest."

Magnanimous! In fact, the charitable neighbor did not really want Subbiah to want any interest. As was well known, it was against his principles to pay any interest on the amount he borrowed. On the other hand, Subbiah never preferred either to borrow or to lend. In any case, he never lost caution.

"Sorry. I propose to invest the money safely somewhere."

Immediately, the neighbor's tone changed. He had come well prepared with a contingency plan. "In that case, why don't you buy a house? Just three houses from here in the very same street?"

The proposition was interesting. For one thing, the house did not belong to him. It belonged to his aunt, an old widow, half blind and fully deaf, with whom his relationship was not that cordial. The nephew had an eye on the property or, rather, on its prospective sale proceeds. For another, the lonely lady would not like to lose her only dwelling. Subbiah was not so frail as to fall for such a perfidious proposal. He rejected the proposal outright.

"I am not interested."

"I thought, as a neighbor, you would be helpful."

"I am sorry; I cannot help you now."

This time, the neighbor's face changed. Like a borrowed sum, his smile vanished. He left the place, terribly annoyed, muttering some inaudible invectives. His subdued threat, however, was audible as he hurried away, "Let me see how peacefully you live here."

For the next few days, he was not on speaking terms with Subbiah. One day, Subbiah overheard his wily neighbor talking to someone: "I tried my best. But, let me tell you, the fellow is too shrewd."

Subbiah's house and his neighbor's were like Siamese twins, one being mirror image of the other, conjoined by a common wall and covered by a common tiled ceiling. The inside *mutram* (courtyard), partitioned by a wall, was open to the sky. One midnight, the noise of a stone hurtling down the roof woke up Subbiah; more stones followed. Someone was pelting stones from outside, aiming at Subbiah's roof. Subbiah opened the door and went out on the street to catch the pelter. There was nobody. Maybe, the screeching noise of the door opening had alerted the miscreant. The petrous drops continued for a few nights. The neighbor volunteered his help to fight the hooliganism. When Subbiah mentioned that he had already reported the matter to police, his neighbor's face turned stony. The lie stopped the stone fall.

31

• Face It

Arvin fast-forwarded the rewound memory. Subbiah's fixed tenure on this Earth came to an end on the due day. No matter what Arvin did or didn't do, his dad's end could not have been deferred or averted. Still, Arvin did not help nursing a guilty feeling that he could not arrange for better medical treatment for his father at Bombay or at Madras, nor could he attend him during his last days. If only Ramananthan had been a little helpful, he would have had the satisfaction of having served as a dutiful son too. Even now, Ramananthan could help. Arvin sought transfer to Madras for a year or two so that he could take up the mantle of the eldest son in the family.

October was a popular month because of *Durga Puja*-related festivities and consecutive holidays. In an office, the first half of a year, prepuja, was devoted to cultural program preparation, and the second, postpuja, was for performance evaluation.

Octobers rolled by. One *Durga Puja* passed, then another, followed by one more and one more. *Durga Puja* came and went religiously. Years rolled by continuously. Yet, Arvin was stuck firmly. No transfer was in sight. It did not take much time for Arvin to carve out a niche for himself in the office despite all odds against him. As the years, his bosses, too, rolled by; one after another came and went, but Arvin remained as the poetic brook.

The Calcutta office proved to be somewhat different. Arvin virtually had a cultural shock. He had been forewarned: "Do not irresponsibly blame anyone for coming late. Blame it, if you so wish, on tram, bus, lift, or something else. Unions here are unique. Typically, there are three. Whether and when they're in conflict or in unison, one can never make out. Similarly, who leads whom, none can get a lead."

Even some bosses, Arvin found, were enigmas. One was typical. He would be mostly out of the office during working hours, attending meetings and meeting people. Just in time would come his instructions for officers to wait for him after office hours. Two or three hours after closing time, he would barge in, vivaciously saying, "Okay, guys, you may go. We shall see tomorrow." For faithful but frustrated staff, this would be another such day. He thoroughly enjoyed his aristocratic style. He also reveled in what other bosses would try to keep out—trade union issues. He proved to be an ache for the head of the organization.

With one more promotion in due time, Arvin became a manager. In other words, he joined a class supposed to be part of the management. That everyone of the organization, irrespective of cadre, is engaged in its management was not inculcated or internalized. That all managers are workers and all workers are managers was an unheard-of concept.

There seemed to be constant endeavors to search for issues and, if none were found, to imagine some. From late marking of late comers to nongranting of overtime for nonperformed or even nonexistent work, from the quantum of food served at lunchtime to a mysterious appearance of a cockroach in the food; from the unceremonious shifting of a clerk to a new desk though in the same building or even floor to a lift going out of order unannounced—anything could emerge as an urgent, life-and-death issue to confront the management, to *ghero* a marked official. If not tackled tactfully, the issue could translate into a gate meeting and, eventually, escalate into a wider industrial action.

Anything new proposed ran the risk of being opposed. When handheld calculators were sought to be provided to staff, incredible were the objections raised even by some officers. "The staff is accustomed to calculations by hand-operated FACIT machines. The keys in the electronic calculators are so feather touch that the staff may get the wrong results—so also, if the battery gets discharged. How will you fix accountability? With the instrument being small and some staff being aged, ocular error could occur while pressing the keys. The calculators may be stolen, and so on, and so on." Taking a calculated risk, calculators were introduced. The calculation did not go wrong. The calculators were accepted—in the course of time. And, better models were soon demanded.

Committee meetings would demand preparation of hundreds of sets of papers, each set containing a good number of pages. First, a paper on a subject would be draft-typed, and after its approval, it would be stenciled, and then copies were taken. Despite all preplanning efforts, papers would get prepared at the eleventh hour. Stencil cutting by typists took time or, rather, overtime. As an efficiency-enhancing measure, on Arvin's suggestion, an electronic stencil-cutting machine was installed. It was possible because Arvin's current dynamic boss was receptive to new ideas. The electronic stencil cutter would not be cutting for long in this environment; it lapsed into coma in a predictable fashion.

A misplaced fear, or a myopic vision, or a mental block takes time to cure. None could then have possibly visualized that this office would be totally computerized one day.

Today, it is.

32

• Peace Besieged

"We will not allow you to leave the office now."

Once, in a gate meeting-less afternoon, Arvin got a phone call that his child had suddenly taken ill. He was coming out of his office, with his briefcase, to go home early to take his child to a doctor. A bunch of nonofficer staff members gathered and surrounded him, blocking his way, demanding immediate discussion on certain issues that seemed to have popped up from nowhere. Arvin sought to know their real issues, if any, so that they could be discussed to find a solution.

The issues were as silly as their behavior. In fact, they were nonissues. Still, Arvin assured that the issues could be discussed the next day and resolved. The agitated staff members appeared to be keen in blocking his way rather than finding a way out for their perceived problems. No amount of persuasion or cajoling by Arvin was of any use. The then observed etiquette, in the context of frequent *gheroes* of some officers in key positions by union members, that demanded that officers show their solidarity and come to the rescue of any beleaguered colleague. However, Arvin observed that all his officer colleagues were minding their desks and working with unusual devotion. None of them seemed to be inclined to commit any dereliction of duty by bothering about a besieged colleague.

One of the obstructionists advanced menacingly, with clenching fists and grinding teeth, spewing a string of invectives. Holding his briefcase and his tongue, Arvin kept his cool and stood calmly. Two staff members, senior-most age wise, physically restrained the advancing Denis. The crowd parted; Arvin waded his way out.

The next day, someone from the staff, not Denis, apologized privately in Arvin's office. A few officer colleagues feigned ignorance of what happened on the previous day, and some shed copious verbal tears. They could put a crocodile to shame.

A report was sent to the headquarters for taking necessary disciplinary action. Was it dispatched, inadvertently, to a black hole?

Later, Arvin was told that the incident was too trivial to be taken serious note of. He learned of what happened when a senior executive had a much worse experience.

One day, when a very senior officer was in his all-wooden office in an upper floor in HQ, a boxer-like stranger entered without knocking on the door. His target was not the door.

"Are you Bharanidhar?"

"Yes, please. May I know your good name?'

The executive stood up from his seat and courteously extended his hand for a handshake. The visitor pulled the extended hand and punched Bharanidhar in the face. Having delivered the forwarded message, the courier coolly left, leaving the officer in a state of stupor.

Many surmised it was an internally induced external assault. Speculation and words of sympathy were floating around for a few days. Then, everyone forgot the incident, except the officer carrying on his nose and in his psyche an indelible imprint made by the metallic wristlet of the hard-hitting intruder.

When he heard this incident, Arvin felt his nose involuntarily. He felt happy that it was undented.

33

• Games Some Juniors Play

"May I come in, sir?"

"Please come in."

"I am Guru."

"Glad to meet you, Mr. Guru."

"It's my pleasure to work with you."

"Thank you."

"You are new to this place. Be careful. You cannot trust . . ." Looking around, Guru continued, in low tone, "the local people. But, you can count on my support."

Arvin heard his loud inner voice, *Beware of this sly guy!* Before long, the guy's character was revealed. Reasonably intelligent but unreasonably arrogant, the officer Guru seemed to be suffering from a virulent attack of some virus, which was later identified as inferiority complex. Though relatively a fledgling, he could not come to terms with his working under Arvin. In his own exaggerated opinion about himself, he was "far more experienced." He would not tolerate his assumed authority being subsumed by a *Madrasi.* Such ego clashes were not uncommon, but normally, they would be kept within the limits of decency. Here, Guru would not recognize, much less respect, such limits. The cold war was prolonged and multipronged.

In those nascent years, credit proposals even for small amounts had to be individually scrutinized and sanctioned. Instead of submitting files as and when he completed scrutiny, he used to accumulate hundreds of files almost for a whole week and then transpose the hillock of files to Arvin's table at the end of office hours on Friday. His motive, as could be deduced, was to irritate, inconvenience, and test him, forcing unquestioned sanction of all proposals. Whatever it might be, Arvin could not object to his clearing a heap of files. He could probably ask why he had not submitted even a single file for a whole week, but Guru would have umpteen reasons in his armory.

One Friday, having done his dumping act, Guru watched Arvin for any immediate reaction. There being none, Guru came to Arvin's office and nudged open its door with a giggle, "May I come in, sir?"

"Please come in."

"I have submitted a number of files today; some are very urgent. I am sorry that now you have your hands full. For you, this is child's play. In any case, I have scrutinized all of them very carefully; you may blindly sign them."

"Thank you, Guru; you have done your job. Now, let me do mine."

Arvin sat late on that day and worked almost the entire weekend, studied all the files with extra care, sanctioned many, raised queries on some, and rejected a few; he also recorded critical comments on the perfunctory scrutiny of a few cases. Guru did not expect this. After a few days of exchange of notings and counter notings, Guru realized his folly of throwing a noose of records around his neck. He started waving the white flag. He was striving to placate Arvin. "I am sorry, sir, if I have offended you in any manner. Let us be friends from now on."

Is the flag really white or grey? Arvin was prepared to take him at face value. The face was foxy. "Okay, Guru, I am glad if you have realized your folly."

34

• Froth of Leadership

"Arvin, what do you know about the bloody law?"

In Calcutta, as in Bombay, Arvin, by virtue of his capability, affability, and reliability, endeared himself to all his bosses, one after another. Though with some, it was not a cordial beginning; they had been, as it transpired later, either misled or mistaken. Some verbal duels were enjoyably professional. Once, there arose between Arvin and a boss, in the early days of their association, a difference of opinion on an issue—a matter of interpretation of a legal provision. Sharp in mind and sharper in tongue, Saul was sarcastic. He proclaimed his own knowledge of the bloody law.

Arvin was also acrid but polite, "Sir, I also know the bloody law."

No daggers were drawn, yet the law became a bleeding victim. Normally, in a government-sponsored organization, any other boss would have taken it amiss. As a rule, a boss should be regarded as omniscient. Disagreement with a boss could be construed as no less than disobedience. You had to agree willy-nilly with your boss that crows are white. It may be a white lie or the boss may be colorblind; it didn't matter. You readily agreed, and you could chuckle later. It was the official dharma. Arvin violated the dharma.

Though an awe-inspiring executive, Saul was a sporting person too. "Okay. Let us bet a bottle of beer." Saul threw down the gauntlet with a spirit of sportsmanship. Arvin, a nondrinker, picked it up with all humility.

"Okay, sir. Agreed."

This incident was soon totally forgotten.

Arvin provided good support to Saul for accomplishing significant developmental work, whether it related to reenergizing a potent but dormant forum or establishing of a new organizational outfit. Arvin enjoyed working with Saul.

One Sunday evening, Arvin received a call from Saul. "Arvin, please join me for dinner at my place at 7:30 p.m.; bring your wife too."

"It will be our pleasure."

When the Arvins went to Saul's place, there was another guest already present. Bossy Saul was a cozy host. Pleasantries over, friendly conversation ensued. Saul told the other guest about the divergence of opinion between him and Arvin on the interpretation of a particular legal provision, leading to the bet. He also told him of his interpretation and Arvin's.

"Sanjay, you are the legal advisor. Tell me who is right."

The LA smiled. After a minute of studied silence, Sanjay asked, "Arvin, do you like beer?"

Arvin admired the legal advisor's polished manner of pronouncing his verdict. Suddenly, Saul left the place. *Was he upset?* After all, he was Arvin's boss; how could he tolerate losing face in front of his junior? Arvin was uncomfortable. Saul returned in a few seconds, his face wearing a beaming smile and his hand clutching a bottle of London Pilsner. "Here is the bet you have won!" Two more LPs were brought by a servant.

"Cheers!"

"Cheers!"

"Cheers!"

Arvin won the bet and lost his teetotaler-hood.

Here is a boss who engages his junior in an intellectually stimulating debate, does not mind his junior's disagreement, challenges him, throws a bet, refers the point of difference to a third person—an expert in the line—accepts his verdict, and honors his bet. Wow! Arvin relished the froth of Saul's leadership quality. Dinner over, the guest left for the guesthouse. Arvin and his wife got ready to leave.

"Arvin, it is eleven-thirty now; how will you go?"

"We will take a cab."

"Arvin, wait a minute."

Saul went inside and, in a minute, a man emerged out with him. Saul came out with his Fiat's key.

"Come on. Let us go; I will drop you and come back."

Arvin was touched by Saul's gentility.

Saul's personality stood him apart. He was dynamic and heroic, witty and gutsy, with fire in his belly. He carried much higher responsibility than anyone of his age and position normally did. He had the qualities of a good leader. Possibly, he would have turned out to be a successful captain of the institution, capable of sailing it through the storm of changing paradigms that was to brew. But, the institution was not so destined.

35

• A Dictator

The office got a new leader, Kirmani, whom Arvin had seen but not worked with before. When the change of guard took place, Arvin was far away in a neighboring state on an inspection duty. At the site of inspection, Arvin had a phone call. Was it a telephone receiver or telescopic gun? His ear was pierced by a volley of firing questions.

"Mister Arvin, how do you think of your self—an executive director or a chief executive?"

Arvin did not think it necessary to clarify the obvious—that is, he was neither. Instead, he asked, "Why, sir?"

"I am told that you have taken a secretary along with you."

His shocking tone sounded as if Arvin had eloped with a pretty secretary.

"You must know that even very senior officers are not entitled to this privilege."

"Sir, let me explain why I was allowed—"

"I do not want to hear any of your explanation."

In dictatorial tone, Kirmani ordered, "Send back the secretary immediately."

"Okay."

The phone went mute.

Arvin sent back the secretary, a middle-aged man, by the next available train.

On completion of inspection, Arvin came back to office. The first visitor to Arvin's office was Guru.

"Sir, how was your tour?"

"It was fine, thank you."

"Our new boss seems to be prejudiced against you; he is damn angry with you for taking a secretary with you. I have spoken well about you. I told him that you are a competent officer. You can dictate a report, which many even very senior officers can't do. In any case, be careful with him. Better not go to meet him until he calls you."

"Thanks, Guru."

The cat itself let it be known, unwittingly, that it was inside the bag.

Arvin called on Kirmani without waiting for his call. The moment Arvin entered Kirmani's office, a verbal faucet was turned on. A stream of accusations flowed. It was obvious that some one—*who else other than a sincere friend*—had prejudiced Kirmani's mind with malicious misinformation.

"Can I talk now?"

"No, I don't want to hear anything."

"Please hear me. None should be condemned unheard. Obviously, you have heard something against me from someone. Please listen to anyone. In fact, you should. As the head of the office, you should keep your eyes and ears open but not selectively. In all fairness, you should listen to me as well. After hearing me and watching me for some time, you may form your own opinion about me. Till then, please do not jump into any conclusions."

The weather improved; the shower stopped.

"Let me first clarify the secretary issue. I do my job in all sincerity, not in anticipation of any approbation nor in fear of admonition. I do it for my satisfaction to the best my ability. I am not enamored of any privileges. Inspection of the institution used to take six to eight weeks, and drafting the report took another four. The process of scheduling and conducting an inspection, then submitting of a draft report with local editing and approval by the head office, then forwarding it to the institution concerned all used to take as long as a year, if not more. Before the institution could take appropriate action on the findings of one inspection, the next would become due. Such inspections do not serve their intended purpose. Mr. Saul wanted to squeeze the process. We discussed. I promised to halve the time for inspections and report drafting, provided administrative services were made available. Mr. Saul agreed. Our view was that administrative services should be counted as a facilitating tool rather than a privilege or a status symbol."

Then, he gave a brief account of the office atmosphere.

"I am sorry, Arvin; I didn't know the background."

The cloud cleared; sunshine started.

"May I come in, sir?"

No sooner had Arvin returned to his office than Guru presented himself.

"Welcome."

"Did Kirmani say anything? How was his mood?"

Arvin looked into Guru's eyes. "You seem to be very curious."

Discomfort was discernible in Guru's face.

"Guru, will you please submit your pending list?"

The message was clear. Guru left the office for his work station.

Many incidents took place thereafter. Kirmani was impressed

with Arvin's devotion to duty and conscientiousness. The Arvin–Kirmani relationship grew cordial. Guru was rather disappointed but not disillusioned. He was convinced that he must change his strategy. *Whatever he wanted to do, he must do under the cover of anonymity without directly antagonizing Arvin.* He did not realize, however, that the cover might prove to be flimsy. Occasionally, Guru would come and talk to Arvin sweetly with a flattering flavor. As Arvin could guess intuitively, Guru would have planted somewhere some mischief that he thought a bombshell. The bomb would, however, fizzle out. Repeatedly, egregious Guru made vicious attempts against Arvin. And, he failed repeatedly.

36

• Blessing in Disguise

"Mr. Arvin, Naganathan has come from Pune; there is a puja at my flat this evening at seven. Please come with your family," invited Bowmic, a junior colleague of Arvin.

Arvin had no other engagements on that day. There was no need to ask for the details of the puja. It would be spiritually good to attend any puja, so long as it was not performed by dubious swamijis. Arvin was a believer; so was his wife. Bowmic's flat was in the same building where Arvin lived. Arvin had heard about Bowmic's spiritual experience. He, therefore, readily agreed.

At 6:30 p.m., when the Arvins were getting ready to go to the puja, the door chime rang. Chatterjee dropped in unannounced. The Arvins were discombobulated. *Will Chatterjee be in the way of our attending the puja? May be. But, decency demands that a guest should be entertained.*

"Aashoon."

Chatterjee liked coffee.

"*Kaafi kaabe?*"

Malar offered him some snacks and a cup of south Indian coffee. After a little general conversation, Chatterjee poured his heart out: His wife had left him or, rather, his home a few days back in a huff over a silly dispute. Her whereabouts were not known. Chatterjee was nearing retirement; at this age, estrangement with his wife was an extreme embarrassment for him and his three grown-up children. His nosy neighbors had already started spreading juicy rumors. They seemed to have been starved of vicious gossip for a long time. Now, they were delighted. The moisture in Chatterjee's eyes was visible through his specs.

"I am sorry, Chatterjee; don't worry. Never lose heart. I believe and you believe in God. Trust Him or Her. Pray. Everything will be all right soon. It is just a matter of coincidence that, right now, we are going to Bowmic's place for a puja. Why don't you join us?" Without any hesitancy, Chatterjee agreed to accompany the Arvins. On the way, Arvin narrated to Chatterjee what he heard about a Bowmic–Naganathan episode.

"Bowmic and Naganathan were colleagues in their previous employment. Naganathan was a devotee of Lord Balaji of Thirupathi. Every Saturday, he performed a puja at his home at Pune, worshiping a framed picture of the deity. The picture was cleaned, sandal paste and *kunkumam* affixed, and garlands of flowers adorned the frame. His wife prepared edible offerings to Balaji. For about thirty minutes, Naganathan would recite prayers. Then, the offerings, *prasad*, were distributed to those present. This he did week after week without fail and with full faith. Over time, some occult powers accrued in him. He started reeling out predictions at random to those present. The word spread by mouth. The weekly puja attracted many visitors with or without invitation. Some visitor-devotees would bring their own preparations for offer to the god. Bowmic was one of them. Initially induced by curiosity and later propelled by growing faith, Bowmic became a regular attendee. That he was a Bengali never inhibited him. Even his relations and Bengali friends' teasing remarks about a Bengali worshiping a South Indian god had no impact on him. A man of real piety, Bowmic was beyond such narrow, petty considerations. In any case, he knew *Ma Kali* would not mind.

"It is a pity, Chatterjee, even gods and goddesses are not spared of abominable identification with one or the other region or community or caste. People do not realize that the different forms of gods or goddesses are but the manifestations of one Supreme Being. So be it.

"Once, Naganathan was immersed in his prayer with closed eyes during puja. Many devotees, including Bowmic, brought offerings to Lord Balaji. Mrs. Naganathan was arranging them before the lord. Chanting of hymns over, Naganathan opened his eyes but immediately went into a trance and demanded to know the whereabouts of the offering brought by Bowmic! Mrs. Naganathan shivered, realizing her ignorance-based blunder. Falling flat before Naganathan, who was still in a cataleptic trance, she begged for His pardon. It transpired that she had, deliberately but discretely, hidden in the kitchen the delicacy brought by Bowmics. No one noticed. Surely, Naganathan could not have, as he was fully engrossed in puja. The pious woman had presumed that it would be profanity to place the item before the divinity. Why? As per the conventional reckoning, Bowmic, not belonging to God's own community, could not claim apotheosis of purity or spirituality. Tradition-bound Mrs. Naganathan could not be blamed. Even some spiritual teachers are not free from such outdated prejudices. Now, she brought Bowmic's offerings and placed them before the lord.

"Chatterjee-dada, you know, God is the Supreme Being, Creator, Protector, Leader, Director, and Ruler. He is—as he must be—above all divisions and denominations and common, fair, and equitable to all. Every being is his subject, his creation, and his own part; it is inconceivable that God, by whatever name he is called, will maintain different religion, region, community, tribe, caste and subcaste schedules of human beings for His dispensations. Definitely, He will have no reservations, no preferences, no discriminations. Only karma, the deeds, good or bad, or merit could form the basis for his dispensations.

"Okay. Let me finish the story quickly before we reach Bowmic's flat.

"Soon after the incident, Naganathan made Bowmic wear a sacred thread and taught him *Gayathri Mandiram* in defiance of possible brahminical ire."

When Arvin, his wife, and Chatterjee reached Bowmic's flat, Arvin had finished the narration of the story, sounding apocryphal, yet actual.

They were just in time for the puja. Many had come from outside the building. The puja over, Naganathan took the *prasad* in a spoon and offered it to the framed Lord Balaji. The semisolid sweet disappeared. Those present there noticed it—the unnoticeable devouring of the *prasad* by the lord. They were not mesmerized but amazed.

Naganathan went into a trance. He looked around and told a businessman that he made substantial profit during the previous year and asked him to visit the lord at Tirupathi and spare one percent of the profit for charitable purposes. To another, he said he would recover from his ailment. To yet another, who wanted to know something specific, mum was his word.

Then, he looked at joyless Chatterjee and observed, "Your joy will rejoin you shortly; pray to me every Saturday."

Arvin's turn came then. He looked at him and said, "You won't have any problem."

"Let it be so willed," Arvin bowed and mentioned his pent-up desire to have a transfer to Madras.

"You have not come to me for long. Come."

Recovering from trance, Naganathan showed Aarathi, waved a plate of lighted camphor in a clockwise, circling movement before the lord, and kept it down; the people present, one by one, placed their hands over the flame and gently touched their eyes. Then, to the surprise of the observers, Naganathan swallowed the burning camphor. And, soon, he swooned.

Arvin believed that Naganathan had gathered some spiritual powers. Naganathan was not commercial minded. He didn't expect or accept anything from the gathering. He never flaunted his powers.

Arvin realized that he had not visited Tirupathi for a number of years. Now that he had been oracled to visit the lord, Arvin decided to pay a visit to the holy shrine without further delay. The trip from Calcutta to Tirupathi and back by train and the hours of waiting in the queue, even on special *darshan* tickets for *darshan* of the lord, required a minimum of four days. He proposed to use casual leave for two days, combining weekend holidays. He casually told Chatterjee about his plan. Chatterjee was yet to be reunited with his missing wife. Having already developed some faith in the Lord Balaji, either out of curiosity or on account of his adversity, Chatterjee insisted on his accompanying Arvin.

The train rolled into Tirupathi station. Both alighted from the train. Arvin could not capture the thoughts running in his colleague's mind. As for him, Arvin was excited, like a child expecting to meet its mother, to have the lord's d*arshan* at Tirumala after a gap of a few years. Dragging their wheeled bags, they crossed over a bridge to reach the bus stand outside the railway station. On the way, a few porters, wearing crimson-colored, badge-bearing, sleeveless shirts, mockingly asked them "Where are you going?"

"To catch the bus for Tirumala. Why?"

"Go, go, buses are not running. There is a strike by the transport crew. Even private vehicles are not allowed."

Chatterjee thought that they were joking because they were

unhappy about the wheeled bags stealing their earnings.

"How long is the strike likely to last?"

"Who knows? It just started today. It may last for two days or two weeks!"

The twosome ambled their way to the bus stand. The bus stand was full of buses. As if to justify the nomenclature, the buses were all standing and not running! The drivers and conductors, misnomers at that moment, were seen playing cards inside the buses. Inwardly, Arvin sought Lord Balaji's intervention. Outwardly, both the visitors from Calcutta talked shop to while away time. They could see many devotees returning, hopelessly, from the bus stand.

This sight seemed to be vindicating Chatterjee's stand that the trip was all in vain. Chatterji was upset to see his plan being derailed. He started lamenting, "What do we do now, Arvin? We cannot wait here indefinitely. God knows when this strike will be lifted. We have wasted our casual leave." Out of frustration, he charged, "Your South Indian god is irresponsible."

Arvin was amused at his colleague's wry humor and girlish murmur. "Dada, don't get upset. It is on his invitation or direction or command, in whatever form you may like to take it, that I am here. And, you are with me. He will surely show us a way out."

That Chatterjee did not share Arvin's faith was abundantly clear from his incredulous face.

All of a sudden, there was an announcement through public address system: "Attention, devotees! The strike has been called off; the bus service to Thirumala will resume in a few minutes."

Chatterjee and Arvin got the first bus leaving for Thirumala. The TTD bus wound its way up the serpentine road encircling the Seven Hills, with a few passengers, nay, devotees chanting *"Govinda, Govinda!"* When they entered the temple with no special tickets, they found it virtually empty; there was no surging crowd, no urging pushers, no straining, no craning of necks. To their heart's content, they could have a good *darshan* of the Lord Balaji conveniently.

"Chatterjee, you thought that the strike was an impediment; you did not even imagine that it could turn out to be a blessing in disguise. At the very first sight of an obstacle, you started losing faith. Never lose faith. Dada, you have overlooked one simple factor. It was He who directed me to visit His abode, and you joined me. He would not have let us return without His benign darshan."

"I am sorry, Arvin."

One Sunday evening, after a few days of their return to Calcutta, Arvin was at home. The doorbell chimed. When Arvin pulled the door open, he was surprised to see Mr. Chatterjee and his wife.

Chatterjee took off his spectacles and wiped a drop, a tear of joy, dribbling from his eyes.

37

• Tantalizing Transfer

Six years—not six months—passed. Four Heads, one by one, had come and gone. Arvin remained stuck, without any intervening superglue, in Calcutta. There was not even a whisper—in fact, there was diabolical silence—about assured transfer to Madras. Meanwhile, two more officers from Bombay had been quietly accommodated. Ramananthan advanced, as usual, some administrative or platitudinous reasons every time for not reckoning Arvin's case. According to the administration, decisions were taken on a case-by-case basis, or in others words, on a face-to-face basis. Perhaps, the fault was in Arvin's face. Madras continued to be an elusive mistress.

One smoggy morning, Arvin woke up with a fever. Still, he went to office on that day. The fever intensified. A blistering rash appeared, sporadically, first on his face. Soon, it blanketed his body. It was chicken pox. How could it be? He had been vaccinated against chicken pox and was also once afflicted by chicken pox in his school days. Yet, the doctor confirmed it. The virulent attack knocked him down for three weeks. There were no elders at home. None could be invited from outside for help. Malar was attending him while managing their two school-going children. One after another, the children, too, were infected. It took a month and a half for the entire family to be up and back to normalcy. Arvin was the worst affected. The pox dotted scars on his body and sapped his energy. With a Mother Theresa's tender, patience and devotion, Malar managed the situation admirably well. With God's immunizing grace, probably won by her devotion, Malar was miraculously spared by the infectious pox.

When Arvin resumed duty after a month, Kirmani could not believe his eyes and exclaimed, "Oh God, why did you come to office now?"

"Go home," advised Kirmani. "Take a week or two more. Forget the office. Take care of your health."

Once again, Arvin made a representation to the executive director for a transfer to Madras. It was forwarded by Kirmani, with his own strong recommendation. It met with the same fate as his earlier representations: careful consideration and the usual regret! Another six months crawled by.

The tantalizing transfer reminded Arvin of the Greek mythological story of Tantalus being plunged, as eternal punishment, into a river of Hades up to his chin with an edible fruit hanging in an overhead bough at a reachable height. The story goes, whenever he stretched his hands to pluck the pendulous fruit, a wind would blow the bough out of reach, and whenever he dipped to drink, the water level would recede. Arvin's predicament was no less pathetic. When he kept quiet, the administration was mum; when he represented, it regretted its inability. The desired transfer continued to be out of reach, while he remained stuck in Calcutta. Tantalus had offended the Greek gods. But, Arvin did not offend even mortals, greater or lesser.

At last, Arvin received a transfer order from HQ, Bombay. The order was for his transfer out of Calcutta. The news of Arvin being transferred spread as fast as today's junk mail.

"Congratulations, Arvin, at last you got what you wanted; patience pays. You must be happy."

After six years and six months, the bough bowed. Alas! The fruit, however, was changed by a magic wand into a bitter one.

38

• "Come What May, I Won't Go."

Arvin could not shut off the flooding painful memory: After five years in Bombay, Arvin was transferred to Calcutta against his will. He could not bring his ailing father, as planned, for treatment. He lost his loving father. The dangled leave vacancy promotion receded, like a mirage, as he reached Calcutta. The assurance of a transfer to Madras in six months vanished in no time with no trace. He had been awaiting the assured transfer for six long years. One by one, his colleagues were being accommodated in Madras, while his representations met with a consistent response—regret. He was being hailed as an intelligent, efficient, capable officer. He was the recipient of spontaneous written appreciation from senior executives for his innovative contributions. He had been picked up for deputation to some outside organizations for executive positions. (Though, it is another story that they did not materialize for mysterious reasons.) Normally, such an officer would be favored by any enlightened management. He did not hanker for any favor; he only longed for fair treatment.

At least now, he hoped, *the administration will be considerate to accommodate me in Madras.* But, as a bolt from the blue, came the *transfer* order. The order was for his transfer not to Madras but to

Gauhati. Assam was then in a state of turbulence. So-called outsiders were treated as outcast, unwanted. The incumbent in-charge of the Gauhati office, a gentleman from West Bengal, was a sitting duck. Before his fate was sealed, he was sought to be saved by transferring him out of Gauhati. A humanitarian thought indeed. But, some other duck had to be placed instead. Who could fill the bill? A pucca priest as he was, Ramanandan could readily spot one. Who else? Arvin! How could he be overlooked? Sincere, soft, southern, an order abider and no string puller—what more purity was needed for a sacrificial lamb?

Arvin has been wounded enough; now, rubbing some salt into his wound should not hurt him more. He has been true to the salt all these years. Let us not bother about the silly principles of motivation, recognition, reward, or fairness. This seemed to be the unwritten code of the administration.

Even God appeared to be indifferent to his devotional pleas. Lord Balaji had called him to his shrine at Tirupathi, and he had religiously obeyed, but still He was testing Arvin. Why should Arvin alone be subjected to such teasing or testing, human or divine? *Why me?* wondered Arvin. None could give him any sensible answer. *Karma?*

For whatever it was worth, Arvin sent one more strongly worded representation to the chairman at Bombay through proper channels. The channel, though proper, seemed clogged. He was not sure of his representation reaching its intended destination.

Simultaneously, he also made a silent, mental protest to Lord Balaji, who would surely hear him. Here, at least, there was no question of jamming the communication channel.

The headquarters—administration, to be more specific—became quarters for annoyance, aggression, and desperation, progressively in that order. A series of messages, both formal and informal, some masquerading as friendly advice, flew to Arvin. The pith was this: "Arvin is a nice, efficient officer; he should not spoil his own career. Let him go to Gauhati immediately; he may be shifted later to Madras."

Arvin had been bitten once—and so badly.

Meanwhile, Kirmani, convinced of the unfairness of the treatment being meted out to Arvin, tried to use his good offices to get him transferred to Madras instead of Gauhati. He spoke to the concerned personnel at the corporate office and conveyed his protest in writing. His good offices were not good enough. His arguments did not cut much ice with the powers that be. He met with a cold response. There were "friendly messages" from some senior colleagues rooted in Bombay for ages:

"Arvin, don't be carried away by Kirmani's support. He is backing you purely with selfish motive. He wants to retain you, in his own interest, for exploitation. Better go to Gauhati. We will certainly get you transferred to Madras from there. Please cooperate."

It was strange. The counseling colleagues, happily sitting in a circle of influence at Bombay, had not bothered to utter even a word of sympathy for Arvin's predicament, let alone raising a little finger or at least a low-pitch voice to help Arvin in getting his transfer to Madras.

The administration, good at chess, made its next move, which was not unexpected. Kirmani received an admonition, an order of transfer.

"Don't worry," Kirmani consoled Arvin, "I shall do whatever possible. I will not move from here until you get your transfer to Madras."

He did whatever possible from his side. He could not stand the pressure. He had to move. He did.

In Kirmani's place, came Indveer, with a specific, incentivized mandate. Successful execution of the mandate, it was rumored, was the litmus test set for him. He would not like to fail this time in getting his elusive but now impending promotion.

Support came from unexpected quarters. The local officers' association registered its strong protest against Arvin's transfer to Gauhati. While demanding, in the same breath, that the incumbent in-charge of the Gauhati office should be shifted forthwith.

Throw one stone to get two mangoes? Or, is one a pellet to hit another?

Any new in-charge at Calcutta would, as a rule, get a rousing reception within a few days of his arrival—a vociferous protest on some issue by the union to make its presence and strength felt at once. Arvin's issue was solid and handy. Indveer had a housewarming reception. It was an opportune time for Indveer to begin his given task. He called Arvin and asked him, ostensibly in a pleading tone, to go to Gauhati. "Mr. Arvin, I am told you have not obeyed the HO order. Please go to Gauhati immediately. This is my personal request."

"With due respect to you, sir, I am sorry that I cannot agree to your request, personal or official. Let me tell you my story."

Arvin poignantly recapitulated the back episodes of his serial story and regretted his disinclination to commit hara-kiri. Adamant Arvin robbed Indveer of any vestige of his clemency. Lightning and thunder followed. He accused him, in an authoritarian tone, of instigating the association to agitate in support of his case.

"I have not asked the association to intervene." Arvin iterated, "Believe me."

"You're bluffing," insolent Indveer charged with a pugilistic face.

"Can you swear in the name of any god you believe in?" Doubting Thomas demanded Arvin, a senior officer, a sincere performer, a wronged colleague, to swear in the name of whatever god he believed in.

"Sorry, sir, it is up to you to believe me or not."

"In that case, go and ask the association in writing not to take up your case."

Crafty *Chanakya*, if alive, would have certainly envied Indveer.

"Extremely sorry, sir."

Arvin was no longer unduly malleable. He had been sufficiently treated and tempered by experience. He sent his representation, again, to the chairman, this time—properly or improperly—directly to him. The chairman, new to the institution, had come from outside with a reputation as an upright, independent, no-nonsense banker. Arvin had had no occasion to meet him.

Wireless messages flowed, through different streams, to Arvin: "This chairman will not tolerate any nonsense. Arvin should not have sent his representation to him directly in violation of staff regulations. If he does not go to Gauhati, he may have to go home—forever. Even now, it is not too late; he can move to Gauhati."

There is a limit, a breaking point for anything, be it elasticity or gentility or patience or endurance. Beyond that point, foolishness sets in. Arvin sensed the invisible fencing. He stopped intuitively. He remained not cowed, unbowed. "Come what may, I won't go," resolved Arvin.

A week later came a telex message to Indveer: "Arvin's representation is being put up to the chairman. Relieve him. He should take charge of the Gauhati office immediately."

Arvin became sick of the sickening administration policy and practice of the august organization, which he once preferred to join. The administrative needle had pricked him so deep as to penetrate the soft layer and touch the hard core. He had become thick-skinned but not a pachyderm. He was forced to entertain the thought of leaving the organization for good. As a prelude, he proceeded on long leave and began an Anjaneya puja to last for forty-five days.

Arvin stood relieved from the Calcutta office. As *Thrisangu*, he was hanging in space, neither here (Calcutta) nor there (Gauhati). Surely, he was going through hell.

Arvin, not yet forty, had just become a senior-grade officer. Career-wise, he had a flight of steps ahead leading to the top, which he was confident of climbing. Malar was only a homemaker, not a wage earner. His two sons were too young, still in high school. He had not acquired a house or a flat of his own anywhere. Less than fifteen years of service in a parastatal organization had not resulted in accumulation of savings adequate for the rest of his life. There were no worthwhile handshakes available from the employer. Those were the days of low tide. Adventurous job surfing was not in vogue. He had no alternative job lined up. Perched in these circumstances, no sane person would even think of a suicide jump into unemployment.

Arvin was in his full senses and was prepared to quit his job. His pent-up frustrations were seeking desperate release. He had only his faith in God to fall back on.

A month into the puja, Arvin had an unusual visitor at home—a general manager (personnel department) from Bombay.

"Please come in."

"Arvin, you won't believe, but you have tremendous goodwill at Bombay."

"I am glad to hear this, thank you."

"Your representation is very well worded. But, you could have avoided citing specific names."

Arvin had cited the names of officers who had been accommodated by the administration.

"If the names are wrong, I am sorry."

"No. Not at all. Still, why make any personal references?"

Intriguing was the poser. Mum was the answer.

"You have documented your case well."

"Thanks."

"You are an excellent officer. We will certainly shift you to Madras."

"Thank you so much."

"You don't know the present chairman."

"You're right; I don't know him."

"May I suggest something in your own interest?"

"Of course. Why not? Please go ahead."

"You better go to Gauhati—just for a month. I promise you will be sent to Madras in a month's time. I give you my word."

Arvin was very well aware of his own interest and the real value of the visitor's promise. "Sorry. I have a vocabulary collected. To me, the *words* are meaningless."

"Mr. Arvin, we are trying to save one of our colleagues. Don't you think it should be done?" The visitor tried to be clever, knowing very well Arvin's compassionate disposition.

"I, for one, fully agree our colleague at Gauhati must be shifted for his safety. Certainly. Quickly."

"Then?"

"Shift him. But, don't place another outsider there for the time being, at least until situation improves. If West Bengal falls outside Assam, Tamil Nadu...? What you propose is only a change of offering at the altar."

"You are being posted as an interim arrangement. We are looking for a suitable officer for a long-term posting."

"Touch your heart, and tell me if what you propose is fair to me. I need not recount to you what you—by *you* I mean the organization—has done to me. You are adding insult to injury. Is this the reward for sincerity and efficiency? Pardon me for shedding my modesty. After six and half years, you are sending me to Gauhati instead of Madras to place me as a target for attack as yet another outsider. Do you think I will not be treated as an outsider? Or, am I expendable? May I suggest one thing? Why don't you advise the present number two there, a local man, a senior officer, to be in charge of the office as an interim arrangement and rescue the current in-charge? Is the mighty organization, with all its resourcefulness, helpless in ensuring the safety of its senior officer?"

"Arvin, we can't. He is unfit." He realized his indiscretion, but it was too late. *Tongues do not have any backspace key.*

"Tell me, sir, can he then continue in service?"

The visiting senior's face reflected, like a neon billboard flashing rapidly changing messages, his changing moods—cornered, embarrassed, irritated, infuriated, controlled, calmed, and collected. He then said, "You are becoming argumentative, Arvin. Consider me as your elder brother. Listen to me. Go to Gauhati."

"Sorry, brother."

An hour of discussion, debate, expressions of sympathy, and exhibitions of empathy, culminated into the administration of this advice to Arvin: 'Please, better move to the new center, or else . . ."

The threatening message was loud and clear. Arvin remained stolid. He only listened to his inner voice: *You have been wronged enough. Don't be foolish and keep on bending. Never lose your guts. Fight unto the logical conclusion. God is with you.*

The visitor went out with a sullen face. Weeks passed. Anxiety prevailed.

39

• The Road Last Traveled

One smog-free morning, at home, Arvin had just finished his daily prayer when he received a call from the Calcutta office.

"Arvin, congrats. You need not proceed to Gauhati. Cut short your leave. Resume duty. Immediately. Today."

Arvin could not believe his own ears. *A miracle? How did it happen?* It was indeed a mystery. It was an oral instruction. Arvin did not receive, nor was he shown any, written order cancelling his transfer. Certainly a cancellation order ought to have been passed. Or else, the original transfer order would subsist on records. *Am I being fooled?* Arvin was skeptical.

Sporadic leaks gathered into a puddle of an untold but widely guessed story.

On reading Arvin's direct representation, the chairman asked for the background of the case. Administration thought of but avoided recourse to misinformation, misplacement, or displacement of relevant records. For, if exposed, it would incur the new chairman's displeasure. But, at the same time, if it put up the case faithfully, with relevant previous references duly flagged, the injustice done to Arvin would surely come to the chairman's knowledge. As a strategy, therefore, the administration wanted to have Arvin pushed quickly to Gauhati, by any means, fair or foul. Once this was done, the file relating to his representation could be submitted to the chairman, solemnly stating, with the soul of wit, "Mr. Arvin's representation and related papers are placed below. He has since joined the Gauhati office. No further action is called for. This is submitted for information, please."

In his busy schedule, the chairman might simply record on the brief covering note, "Seen. Thanks." Then, he would initial and return the file, which would retrace its route down. The issue would get happily closed as a fait accompli. And, Arvin would remain stuck now in Gauhati for another six years or more, solving the administration's problem.

This was the administration's plan.

Unexpectedly, however, Arvin turned out to be a nut unusually hard to crack. He refused to move. He stayed in Calcutta on long leave. As a result, the administration submitted to the chairman the representation of Arvin, with all back papers, and with its own contrived arguments for its outright rejection. The chairman read the entire story of unjust harassment to Arvin and ordered the cancellation of his transfer to Gauhati.

The story was purely conjectural yet highly credible. Not even an iota of suspicion hovered about possible string pulls or phone calls. For everyone was aware of the merit of the case and the steely spine and the balanced mind of the chairman.

Arvin, however, knew of the intervention of an invisible hand too. Anjaneya did not wait for completion of the forty five days of puja to be pleased and act through the good soul of the chairman. Arvin would never lose trust in Him. Arvin did not try to peek into the mystery. Cutting short his long leave, he resumed duty. Soon, he started traveling as his job demanded.

The Indian Airlines plane landed at 1:30 p.m. Outside the airport, a *Willis* was waiting to take him to his destination.

The jeep looks new; the driver appears good. Hope the journey will be safe, so thought Arvin. The driver turned out to be a friendly chatterbox.

"*Saab*, 125 kilometers. Five hours. Pray no problem."

"What problem?"

"A fallen bald, bold, na, na, boulder. Today rainin'. *Saab,* land sliding, road blocking! Vehicles trapping! No going—front or back! Sometime, road closed four days. No worry, sir. Twenty years I drive. No accident." The driver butchered the language and rattled the occupant of the vehicle.

It was a narrow, winding road, rising, falling, and turning with bends of all shapes and angles, hedged by high, rugged hills on the one side and accompanied on the other by the deep, swift *Teesta* hurrying to hug *Brahamaputra.* Travel on this road was thrilling and chilling at the same time. You could have an eyeful of beautiful and serene natural surroundings. Your heart leaped in joy, in tune with the bodily jolts caused by the jumping jeep. You need not be a musician to enjoy the accompanying euphonious sound of the music of gurgling water brushing the pebbles of tranquility. But, you may forget to realize that a small error by the driver, and you and the driver would hurtle down, like rolling balls within a rolling ball, down and down, down and down, hundreds of meters into the rocky riverbed, a veritable deathbed.

A fleeting thought crossed Arvin's mind, *You have options: Drive safely, diligently and skillfully and reach the peak. Or, drive madly, recklessly, and impatiently, and fall into abyss. Choose your option carefully. Never lose your balance.* Arvin jotted down the thought in a pad that he always carried while traveling, as it might be useful for a talk on *management*.

In fact, Arvin was not new to this road. He was transported mentally to a year back—the first time when he traveled by this road. It was along with his senior on an official visit—a momentous visit on multiple counts. He met the royal head of the state, offering him, as guided, a small piece of cloth, with bowed head, as a mark of respect; he had an audience with a spiritual, noble leader then camping in a monastery. The most memorable experience was a blissful glimpse of a visual extravaganza. It was mistless dawn. Arvin was waiting on the rooftop of his hotel. A red-faced Tom was getting out of heavenly bed at the crimson-hued eastern corner of the blue sky. Both were keen to see something spectacular. Arvin remembered his visit to Kathmandu and the hour-long helicopter tour over the snow-covered peaks of the breathtaking Himalayan range and how the excitement of the tourists had surpassed even that of Edmond Hillary. Now, he was waiting to have a similar experience. Oh God, the glittering glimpse of silvery crest of deemed-divine, deeply-revered, and lofty *Kanchedzonga*, slowly revealed by the parting curtains of the clouds, was an unsatiable feast to the eyes.

At the earthly level, he found the hill people plain, simple, and honest to the core. The jurisdictional extremities of some of the national laws had not tickled the place. Still, there was no lawlessness. Perhaps, fewer laws meant more orderliness. It was a biting-cold winter. He could not hold his pen and write legibly. In contrast, the people were so cordial. One could feel the human warmth in the bosom of cold Nature.

Arvin did not even imagine then that he would become a frequent traveler on this route. His nomination to the board of an organization made him one. Board meetings were always scheduled at seven in the evening for logistical reasons. Keeping company with the agendas on the table, there would invariably be a glass of a locally distilled produce neatly placed in front of each seat for climatic reasons. A "small" of icy liquid would go down the members' throats, warming them up for solid deliberations on the large number of listed items of business.

A sudden jolt, following a screeching noise of tires, jerked Arvin out of his reverie. The driver had stomped the brakes. Arvin's heart leaped into his throat. It was raining still.

"Driver, what happened?"

Arvin peeped out. There was no obstacle in the way—no boulder, no landslide, no traffic jam, no accident, no stop signal. Why had he stopped the vehicle so suddenly? There was no apparent reason for the abrupt stop. Why had the driver fallen silent? Did he see a vampire? Or, was he possessed? The driver was lifeless, silent, and, still, like the vehicle. An eerie thought momentarily seized Arvin: Breaking the suspense, the driver s-l-o-w-l-y t-u-r-n-e-d and, as in a Hitchcock movie, showed his ghostly face! Seconds slid away. The driver recovered from his meditative posture and reignited the engine.

"What happened?"

The repeated question now evoked a reply. He pointed out a pair of snakes, which having leisurely crossed the road in a zigzag way, were now entering a bush.

"Sorry *Saab*, if I not apply the brake, I commit a sin."

"What sin?"

"I crush join snakes. We worship snakes."

The driver was happy. By his presence of mind and sudden brake, he had avoided crushing and killing a pair of copulating cobras. With a smile of satisfaction, he resumed his driving duty. Had the driver known the causal name of the traveler, his respect for him would have turned into reverence.

At six-thirty, Arvin reached his destination. With the meeting over, he traveled back the next morning to Bagdogara to catch his flight to Calcutta. He thought he would be a frequent traveler to this eye-pleasing route. How would he know that this would be his last?

40

• Happiness Robbed

When Arvin returned from Gangtok, a surprise was waiting to receive him—a long-awaited order of long-term transfer to Madras! Arvin's happiness was beyond description.

In his office, Arvin was busy clearing files. A telephone ring disturbed his concentration. Arvin picked up the receiver. The in-charge of the Madras office was on the line.

"Mr. Arvin, you are w-e-l-c-o-m-e. I am personally happy about your coming here. Really. But . . ."

There was a hesitation-laden, curiosity-creating, deliberate silence.

"Sir, but, what? What is the issue?"

"Arvin, don't think I am discouraging. Let me tell you, quite frankly, and don't mistake me." He was trying to say something obviously unpleasant, but did not know how to put it.

"Arvin, for your information, this is not a garden of roses. The office is riddled by *Bee and Enbee* divide. You may not feel comfortable. You may regret your decision to come here. Anyway, it's up to you. Think it over."

Bee and Enbee? One need not consult any manual. It was well known. Bees have two major denominations. Arvin recalled having read somewhere an interesting observation made by Paul Erdos, a Hungarian mathematical prodigy of international repute, when he came to Madras:

"This is the city of Madras.
The home of the curry and the dhal,
Where Iyers speak only to Iyengars,
And Iyengars speak only to God."

Arvin thought the mathematician could have as well added, without any risk of being asked to prove, "Though God listens to all!"

Erdos perhaps had no occasion to deal with the denominations of *Enbees*, which are too many. The so-called community divide and ethnic conflicts were not exclusive to the state. Perhaps, relatively, it was more pronounced. Arvin knew it too well. But, one cannot renounce one's native country or state for such reasons. The real reason for Arvin being dissuaded from coming to Madras must be something else. For one thing, a cliquish group did not relish any newcomer into its bastion. For another, Arvin's acquired toughness was discomforting to some. This was all part of the occupational game one had to sportingly play. Arvin was not looking forward to be in a garden of roses. No office, for that matter, could claim to be a flowery bed. Even roses were not bereft of thorns. Arvin's earthly experience had grown enough to ward off or tackle any prickly thorns.

"Thank you for your tips. I never wanted to be in a rose garden, even if one exists."

"As you wish."

The Arvins landed in Madras, as he wished. He could attend to some pending family matters, and the months rolled by. The forewarning proved to be right. The office was indeed not a garden of roses; it was a park of prickles. Unyieldingness to unreasonable demands evoked agitation—protests, banners, caricatures, gate meetings, office stormings, and the like. Arvin shouldered responsibilities to support the head of the office in enforcing discipline and ensuring the organization's long-term interests. Madras was no less difficult a center than Calcutta. Though not brambles, both were veritable beds of prickly pins. The pins were either discreet or daring. In any case, no office could be a cushioned couch for resting; it must be an arena for action.

There was no truculent Guru to be handled here. But, sophisticated submarines could be spotted here and there, now and then. Agile, active performers were many. Reliable were one or two live wires good for any task. One should not, however, be oblivious of a live wire's potential of subterranean communication or distorted messages up and down.

The pins, for that matter, were strewn not necessarily in the office but at home, in the street, in the surroundings, everywhere.

One morning, it was fine when the Arvins woke up. It was not so a few minutes later. When Malar opened the Godrej, she found some ornaments missing from the locker inside. How could it happen? It had not been broken open. The keys were in the usual place. No outsider had come. The mysterious disappearance of the jewels baffled the Arvins. Malar could not bear the loss; she wept and wept. There was no full-time servant at home. A part-time maid came in the morning for an hour. She was yet to come for work on that day. It was normal to suspect a servant in such circumstances. Just because one is poor, Arvin used to say, he or she need not be dishonest. Mostly, the poor were more God-fearing and honest than presumed. In fact, as Arvin believed, education and affluence may not be a foolproof index of one's character. The maid had been working with Arvins for many months now. So far, nothing was missing from the house. Humble and quiet, she was not given to gossip spreading or nagging.

In any case, she may be asked; once the matter is reported, the police will surely interrogate her.

As soon as she turned up, she was questioned but not in an accusing tone. She claimed to be innocent, and so did she look. She started inquiring into the details of the missing items.

"Where did you keep them? How many grams? Was the cupboard broken open?" They were all innocent, inquisitive questions.

She consoled Malar: "No worry, Amma, you'll get back your things."

Now, Malar was gaining her confidence about the innocence of the maid precisely when Arvin was losing his. Arvin thought it better to report the theft to the police, though some neighbors considered it a wasteful exercise. Following the usual visit by the police, a statement, fingerprints, and so on, were all taken. Two days passed. Nothing happened. The third day, when Arvin went to the terrace of the house, he went around to look for possible clues. Behind the overhead water tank were deftly hidden the boxes that once contained the missing items. They were all empty.

How could the boxes come here? Someone has opened the cupboard, taken all the jewel boxes, brought them here, emptied them into a bag or piece of cloth, hidden the containers, and quietly sped. This cannot be the handiwork of a burglar. He would not have had the time and patience to come to the terrace and do all this. Even assuming that he could have sneaked into the bedroom where the Arvins—husband, wife, two children—were all sleeping and noiselessly pulled the keys from under the pillow. Moreover, from the terrace, he could not have jumped down; there was no easy means of climbing down. In fact, he could not have come in via the terrace; he had not come in or gone out through internal stairs, opening the main door of entrance, for the door was found locked from the inside. So, it must be a case of an insider stealing.

Arvin started interrogating Malar to the point of annoying her. "When did you see the jewels last?"

"A week back."

"Where do you keep the keys in the daytime?"

"I leave them hanging in the cupboard."

"Both the outer and locker keys?"

"Yes."

"Why?"

"Because I am an idiot." Malar was upset. She started blaming herself for the loss. Arvin pacified her but proceeded further:

"I keep on opening and closing it for removing or keeping dresses."

"Okay, what are all the duties the maid performs upstairs?"

"She wipes the floor and washes clothes in the attached bathroom."

"Where does the maid get the clothes dried?"

"On the terrace."

"When the maid works upstairs, where would you be normally?"

"Downstairs—either in the kitchen or in the drawing room."

Initially irked, Malar was convinced of the deductive usefulness of the dialog. The pointing direction of the suspicion needle was now clear. Malar was excited and agitated; she wanted to immediately call the maid from her hut to question her. Arvin advised her to be patient. He brought those boxes down to the drawing room and displayed them prominently on the center table. As usual, the maid came. Arvin was watching her. The boxes could not escape the attention of anybody entering the house. The maid looked at the boxes. *Did she see any ghost?* She turned deathly pale and was in a state of stupor for a moment—only for a moment. Like a coiled spring let lose, she quickly regained her poise. No questions were asked. She was being constantly watched by Arvin. That she was nervous was apparent. After hurriedly finishing her day's work, she went. The next day, she absented herself. Arvin's suspicion was sustained.

Arvin could now get a fairly clear picture of how it could have happened.

The maid noticed that most of the time she worked upstairs, Malar remained down. The hanging keys tempted her. She quietly opened the cupboard and the inside locker and took out all the jewel boxes. Then, she locked the locker and the outer door silently and left the keys hanging as earlier. She then had taken the boxes to the terrace along with the washed clothes meant for drying. There, unseen, behind the overhead water tank, she emptied and repacked everything. She had enough packing material and time. Carrying the jewels alone in her sari was easier and safer than the boxes. Malar, all this time, was blissfully ignorant of what was happening behind her back or above her head. She was so confident of the maid's integrity and so busy with her daily routine. Once the day's work was over, the maid took leave of Malar, as usual, and ambled out with the treasure safely tucked into her sari. She must be the insider thief. Otherwise, why should she—who was so confident and bold two days earlier—become so nervous on seeing the jewel boxes and absent herself the very next day?

For such a simple deduction, Sherlock Homes was not required. Nor would a Scotland cop be necessary to nab the culprit, thought Arvin. Arvin went to the police station, presented his own logical deduction, and made specific mention of the name of the suspect. And, he went to his office, thinking that the rest of the job would be easy for the police.

No sooner had he reached his office when there was a call from home. Malar was on the line. She sounded perturbed. A score of people from the nearby slum had gathered in front of the house and were vociferously protesting against the arrest of the maid. They were demanding the withdrawal of the complaint. Malar was unnerved. She wanted Arvin to rush back home. He comforted her and told her not to get panicky. "Be calm. Don't show your nervousness. Tell them to wait; I am coming with the police. If necessary, call our neighbors for moral support."

Arvin called the police station to find out the factual position and also to report about the scene at his house. He learned the maid had not been arrested; she had been taken only for interrogation. She was now in the station. He then went to his house along with two of his colleagues. By the time he went home, the crowd had dispersed.

Now, Arvin went to the police station where he found a gentleman in a spotless, white and white, dhoti and shirt, with a thick, golden minor chain dangling around the neck and over the shirt. He sat before the inspector and demanded they let the maid go.

Who is this chap? How is he concerned with this case? Is he a lawyer?

Arvin got the answers in a minute. The gentleman was a person living in Arvin's neighborhood. He had never met this neighbor. The maid's daughter was working in his flat. At the insistence of his maid, he had come to protect her "innocent mother," a downtrodden. He was vouchsafing for the integrity of the suspected servant maid. His demagogic demeanor was striking. He was belaboring to convince Arvin that the maid was not guilty. He pronounced his own judgment. The cadence of the conversation between the inspector and the gentleman was such that it left no doubt in the mind of an observer: They must be chums.

It seemed the search of the maid's hut was in vain. She was not so foolish as to keep the loot in her hut. Let free after some questionable questioning, she went straight to the flat of her protector and promptly discontinued her job at Arvin's house.

By persuasion of her friends, Malar had gone to an astrologer–swami to find out the prospects of recovery of the stolen property. After some searching questions and serious calculations, she was told, "It would be difficult to recover them. Forget it. But for this theft, let me tell you, some serious ailment would have afflicted Arvin."

Police "investigation" continued. Meanwhile, days were being stolen by unknown hands. There was no trace of the stolen valuables. *Perhaps, a word from a higher-up might hasten the process*, Arvin thought.

A written word was brought from a sufficiently higher authority: "Please give priority." As a matter of fact, what was really required was not a word from above but a sense of duty below. There was no evidence of any priority being accorded or duty being discharged. Apparently, the thief got adequate time to secure a safe shelter beyond the reach of the arms of the law. Obviously, the immunity would not be free of cost. Was the robber, too, robbed?

"The thief had gone with so much" as Shakespeare lamented. And, Arvin was not prepared "to spend so much to find the thief" with little prospects of recovering the stolen items.

What was lost was lost for good.

41

• Lifetime Happiness

He was in a skyscraper a score of floors above and a few below the ground. Inside the concrete maze, Arvin lost his way. He could not locate a lift or an elevator. He asked some people around. Everyone nodded his or her head horizontally and went ahead bending their heads and minding their business. After some annoying minutes, which appeared to be hours, he located one. With a sigh of relief, he traveled in the lift all alone up and down. He was operating the lift, trying each button and every landing. He could not locate a floor that would lead him to the road exit. He felt miserable. Everything was written in the national language. As a part of his pretravel preparations, Arvin had learned a couple of words in that language—to greet, to thank, to bid good-bye—but nothing more! To his inquiries or entreaties in English, all he could get by way of response was a typical bowing of heads but no guiding hands or helping words. He felt miserable, like an illiterate. Mobile phones had not materialized then. Mapping services were unheard of. An old gentleman with noodle-like wrinkled skin and cadaverous appearance—he must be an octogenarian—approached the stranded man.

This old man may not know English. No. Never under estimate anyone.

Let me try.

Arvin narrated his ordeal to the old man in measured tone and pace so that the old man would understand his predicament. The communication was, to his surprise, complete.

The old man's eyes—jelly in palmyra fruit—glistened with tenderness.

"Don't worry, young man. Are you from India? From which part? Where do you want to go? Come along with me."

Stunned by the good English of the elderly gentleman, Arvin followed him, like a lamb, answering his questions. Both were engaged in friendly conversation throughout their journey from inside the building to the road.

"Young man, what has brought you here?"

"I have come to attend a program."

"Oh, I see. How long you will be here?"

The conversation set Arvin's mind in reverse gear.

This chance of attending an overseas program had flowed to him through the maze of the organization's internal selection process, which was, at times, mysterious, leaving a trace of heartburn behind. Deputation to a program abroad was as much a reward for performance or a means of skill improvement as a grant of favor to a favorite. Arvin was all along accustomed to only being overloaded with work and overpraised with words. The organization's present gesture, though relatively belated, was soporific. It provided him his first-ever break—a foreign travel opportunity that traveled in his way after fifteen years of service. Deepening knowledge and sharpening skills aside, exposure to such a program was expected to broaden experience, more so because the program had been organized by an institution of international repute and the participants were from multicultural backgrounds. The subject of the program was very relevant to Arvin. He learned that, while the methodology of project appraisal and monitoring was essentially similar in different countries, the areas of emphasis varied. For instance, the Japanese banks were then swearing more by multivariance discriminant analysis and were less reliant on the internal rate of return or economic rate of return as on the World Bank. Group discussions centered on the reverse flow of technology to the West and exciting possibilities emerging in the Pacific region. It was at the dawn of the eighties. The split location of the program—Manila and Tokyo—widened the range of experience from "Jeepney" rides to bullet train travel, from sporting multicolored Filipino casuals to donning plain leather overcoats, from stroll on sun-drenched tropical beaches to wading through snow in neon-lit, glittering streets, from sipping San Michel to tasting sake. Plant visits, meticulously planned and organized with clocklike precision, took the participants to a robotic assembly line of Toyota and an automated but beautifully small, notebook-making firm. Both were amazing.

Coming out of the flashback, Arvin replied, 'Well. The program is almost over. I am returning to India this weekend."

"Do you like our country?"

"Of course I do."

"What all impressed you most?"

"The cleanliness, the discipline, the simplicity, the politeness, the respect for elders, the electronic revolution, the advancement in automobile engineering . . . I am simply amazed."

"I like India. I admire its rich heritage, its diversity, its philosophy, its potential . . ." The old man could have simply gone on, like the others, minding his own business, or could have bowed his head and politely walked away or, at the most, could have indicated directions and then left. But, what he did was an amazing instance of surviving human tendency to sincerely help a fellow being. It was the impulse of the elderly man to go out of the way—an extra mile—to help an unknown foreigner to find his way. That impressed Arvin. The age-withered man was a veritable form of sober astringency with a Haiku-like condensed charm. Surely, he must be a practitioner of the three pure precepts of Zen philosophy.

The Good Samaritan took Arvin all the way down a score of floors and out of the concrete maze to the road, called a cab, and told the taxi driver in Japanese to take Arvin to his place of stay. Both took leave of each other as if they were longtime friends. They exchanged their phone numbers. "Thank you. You are so kind. I shall never forget you."

"It's all right, sir. It's my pleasure to do a good deed. Do you know the saying, 'If you want happiness for an hour, take a nap; if you want happiness for a lifetime, help someone.'?"

"Domo arigato!"

"Sayonara!"

Arvin bid good-bye to the good old Samaritan, who disappeared inside the concrete colossus.

The program over, Arvin returned to India. In his absence, there was a significant development at home. A pleasant, surprise gift awaited him.

42

• Landing in Trouble?

Two passengers exited from Air India's airbus and entered the arrival hall of an international airport. Gun-holding soldiers were standing erect, steady and mute, like pillars, inside the airport premises. For the duo, arriving with work permits, immigration formalities got over rather quickly. Even a resident Indian returning after a brief trip abroad would have taken much more time to snail through the immigration counter in Bombay. Their checked-in luggage all arrived intact, swaying slowly on the conveyor belt. None of them had been picked up, as they had been cautioned, by some mysterious hands from beneath the carousel. Wheeling the baggage-laden trolleys, the duo was about to pass through the green channel. A red-eyed official stopped them.

"Gentlemen, nothing to declare?"

"Nothing."

"Any food items?"

"Yes, we have brought some ready-to-eat packed items."

"Let me see. Open the suitcases."

Both obeyed and displayed the cases' interiors. "Please wait."

The officer seemed uninterested in checking. He moved away without uttering a word of clearance. Minutes ticked away. The official was now engrossed in animated conversation with his colleagues.

"Please excuse me; we've been waiting here for almost half an hour. We have come here on an official assignment. A government escort is waiting outside to receive us. May we proceed now?"

"Wait!"

Why should he be so curt? Was this his customary demeanor?

With their suitcases open, the vexed visitors waited impatiently.

If anything is dutiable, duty may be collected, or if any edible item is not allowed to be carried in, it may be thrown into dustbin. Then, we may be allowed to proceed. Instead, why does he make us wait like this?

The duo was ignored. The pillars around remained unblinking spectators. At last, the local escort came in with an official pass to receive the visitors. He could identify the Indian visitors without any difficulty. After showing his visiting card, he welcomed the visitors. He then met the customs official with a handshake. In a dramatic turn, the official told the duo in an apologetic tone, "Sorry, sirs, you may go."

Led by the escort, the duo, Mr. Puri and Mr. Arvin, left the airport.

The duo's organization had won an international consultancy assignment, the first of its kind, emerging successful in a global bidding. And, these two officials had been handpicked to provide their expert advisory services to a banking institution in this country. Hence, they landed here.

The duo had heard of a few horror stories:

Once, an Indian had landed here—in trouble. He had with him a small packet of some whitish, powdery substance. Suspected to be some narcotic substance, the packet was taken to a lab and the visitor to a cell. Neither his family back at home nor the expecting local host had any inkling of the fate of the missing visitor for a fortnight. Cell phones did not yet exist. Clueless, the family and friends of the missing man spent sleepless nights. Later, the substance was found to be not a drug of any sort. The visitor, a faithful Hindu-Saivait, was carrying mere *vibhuthi*, sacred ash, to be worn on his forehead.

Mercifully, the visitor was let out, lighter by a few pounds, poorer by a few dollars, but wiser for experience. "Much worse could have happened in this military regime," he was consoled. Jettisoning, then and there, his aspiration of eking out a living in this land, he returned to his motherland determined never ever to come back with or without *vibhuthi*.

Another instance related to an Indian arriving at this airport, having been whisked away by two locals, who received him. It was too late when the visitor realized that he was not received but deceived with some fake visiting cards; he was discarded on the way as unwanted, bereft of all his belongings, including travel documents. Left high and dry on the highway in the dead of night, he was stranded, stripped of his proof of identity, miserable for hours, till a Good Samaritan came to his rescue.

These tales, believed to be true, had scared the duo even before they boarded the flight. Suddenly, now a doubt crept into their minds. They stole a glance at the escort in the front seat, who had received them at the airport. A chill of realization descended down their spinal cords. The escort was a stranger, huge and dark, with a visiting card, *prima-facie* genuine. Beside him, the driver resembled a menacing wrestler of WWF fame.

Can we trust these chaps?

A few searching questions cleared their doubt a wee bit. The escort, dressed in a darker suit, looked handsome, gentle, and polished. That he had had his education in London was reflected amply in his diction and accent. Friendly conversation ensued. They exchanged information about their respective countries, cultures, and customs.

The Peugeot 404 was speeding on the highway, darting into the gradually darkening night. The speedometer needle was tottering to touch 140. The speed was not felt inside the smooth-running, air-conditioned vehicle.

A good car, an efficient driver, but where are we heading to? The duo's pulse rates raced with the speedometer. The running doubt was haunting the visitors. Suddenly, the vehicle lost its speed, causing a jerk on the duo's confidence. The car started c-r-a--w--l--i-n-g. With their hearts thumping, they were now almost sure of being knifed or shot any moment and dumped, dead or alive, on the edge of the highway in an alien land.

What sins have we committed in this birth or earlier to deserve this kind of an ignominious end? Are we taking too much risk for a few more bucks? No. If anything untoward is destined to happen, it could happen even in your homeland itself. Never lose your courage. Whether brave or coward, you are not going to be spared by your destiny. Why not be reasonably brave, having faith in God?

Competing thoughts raced in their minds. They quietly prayed. Faint shouts and cries pierced through the tinted glass. A few palms tapped the door-glass outside as the speedometer slumped toward zero. Lowering the glass of the side door, the visitors found themselves stuck in a traffic jam. Cars of all makes, of all sizes, of all colors, of all shapes were lined up, bumper to bumper ahead and behind theirs, each one in slow motion nosing the rear of the other. For several minutes, the traffic flow remained frozen. They saw many outstretched palms, not for alms but with some things to sell. Ebony-skinned boys and girls were hawking a variety of wares, ranging from dusting cloth to electronic gadgets. "This is go-slow market," explained the escort.

The visiting Indians were reminded of the traffic jams near Howrah Bridge. The junior of the duo had a flash of personal experience in his mind.

Once Arvin had to catch a Patna-bound mail train at Howrah. It was *Durga Puja* time. Like on *Ganesh Chadhurthi* days in Bombay, more people were loitering merrily in the streets, visiting one *Durga Puja Pandal* after another. Anticipating heavy traffic en route, he had left Alipore well in time by a taxi. Almost near the station, just half a kilometer away, the vehicle was caught in a traffic jam on the bridge. There was no hope of his vehicle reaching the station in time. The experienced *taxiwala* suggested, "*Saab*, better get down and run, or else you will miss the train."

Just like a cop hurrying to catch a fleeing thief, he virtually ran, zigzagging through the maze of vehicles, to catch the train. Panting heavily, he reached the platform just in time to catch the glimpse of the fast vanishing "Last-Van" sign on the train exiting the platform.

Alighting from the memory express, Arvin continued his chat, "A traffic jam? In Calcutta, roads are narrow and rocky. Vehicles of all sorts ply on the road—hand-pulled and pedaled rickshaws, teetering trams, bumpy buses, ample ambassadors, trembling taxies. They all coexist or, rather, corun but not always in comradely mode. Naturally, they create chaotic conditions during the rush hours. But, why traffic jams here?"

"I have visited India; I have seen an ambassador carrying five persons beside a driver. Here, it is a different story. Petrol is cheap. We are, I think, the sixth or the seventh largest oil producer in the world. Till recently, we used to export crude worth $15 billion dollars a year. Now, the volume has dropped. Our network of roads is reasonably good. We all have imported cars. Name any brand, any model. You can see them on the road. Car population is vying with humans.

"Here, half a dozen children at home are not viewed as too many for a couple. But, even two persons, plus a driver, are considered a crowd in a car. People have money. They prefer everything in the luxury of multiples, whether it is cars or houses or wives! People prefer to travel mostly by road or air. Now, you can understand very well why there are traffic jams here. At times, believe me, people may have to start several hours in advance to reach the airport just twenty miles away. To ease the situation, the government ordered that only odd-numbered vehicles should use the roads on odd dates and even numbered on even dates. You may think the traffic flow would have halved. No. Not at all. The car population almost doubled. Now, everyone has a minimum of two vehicles—one per wife, in some cases!"

The chirpy chattiness of the frank escort had a comforting effect. "Do these street vendors manage to sell anything at all?"

"Aa-haa! They do brisk business. Sometimes, people get stranded on the road for hours. They spend their time, and money, sitting inside the car. Let me warn you: You have to be careful in buying here, especially electronic items. They may turn out to be stolen or spurious. I would also like to caution you. Please do not think I am trying to scare you. Better beware of robbers."

"Robbers?" The visiting Indians could once again feel their rising blood pressures.

"Yes. Robbers armed with guns. Do not go for late-night partying. Armed robbers loiter on the busy roads and lie in wait near the parking lots of luxury hotels. At gunpoint, you may be robbed of your cash, valuables, and your car. In the case of such an encounter—may God forbid—better don't resist; surrender. Otherwise, they will snatch away whatever you have—including your life."

"Can you not keep a pistol for self protection?"

"Aa-haa, you can with proper license. But, remember, the robbers are very smart; they wear bulletproof vests—high-end vests that can challenge even bullets from an AK-47. Your pistol will only add to his armory."

"What about the police? Is it not possible to report the matter to police and recover the loot?"

"Possible, provided you are still alive. The victims normally recover the loss partly from insurance companies; this, the robbers know too well."

"Amazing."

"Wait a minute. You may not believe that some private concerns pay their executives robbery allowances, in cash, to be kept handy at home, so they can hand it over to demanding robbers."

"What?"

"Yes. It is a matter of cash. The robbers come with vans to carry their loot. Valuables take time to sell, you know. The robbers require instant cash for their immediate needs. They pocket the cash and carry the valuables. In case the victim does not have cash, the frustrated robber may shoot him down. The local employer would not like his expatriate executive being executed by a gang of robbers. The bullet may leave a gap in the brain of the organization, too."

Whatever courage the expatriates were slowly picking up was now fast dripping out, like blood through a bullet wound.

"You said the people are rich; why then this robbery?"

"Aa-haa, like yours, ours is also a country of contrasts. We have continental breakfasting, globe-trotting rich, and yam-eating, job-seeking poor. Our population is exploding. Unemployment rates are high. The dismal poor despise the venal rich and take to robbery. This is a serious social issue."

"By the way, tell me why you still have hand rickshaws in Calcutta. A man ferrying a man; is it not shameful?"

The escort executive, having visited India many times, was fairly knowledgeable about the Indian cities.

"I look at it differently. To me, a man riding a man is inhumane. Some, sitting cross-legged with regal postures, travel like princes in palanquin. The way in which they urge the puller to hurry up even on an ascending slope of a bridge, smacks of their cruelty. This I deplore the most."

"Why do people like this kind of transport?"

"It is a cheap means of travel, if not cheaper than a tram. It is eco-friendly—no gas, no petrol, no diesel, no pollution. It is a convenient mode. It can rescue the stranded in times of floods and *bundhs*. It can easily negotiate in narrow lanes and by-lanes. It is ubiquitous—available at a hail's distance. Even a postman cannot beat a rickshaw puller in familiarity with the locality. Rickshaws are not the unique legacy of Calcutta. They were in vogue in metropolises like Tokyo, Paris, and Shanghai. But, they gradually disappeared. In Shanghai, Mao banned them as symbols of imperialism some half a century back. But, in Calcutta, they still survive as a bourgeois conveyance of convenience."

"Aa-haa, why? Why can't the government abolish it?"

"Most of the rickshaw pullers are poor migrants from neighboring states. They eke out livings in Calcutta and raise and support their families left behind on their native soil. This is their means of livelihood. They run on the roads, hauling their rickshaws and lay on the pavement, cooling their heels. They have not tried their hands at any other jobs. Abrupt abolition of hand rickshaws will surely invite red-eyed protests from the pullers and the pulled alike. Maybe one day, after a decade or two, circumstances may compel or induce this legacy to move to a museum."

Gradually, they were released out of the gridlock onto a free road; the car regained its speed. The duo failed to regain their confidence fully. They were conjuring up all sorts of misfortune that might still visit them en route. Suddenly, the car screeched to a halt. *Oh, God!* Two armed, muscular men marched menacingly toward the vehicle. The escort obligingly got out of the car.

Is it going to be an encounter with armed robbers? The first? Or, the last?

Overcome by angst, the visitors remained seated inside the vehicle, with bated breath, hoping for the best. The armed chaps snapped to attention, with salutes.

These robbers seem to have military discipline.

The escort came forward and opened the rear door of the car.

"Please get out." There seemed to be stress on *get out.* Mentally prepared even to kneel down, they got out of the vehicle.

"We have reached your residence; these two are your guards."

Heaving a sigh of relief, the duo smiled. They were in front of two sprawling bungalows.

The duo was led to the first house by the escort.

"Mr. Puri, this is your official residence. The adjoining, identical house is for your colleague. This is Victoria Island, an island of aristocracy. The houses are centrally air-conditioned, fully furnished, fortified by grills, and guarded round the clock by armed security personnel. A domestic servant has been arranged for each. They will report to you tomorrow morning at six. We have provided two brand-new cars of same make and model to each of you, with drivers—Edward and David. Both are good drivers and reliable boys. We want you both to be comfortable. If there is anything more you need to be more comfortable, please do not hesitate to tell us. The guards and the drivers will extend the necessary help in arranging things at home. Now, let me take leave. We shall meet tomorrow at eight in the office, just fifteen minutes' drive from here."

"Thanks a lot."

"Good night, Mr. Puri, Mr. Arvin."

"Good night. Good night."

43

• Vigil on the Guards

"Arvin, I suggest we stay together. I'm afraid that staying all alone in these houses with armed fellows around all the time will not be safe. I don't see any houses within earshot."

Arvin was debating in his mind, *Will it be prudent? Teamwork is a must for the success of the assignment. But, why live together at home? It is, after all, the selection process that has thrown us together in this oversees assignment. Probably, the person of his choice was unavailable or unapproved. Otherwise, he would have picked one of his cronies as his teammate. His biased, narrow preferences are too well known. But for want of self-confidence, he would have grabbed this opportunity exclusively for himself. In any case, having taken up the assignment, we both have the joint responsibility to make it a success.*

Arvin also recalled his parting speech at the farewell. In conclusion, he had observed, "The continent to which we are going may no longer be dark. Yet, we are totally dark about the country we are heading to. With your good wishes and back-end backup, we shall make this prestigious assignment a grand success."

His musings continued, *Personal prestige apart, the image of the sponsoring organization and the home country is involved. Official and personal relations should better be kept apart. We must stay in the respective houses allotted to maintain the status and not to breed contempt.*

The undercurrents of such thoughts rendered Arvin mute. Puri sought to unmute Arvin, "Arvin, why do you hesitate? This is an alien land. We don't know anyone here. Better, we stay together."

"I understand this is a safe place. The army barracks are nearby. The houses look like fortresses. Moreover, we have to maintain certain degrees of status and dignity. Our staying in the same house may not be appropriate."

"No, Arvin. Be practical. We can save more. If we surrender one house, we can even bargain for a hike in our compensation package."

"To be frank, I am not in favor."

"Okay. Let us stay together for now, at least till our families join us. To tell you the truth, Arvin, I am somewhat scared to stay alone."

"All right, we may stay together for a month or so, by which time we may get used to the surroundings. Hopefully, our families also might join us by then. But, let us not surrender the other house."

It was the first morning at the new place. The doorbell chimed. Puri peeked through the peephole.

"Arvin, Arvin, come here. Quick."

"What?"

"See. See."

Puri moved aside so that Arvin could peep through the magic eye. Arvin caught a glimpse of the hazy figure of a tall, hefty, dark, uniformed man with a rifle slung on his shoulder.

"He is our guard."

With night latch unfastened, Arvin opened the door, partly.

"Good morning, Master, I am James. I am your daytime security guard."

"Good morning."

Puri turned to Arvin and asked him in a low tone, "What is the guarantee that these guards will not train their guns on us? Let us be watchful."

The guarded thus started keeping vigil on the guards.

44

A Haunted House

"Arvin, are you ready? It's seven-fifteen."

"Just a second, please."

Both Puri and Arvin came out of the security of the house. Two sky-blue cars were waiting side by side, like identically dressed twins poised for a running race, to take them to their office. The respective drivers opened the rear doors of the cars for their "masters" almost simultaneously.

"Arvin, let us go in one car. In my car."

"Why?"

"Arvin," whispered Puri, "only for our safety, at least for a few days."

Amused at the psychotic fear of Puri, Arvin agreed.

"David!"

"Master!"

"Follow us."

"Yes, Master."

An empty car followed a crowded one.

Arvin understood Puri's mind. Puri was not really seized with a fear to travel alone, nor was he concerned to conserve energy or contain the fuel cost for the host.

"Good morning."

"Good morning."

"Glad to meet you."

"Welcome."

There were greetings and handshakes.

A rousing reception was held for the expatriate experts at the entrance of the Pioneer Commerce Bank.

"This way, please." The chief executive officer of the institution, who had recently taken over the reins of its stewardship, conducted the expatriates to the board room. A formal ceremony followed. Introductions over, speeches flowed. The experts were eloquently apprised of the genesis, the objective, the activities, the organizational setup, and the current state of affairs of the institution. The CEO then indicated the areas in which he would look forward to the expert advice.

"Gentlemen, we look forward to your help in establishing sound principles, policies, systems, and procedures in the areas of loan sanction, disbursal, and recovery and instituting a good management information system. It will be nice if you can also draw up a good manual of instructions for the benefit of our staff and provide them proper training, both in classroom and at their desks."

The experts assured the host of their best services. The informal chat later touched upon the operative environment. The advisors were given copies of annual reports, brochures, and so on. "It must be clearly understood that the loans shall be repaid," bold print in the brochure proclaimed. The outside experts were reassured that it was not a redundant statement of the obvious. "Otherwise, it would be taken for granted that the loan is just a grant."

The experts could not help contrasting this with their home environment. Back at home, honestly speaking, there was no such gross misunderstanding to be cleared up front in black and white, but the perfect understanding would not, at times, translate into abiding observance for various reasons, including borrowers' recalcitrance or delinquency or the lenders' tolerance or helplessness.

"Mr. Arvin, long time, no see. I would like to talk to you."

"Nice to see you, Mr. Irvin. Is two weeks a long time?"

"Aa-haa, Okay. Tell me, don't you want an independent residence or a chauffeur-driven car?"

"Of course, I do. Why? What's the provocation?"

"We understand that one house and one car are enough for you both. I thought I would check with you."

"Mr. Irvin, if you don't mind, may I know who gave you such an understanding?"

"Aa-haa, your own colleague. In fact, we're surprised. He wants to surrender your facilities. He may be the leader. But, for us, both of you are advisors. It is for you to tell us if you don't want any of the facilities."

Suppressing his shock, said Arvin, "Thank you, Mr. Irvin. There is no question of surrendering these entitlements. I would like to have the house and the car, as per the terms of the agreement."

"Okay. No problem. For your information, we have taken pains to locate these houses, befitting your status, and taken them on lease for three years. We shall abide by the terms of the contract. You must feel comfortable; that is what we want."

"Thank you. So nice of you."

"Arvin, I think you have not booked any flat in Bombay. You could have. Did you not expect this assignment?"

"I was not quite sure of this assignment."

"In two years, you can make considerable savings."

"Of course!"

"Arvin, you should be ever grateful to me for this opportunity. If I had not agreed to take you as a coadvisor, you would not be here."

Puri did not even pretend to say this in a casual manner or in a lighter vein. Arvin knew, for sure, Puri had absolutely no say in the matter. He could see the curtains of civility slowly sliding open to reveal the soiled interior.

"Thanks a lot."

"Arvin, our families will be joining us soon. Why don't we stay together in one house? The bungalow is spacious; it can accommodate two families easily. By the way, we can also make do with one car. We can share the domestic expenses and save more. What do you say?"

Why is he so persistent to share the house and vehicle? Fear can no longer be the reason. Cost savings cannot be his sole motive. He cannot tolerate my enjoying the same facilities as he does—an independent bungalow, a chauffeur-driven car. Perhaps, he feels that his status, as leader will be shadowed. How silly.

"We may better stay in our allotted residences."

"Don't be silly."

"Am I?"

"Don't be upset. Think it over. I'll tell PCB that we both can manage with one residence and one car."

"Please don't do that. It is not proper. They will not relish it. Don't mistake me; you may go down in their esteem."

"Don't worry. I'll tell them that this is your wish."

Flabbergasted, Arvin tried, in vain, to look into the ever-elusive pair of eyes. Puri would never look at anyone eye to eye, as if the other person suffered from Madras eye or had the gifted powers of *Vali of Ramayana.* It seemed as though he didn't to want to get the infection or lose half of his strength. In fact, by lowering his eyelids—the shutters of his mind's windows—he tried to hide his real intentions.

The conversation with Mr. Irvin quickly flashed into Arvin's mind. It was amply clear that Puri had already misinformed PCB. No doubt, Puri was determined to undermine Arvin's status.

"Mr. Irvin has already spoken to me. I have told him clearly that PCB must go strictly by the terms and conditions of the consultancy contract."

"Oh, I see."

Puri tapped his fingers restlessly on the table.

Kinesics is useful for many occasions, be it a social intercourse or a business interaction. This language has no dictionary. Yet, it is not too difficult to learn. All it calls for is careful observation of a person's mannerism on a continuing basis. This language is often person specific. Body language, if followed, can often convey more than verbal communication. In fact, it is possible for a diligent person to read the mind of someone else and infer if the other person lies or what he or she actually means.

By now, Arvin understood Puri's body language. Puri's fingers drummed to the turbulent tunes of his mind.

"I have decided to shift to my house today and start traveling in my car tomorrow," declared Arvin. Puri was startled. He did not expect this defiance. He had expected Arvin to be acquiescent. Collecting himself quickly, he muttered, "Okay, as you wish." Obviously, it was against his wish. Puri's face tightened and, in a huff, he left the place.

45

• A Systematic Swiping Plan

Puri rang up his family and talked to his wife, sons, daughters, and brothers. An hour later, disconnecting the phone, he told Arvin, "I have asked my wife to tell your family that you are doing fine here. Both our families are preparing to catch a flight next week to join us."

"Thanks."

Thirty minutes passed. Suddenly, Puri returned as if he had forgotten to tell Arvin something. Obviously, he had seen a glint of happiness in the face of his colleague.

"Arvin, you seem to be overjoyed. Don't be overexpectant. It may so happen that your family may not be able join you here. One must be prepared for any disappointment."

Childlike? Is he the same human who is talking, often, with natural, undisguised excitement about the imminent arrival of his own family from Bombay? Is it his intention to be a spoilsport? Or, does he want Arvin not to be as happy? Or, is he trying a trick to stop Arvin's family on the track? Or, is he becoming a preaching philosopher?

Arvin was perplexed at the behavior of his sermonizing senior.

At the PCB's office, Puri said, "Arvin, we need not occupy two offices separately. I'll ask them to provide one more table and chair here. You may move in here."

One must admire his dogged pursuit of his aim.

"Why do you want to do that?"

"We can discuss and work together."

He opened the table drawer and, like one urgently searching for a missing paper clip, kept looking into it, obviously to avoid eye contact with Arvin. The purported purpose of Puri's proposal, as Arvin sensed, was far from truth.

"The areas of work have been defined. My office is only a few yards away. Whenever necessary or whenever you want, we may meet and discuss. Give me a call, and I will be here in a minute."

Puri fell silent. The silence was an unmistakable mark of annoyance.

Arvin could not believe his eyes and ears.

Has Puri turned a new leaf? Soft? Soothing?

Puri was straining himself to please Arvin.

Is the happiness flowing from his imminent family reunion responsible for this involuntary transformation?

Arvin remained unmoved by the newfound kindness of his boss.

"Arvin."

"Yes."

"Our families are arriving this Sunday."

"Yeah."

"We may need each other's help and cooperation."

"Yes, of course. You can count on us."

"Let us be good friends."

"Surely."

"Arvin, sit down here. Let us have a chat. You know, this is a God-sent opportunity . . . to have a decent earning. I don't know what sort of opinion you carry about me. I have no prejudice whatsoever. In fact, when your name was proposed as coadvisor, I didn't know you. You are not one of us. Anyway, I am happy you have come with me. Don't think I am flattering you; you are so intelligent, so knowledgeable. Even after this assignment is over—why, even after retirement—our friendship should continue."

Puri rambled on and on, bending Arvin's ears. Arvin could not trust his ears. *Is it a miraculous transformation? Or, is it a prelude to something sinister? Better be cautious and, yet, open-minded.*

"Thank you. Genuine friendship will certainly last long."

Having paved the way with friendly overtures, Puri now moved closer to his point, "Arvin, PCB says we have to open a bank account outside to credit our fee."

"No problem. We may open accounts with a bank in London."

"Precisely, that is what I too thought."

"Arvin, consider what I am now going to suggest."

"Yes."

Puri suggested. A bell rang in the mind of Arvin.

Arvin recalled an educative experience he had in the early bachelor days of his career.

Once, in the middle of a month, a colleague, Anand, sought some amount for certain urgent purpose with a promise to repay it on the next salary day. Such a help in need between colleagues was normal. Arvin readily obliged. The word was kept. Perhaps the need was met. So, Arvin was considered as a friend indeed. The friendship continued. The next two months witnessed similar accommodations.

It happened again the middle of the next month.

Anand approached Arvin with a similar request. But, this time, the proposal was for regular, revolving credit. Yes. He wanted Arvin to give him a certain amount, roughly a half of his take-home pay, in the first week of every month to be repaid on the next salary day.

"Arvin, you are a bachelor. Can you not spare a part of salary for two weeks?" It was a logical poser. This time, Arvin did not readily oblige the glib talker. The innocuous proposal set him thinking,

Anand is not known to be a spendthrift. What can his plan be? To avoid withdrawal from his account during the core period of each month? Not to lose interest as per the bank rules? A petty-minded strategy? Or, a penny-wise, pound-wiser policy? Or, most likely, Anand may be in the private money-lending business. Maybe, he is simultaneously tapping many of his unsuspecting colleagues for pooling a sizable lendable fund.

A discreet inquiry revealed that Anand was indeed engaged in some side business and owed a lot to many. A "no" in time would save more pain later. Arvin heard a voice from within, *Whether a lender or a borrower, never lose prudence.* It was better to shed the false friendship fast rather than to miss it with the wallet later. The request was politely declined. And, Anand, as expected, ceased to be as friendly as he was. Probably, he was on the lookout for a new, naïve friend to hook.

"Arvin, Arvin, where are you? Lost in thoughts? Let me elaborate my idea."

"Sorry, I was thinking something else."

"Do you know a certain minimum amount is required for viable investment?"

"I know."

"I suggest we need not open two separate accounts."

"You mean we can have a joint account?"

"No. No." A smile ran along the hurried response.

"Then?" Curiosity hung in the question.

"Relax. I'll clarify. Arvin, let me open an account. Your fee can also be credited in that account."

"What!" The exclamation escaped his control. "I don't understand how my fee can be credited to your account."

"Simple. Let me tell you how. You just give PCB a letter authorizing it to do so. That is all."

"I'm afraid it is not that simple. I cannot, and even if I do, PCB will not accept such a mandate."

A rehearsal of the digital dance commenced.

"All right, you have your own bank account and give the bank a standing instruction to transfer the balance above a certain minimum every month to my account. Simple."

Muted Arvin wondered, *Is it that simple?*

"The savings will accumulate and be invested. In two years' time, the investment will swell."

Arvin was taken aback by Puri's risqué remarks. *Anand was an ordinary person acting smart. He pales in comparison to Puri, who seems extraordinary.*

Arvin could not help comparing.

"Don't you trust me?"

"There is no question of trusting or distrusting. It is an issue of propriety."

The actual digital dancing began. Abruptly, Puri got up and started pacing up and down in the room. He resumed his seat.

"Why do you use big, big words, Arvin? I do consider you as a family member."

"Thank you very much."

Arvin had already cut his teeth. He was noncommittal.

"If you are not interested, tell me so. We will forget it."

This is one tactic some use very effectively. This plays on psychology. The weak-minded may fall for this kind of confidence trickery.

"Yes, you guessed right."

The ready response rattled Puri.

"Why? Why?"

While the dance gained pace, tactics changed. Puri was a shy person. By nature, he could not be very jovial or sociable. Arms-around-the-shoulders bonhomie was not his cup of tea, nay, coffee. The maximum he could do was to wear a subdued smile and utter sweet, persuasive words with rare eye contact.

"Arvin, think it over. What I am suggesting is for our benefit."

"I appreciate your suggestion. But, I think there will be some tax implications."

To be honest, Arvin did not appreciate the suggestion. He only tried to be as gentle as possible.

"Don't try to fool me."

Who is trying to fool whom? Let me be more direct and put him to a litmus test. "If you don't mind, let me make it clear. Crediting my salary into your account will create complications. For mere argument's sake—though I won't agree even if you do—would you be agreeable to have your fee credited to my account? I mean, if you were in my place.

"How dare you?" One could almost read Puri's quivering lips.

Puri's frustration was evident from his frowning face. From the sheath of subtlety emerged his sharp dagger of direct intimidation. "Mind you, I am the senior, the leader. If you do not agree with me, well, it is all right; you will be the biggest loser. I can very well ask our institution to withdraw you from the assignment anytime, even immediately."

Indisputably, Puri was the senior of the two—in age and position. Seniority and leadership are, after all, two different things. Conscious of the first, Puri was well nigh devoid of the second. Puri, it seemed, had thoroughly misunderstood the concept of *transactional leadership.* One comes across, in official life, many such characters who are akin to a rolling coin; their unstable static equilibrium gets disturbed even by a whiff of disagreement to toe their line. They fall down with their ugly faces up.

Arvin had seen many bosses. Some were firebrands but fair-minded, some were taskmasters but credit givers, and some were sweet talkers but backstabbers.

Puri was unique. He seemed to be worse than some bullying bosses Arvin had ever met. Many bosses had picked his brain, but none ever attempted to pick his pocket too. Puri's resolute move to force Arvin to surrender his earnings revealed the unseemly side of his character. If told, none would believe that Puri had made such a preposterous demand. If Arvin obliged, none would believe him to be so wet behind the ears. An instant "no" would protect Arvin's interests but invite Puri's wrath and harassment. Puri might even try to carry out his threat.

Let him do whatever he can. A senior usually enjoys an edge. He may abuse the weapon he has—confidential reports, the weapon of career destruction. Worse come to the worst, I may have to go back. So be it. There is no question of yielding to unfair demand. No deal.

Ignoring the idiosyncrasies of his boss, Arvin decided to concentrate on his job to uphold his and his institution's image. While Puri might seek vengeance and speak ill of Arvin to headquarters, Arvin's performance should speak for him. Arvin was firm, "I will not bow before Puri with offerings. After all, Puri is not the Lord *Paramatma*." One may believe in the philosophy of *atmanivedan*, absolute surrender to the Almighty for salvation. But, it would be disgusting for a person to surrender to another for career survival.

Arvin did not like to share his predicament with anyone around. *This is not linen that is fit to be washed outside.*

As a person, Puri had occupied a sublime position in Arvin's heart of estimation. In close quarters, Puri had normally portrayed himself as a different person—a God-fearing, devout Hindu; a person of humble origin, orthodox upbringing, and honest disposition; a simple, shy, sensitive man; an ardent worshipper and a regular reader of Scriptures. Arvin had, at times, felt so happy to be in such a *sat-sang*. Alas, what a steep fall! After all, piety is what piety does. Puri fell down with his ugly face up. Many unpleasant epithets vied with each other in rushing into Arvin's mind but were promptly checked from stumbling into his mouth. Arvin would never lose his gentility. Human behavior is individualistic and need not necessarily depend on descent or rearing, education or environment, position or age.

Why does a patently pious man behave like this? Due to bipolar moods or dual personality disorder? Or, is he really well meaning? Does he intend to act as an AMC—asset management colleague? For mutual benefit? Then, it should be by mutual consent on explicit terms. It should not be an imposition by dint of his position. Nonagreement to the proposition by a junior colleague should have been accepted with grace and should not have invoked anger or threat, overt or covert. Would Puri have behaved in a similar manner with any other colleague in my place? Has my politeness been mistaken as submissiveness or my gentility as gullibility?

The more he ruminated, the more perplexed he got. *Okay. If Puri had hatched a systematic swiping plan, it is stopped for now. Let me forget it.*

Arvin dismissed the whole episode as a freak incident. He was clear in his view, *Interpersonal relationships should not be allowed to interfere with interinstitutional relationships.*

46

• Daylight Robbery

Weeks passed. Interactions between the duo were muted, except for meeting job requirements. Puri's family arrived. He was immensely happy. By the same flight, Arvin's family, too, came. So overwhelmed by his family reunion, Puri forgot to tone down Arvin's happiness by cautioning, "Don't be overjoyed; your family may have to go back shortly." Both the families had become friendly during the flight. Children are children, unspoiled by adult egotism. The relationship between the two families grew warmer, while the heads were bogged down in a cold war. Arvin had not told his family about his souring relationship with Puri. He hoped his colleague would not do anything to drive a wedge between them. But, Puri was not what Arvin thought him to be. In fact, he was an enigma.

Abruptly, Puri's family stopped talking to Arvin's. Puri, it transpired, had ordered a cease-talk and drawn a *Laxman Rekha.* The twin bungalows were now barricaded by a wall of silence. In the following weeks, a number of Indian families living in the neighborhood got in touch with the Puri and Arvin families. They all became friendly. Thousands of miles away, Indians came closer, transcending caste, creed, or community. Here, they were no longer North Indians or South Indians, Malayalees or Tamilians, Iyers or

Chettiars. They were all but Indians. Unity seemed to grow more in alien soil thanks to climatic conditions or security reasons. During weekends, they would organize one-dish parties, one dish to be brought in by each family, to share culinary tastes. At times, they would go for joint outings—to a beach or a resort or a sanctuary. Each family would come in its own car or van. Sometimes, two families would travel in one van. Mostly, the vehicles would be self-driven. During such outings, some would exhibit their latent talents—singing, dancing, or joking. The weekends provided a recharging break between the weekdays of work pressure. The get-togethers provided occasions for fun, entertainment, and relaxation.

On one such outing, a few families, including the unfriendly duo, traveled in a caravan of six vehicles. It was more than half a day's drive to a faraway picnic spot. National Airways were less dependable and more costly. "Confirmed booking" was a misnomer. If you were not quick enough, the flight would be filled up on first-come-first-seated basis. You might have to run down the ladder and across the tarmac to board another airbus. A scent of a sandstorm would be enough to see you stranded with no flights taking off. The road was therefore preferred. It was cheaper too. Petrol was as cheap as beer.

The Puris traveled with Prems in one van and the Arvins with the Ajiths in another. It so happened, unplanned. In the course of conversation, Arvin asked Ajith, "Ajith, where is Krish? Has he not joined us?"

"Don't you know? Armed robbers struck at Krish's home last Sunday."

"What? Is he okay? I hope they have not harmed anyone."

"He is okay. His family is shaken. They have lost all their valuables."

Ajith narrated the horror story.

It was Sunday at 11:00 a.m. Mrs. Kamala Krish and Miss Sujatha

Krish were on the first floor, watching TV. Krish was sitting in his drawing room, reading the newspaper. He was absorbed in a reported miracle. A tribesman credited with magical powers had been fired at point-blank. Stretching his palms, he had caught all the bullets. Before Krish could read further to learn whether the wizard gulped down or threw away the bullets, the doorbell rang. Krish got up and opened the door. To face the music? A well-dressed stranger was standing outside.

"Are you Mr. Krish?"

"Yes, please."

"May I come in, Mr. Krish? Your friend gave me your visiting card and asked me to see you."

The stranger handed over to Krish the visiting card.

"Please come in," invited an impressed Krish.

"Thank you, Master."

With a beaming smile, Krish led the visitor to the sofa. Suddenly, the visitor whipped out a pistol. The smile turned into shock. A noise at the door made Krish turn and look back. Now, two more burly boys barged in with revolvers, kicking the door closed behind them. The trio surrounded Krish. Stunned, Krish did not immediately realize that his own visiting card had been used as an entry pass. When the card was presented by an unknown person, unfortunately, no warning bell had rung in his mind.

"Before letting the fellow in, I should have asked him, 'Who gave you my card?' It is my foolishness." Krish was displeased with himself.

"Mr. Krish, please cooperate with us; you won't be harmed." This was big mercy from a merciless chap.

"Hand over the keys, and watch the proceedings." Impeccable was his English.

There was no alternative. He had to cooperate. Krish had heard a number of real stories of armed robberies. He knew how an Indian friend, whose house was attacked by armed robbers, was shot in his thighs as he tried furtively to call someone, inferably police, and had to be flown later to London for removal of the embedded bullet. The aim or hit may not always be below the belt. This was the first encounter for Krish with robbers. He was wise enough to give in, as the most obedient victim. After all, life is more valuable than cash or durables. Hearing some unfamiliar voices, Krish's beautiful wife and lovely daughter came down the stairs. They were petrified at the sight of the weapon-wielding, scary strangers.

"Come on, babes."

One of the robbers ambled toward them.

Krish was aware that, generally, people here, even robbers, would not misbehave with women. This place was different. He had seen how the security staff of a luxury hotel would manage the nimble nymphs seductively loitering in the lobby or at the entrance; they would caringly ask, "Where is your man?"

The implied message was "Don't hang around alone; pick up a man quickly."

Even invitations from some organizations for a social meet would suggest, "You may bring along with you not more than two girl or boy friends."

Boys and girls would meet and socialize freely. There was no teasing; there was no need. Liberal in outlook on gender relationships, the country was virtually devoid of sex-related crimes, as a contrast to the country of Kama Sutra. Still, Krish was scared.

"Please, do not harm them, p-l-e-a-s-e." Krish pleaded in a begging tone.

"Don't worry, Mr. Krish, we will not touch them."

Turning to the women, the chief ordered, "Both of you ladies come here. Lie down facedown. Don't lift your heads till we tell you. If you do, it will be the last time."

The women, trembling, obeyed at once. They knew that these chaps would be true to their words. One chap stood by their side as a sentinel. The gang leader commanded Krish, "Show me the place where you have kept all your cash, including your robbery allowance."

This robbing leader was unmasked, daring, and forthright. Krish had to surrender.

You may lose your valor. But, never lose your discretion.

He showed him the locker. The lead robber grabbed all the cash and other valuables he could lay his hands on. Meanwhile, the third swiftly loaded all durable goods on the van parked outside. The entire operation was over in a few minutes with a clocklike precision. It was indeed a spectacular example of extraordinary teamwork with clear division of functional responsibility and efficient time and motion management. The three thieves quickly gulped a few bottles of beer from a crate found in the storeroom and then fled, gleefully, waving their hands.

"Bye, Krish." The armed robbers left Krish unharmed with a timely parting advice, "Lodge your insurance claim. Good day! See you again!"

Everyone in the van felt sorry for Krish. On their return, they would visit Krish to console him and his family. They did not betray their fear, but the screwing question in their mind was, *When will be our turn?*

47

Family Feud

The van was speeding. A check post barred their way. Gun-holding security personnel stopped the vehicle. They gestured to the driver to open the trunk. A searching operation took place. A few questions were asked: names, where from, where to, what for, and so on. Apparently satisfied, the security guard said, "You may go, good day."

The relieved travelers responded, "Good day."

"Good day," repeated another guard, standing in front of the van, without letting the vehicle go. The response was also repeated innocently. This drama went on for a few minutes till it dawned on the travelers that the vehicle would not move unless the palms were greased. The deed was done. "Good day, Chief." The signal was understood now. There were a few more check posts but no more repeated "Good days."

On the way, at a distance ahead, the van travelers could see by the road side a small crowd rejoicing at something. Curiosity overtaking them, the driver slowed down. People were dancing around a bonfire. A stack of vehicle tires was burning. Visible were some dancing movements inside the hollow of the burning stack. It appeared as if the crowd was peering at a show of dance by a dress-less damsel. The local driver could guess what it was. He stepped on the accelerator. "Master, they have caught a thief. He is being given heat treatment." He said it coolly, with a sense of wry humor.

"Oh, no, it is so cruel. How can this crowd cheer at the searing event?"

"This is common here," a naturalized citizen, Ajit, clarified. "If a thief is caught by the public, this is what happens. There's no trial, just an immediate verdict and instant execution!"

He then proceeded to apprise the newcomers of the local situation.

"This colonial creation is a land of coups. Those in power are in constant fear of a coup. Those scheming for power wait for an opportune time. The avowed purpose of every successive coup is corruption weeding. Many coups have taken place. All coups do not succeed. Some do, some fail. In any case, some heads roll, literally. Either the so-called swindlers or the so-called traitors die, but rarely, civilians will lose their lives. You know what happens if a coup fails? The so-called traitors are tried by a tribunal, tied on polls on the beach, and drilled by machine guns in full public gaze. The next morning dailies flash their drooping bodies for the benefit of those who could not witness the execution. It seems coup attempts and corrupt practices can never be destroyed!"

"Do you know there are some cannibals?"

"What? We have come here to earn our bread, not to end up as meat."

"Don't be scared. Some say they live in remote jungles, tucked far, far away."

"Thank God!"

Some unknown fear started eating the newcomers. The conversation touched upon many such interesting aspects of life and death here.

The well-laid highway road ran alongside the gentle-flowing Niger. The weather was beautiful. The air-conditioning was switched off. The windows were rolled down. The speed was reduced. The travelers enjoyed the crossing natural scenery. Greeneries abounded.

"Look, look at these flowers. How colorful they are! These exotic blooming cactuses grow only here."

Suddenly, Ajit anxiously told his wife not to look at the right side. And, he quickly stretched his hand and covered her eyes. She was surprised. "Ajit, what is this? I'm not a child. Is another thief being punished?"

"No. Something else."

It was obvious that Ajit had seen something that he did not want his young wife to see. *Another act of a vigilante mob?*

The caravan arrived at the picnic spot. Six families assembled. They all gathered in a place for some entertainment. A tribal dance program was just over. The din subsided. The picnicking families started chit-chatting. Conversation turned to Ajit's covering his wife's eyes on the way. "Why, Ajit? What did you see?" Ajit disclosed, in a low tone. He did not want to embarrass the ladies present in the proximity. "Oh. It is then a complex issue for Ajit!" Someone made a friendly dig at him. Every male had a hearty laugh.

Noticeably, the Puris and Arvins talked to others but not to each other; in fact, one avoided even glancing at the other. They seemed to be too uncomfortable in each other's presence to enjoy the picnic fully. An awkward attempt by Mrs. Arvin to strike a conversation with Mrs. Puri proved in vain. Mrs. Puri, a devout housewife, would not like to cross or bypass the *Laxman Rekha.* Even strangers would not behave so estranged. Some well-meaning common friends tried on their own to intervene to bring about rapprochement between them. They were given the cold shoulder by haughty Puri.

"Both have come from the same country, the same city, the same organization. They work here in the same institution, hold high positions, and live side by side. Friendship cannot be one-sided. Why do they, the Puris, behave so childlike?"

The circle of friends seemed to chuckle, as one could guess from their expressions.

The weekend was due to end. The group returned by the same route. They were nearing the locale where, on their way up, Ajit covered his wife's eyes. Ajit looked out. He was visibly relieved. He did not see now what he saw then: an unabashed band of sable, virile boys diving into the river with nothing on.

For a painter or a sculptor, it would have been a beautiful subject—to observe and capture in mind for creative reproduction a silhouette of perfect, carbon-colored, manly nudes with outstretched limbs, poised in the air, against the backdrop of the crimson-colored setting sun, ready to plunge into the crystal-clear water.

The picnic party was back at home. The weekly routine resumed.

"Arvin, how is it that the group is chummy with you?" For Puri, this matter was more significant than a review of the previous week's job.

"Which group do you mean?"

"The one with which we went for picnic."

"Why, what is wrong with them?"

"I don't like them."

"Why? They seem normal, decent."

"I can cut them off from you in no time," said Puri curtly to Arvin without batting an eyelid. Puri said it without raising either his voice or his head.

Some virus is corrupting Puri's mind, surely, Arvin surmised. Arvin was right: Puri did not relish the others being friendly with the Arvins.

"Why are you so upset?"

"I am not upset, Arvin. Wait. You will be upset soon. In a month's time, you will be isolated; wait and see." Simmering fiendishness splashed on Puri's countenance.

We are far away from home in an unfamiliar land for a common purpose. He need not be friendly. Let him be as officious as he can. But, why should he be so inimical, so crude? Is it a matter of chemistry or arithmetic?

Arvin was anguished. Puri strived to be as prickly as possible so that Arvin should either relent or return on his own. Arvin was not, however, prepared to oblige him. He would try to blunt the spike or grin and bear it in the enlightened interests of the employing institutions.

Months ran by, one after another. Arvin was not running away from his responsibility. He willingly shouldered a major brunt of the load. He contributed to the shaping of the institutional policies and laying down proper procedures. He conducted classes to apprise the staff of the refined project appraisal methodologies and monitoring tools. He endeared himself to the officials. The consultancy job progressed well.

Be sincere, be dedicated, and do your best. Bother not about your bullying boss or cunning colleague. This was Arvin's attitude. He would never lose his dedication.

No worthwhile intellectual input was forthcoming, nor was it expected, from the leader. Arvin knew the leader's limitations in the areas of conceptual skill, lateral thinking, and drafting deftness. To be fair, the leader could not be denied the credit for his assumed agility, beaten-track familiarity, and painful drafting (a pencil-and-eraser duel). Arvin did his job with full commitment to his satisfaction. Nothing, nothing including the noninspiring and demotivating leadership, was allowed to interfere with his performance. Pin pricks in personal relationships and pen pricks on official papers, though irksome, were simply ignored by Arvin. That seemed to be the best policy. In fact, he even disregarded a suggestion made by a devil-may-care colleague. His suggestion was to revolt, to blast, to tom-tom. No. it would be an irresponsible response. Some in PCB had already sensed the binary disharmony but were not aware of the details. So long as the contractual job was well performed, PCB would not—and need not—be concerned about anything personal between the advisors. Any open skirmish between them would certainly show their own institution in a poor light; it might jeopardize the assignment itself, with severe damage to the image of the institution. Arvin's serene disposition and exceptional patience, even if perceived by some as a sign of weakness, had always stood him eventually in good stead.

Arvin was respected and liked by PCB. And, outside PCB, the Arvins, far from being isolated, remained a part of the friendly circle, now enlarged. On the family front, the situation became very delicate. The women and children of both were on the horns of a dilemma.

48

• Gentleman's Agreement?

A senior executive from India was due to arrive for a midterm review of the progress of the consultancy arrangement. Both the advisors were seriously engaged in taking stock of things done, listing out the aspects yet to be covered, and identifying the areas in which they would need specific skill support from the home organization.

"Arvin, Saul is coming here next week. He will be here only for two days. Whatever has happened between us, let's forget it. I won't tell Saul a word. Don't say anything to him. If you have observed any weaknesses or inadequacies in me, please, please don't tell him about it. This is a gentlemen's agreement, okay?"

Is Puri trying to bury the hatchet?

Saul landed at PCB. The initial round of meetings was with his colleagues, then later, meetings with the top management of PCB went over formally, officially, and pleasantly. That evening, Saul met Arvin. Initial pleasantries over, Saul asked Arvin about the progress in the consultancy task, his own contribution, and incidentally, but cryptically, how he was getting along with Puri. Arvin gave him a fairly comprehensive account of the tasks accomplished and his own contributions. As for his situation with Puri, he just said, "It is okay."

"Are you sure? Speak up."

Saul then reeled out what Puri had told him in the matter—all contrived lies and distorted stories!

When Puri had proposed the so-called gentlemen's agreement, Arvin had in fact paused for a moment for a mental debate. *Maybe Puri will behave like a gentleman this time and honor his part. Or, true to his natural color, he may turn cunning. It is not unlikely. Still, let me go by his suggestion. If he is again up to his mischief, then I must act.*

This was the line of thinking of Arvin when he agreed to the suggestion of his senior. Even if Puri had not suggested the idea of nonventilation of their mutual grievances, Arvin had no intention of complaining about the leader's harassments and, much less, his shortcomings, which he had observed in many areas. In fact, Arvin had found Puri as a striking example of a mediocre manager.

As Arvin now guessed, Puri's calculations were these: *I am the leader; I can pull a fast one. The visiting executive will hear only me. Even if the matter is checked up with Arvin, he will end up as a weak defender. I can take the first mover advantage. Or, possibly, my action will remain a secret for now, and, by the time the consequences visit Arvin, it will be too late for him to defend himself.*

Puri was only hiding the hatchet. *Now that Puri had breached the agreement he himself proposed, the flood gates must be opened,* thought Arvin. *Let the chips fall where they may.* There was no other sensible option. Arvin opened up. He told Saul all without mincing words. But, he remembered the words of Rudyard Kipling: "Being lied about, don't deal in lies, or being hated, don't give way to hating."

It was revelation for Saul. Shrewd as he was, he could see through the game of the leader. Yet, he wanted to test Arvin's motives. "Will you take up the leadership role?"

"That is not my intention, sir. But for Puri's compelling action, I would not have complained about him. Let the assignment be over successfully. You may, if you so wish, counsel Puri appropriately."

If Saul had been misled to doubt Arvin—indeed, he had been—that doubt now stood toppled by Arvin's ready response. The cloud dissipated. The genuineness glistening in the eyes of Arvin was unmistakable. It was not too difficult for Saul to understand the unfair game being played by Puri for dual purposes—to drive nonobliging Arvin quickly back to the pavilion and to import a substitute of his ilk. For persons like Puri, fairness is just skin-deep. The lesson Arvin learned was this: Don't go by the skin and the tongue alone. Scan the mind and the heart as well.

49

• On the Dock

Arvin had neither missed a step, nor had he been overtaken by anyone in his two-decade career climb. On an average, the first three steps he scaled had taken less than five years each. This particular step turned out to be steep. A new Head, an outsider having come free of any baggage of bias and who distinguished himself by his remarkable dynamism had initiated an organization-wide, morale-boosting exercise soon after he took over the reins three years ago. It instantly energized the slumbering organization. But, his wrist, as tongues wagged, was caught by an insider's hand midway while signing a series of promotion orders. Some arguments, specious of course, were advanced to draw a stop line. The cutoff point at which the pen was held happened to be just above Arvin in the list.

The elevator halted at a crucial moment. The stop button had been pressed by the operator. The lucky ones got off at a higher cadre; the rest would have to wait for a while more. *A while* meant years. Coincidentally, two unexpected developments occurred: One was an abrupt merger of two main streams. Many, in one stream, reaped the benefit of rapid promotions during the premerger regime thanks to post duplications and strength disparities. They now gained higher seniority because the merger was based on current positions.

This was compounded by the imposition of austerity measures. And, this combination resulted in stagnation.

The hand that caused the halt of the elevator was incidentally the same one that had, years back, barred Arvin's leave vacancy promotion. Significantly, it was the same hand that had jotted down, on a memory pad, the following quote from William Penn:

I expect to pass through life but once
If, therefore, there be any kindness I can show or
Any good thing I can do to any fellow being
Let me do it now, for I shall not pass this way again.

Probably, the memory pad was lost soon after recovery from illness. Or, he became hopeful of "passing this way again." Dispassionately thinking, Arvin wondered which hand he was to blame. Was it the hand that intervened or the hand that yielded or the divine hand that rules all?

Defreezing commenced. Promotions restarted. Arvin was now poised for promotion to a level in his career pyramid far up from the bottom and, yet, two more steep steps to the top. He was called for a "chit-chat" with a panel of senior executives. *Discussion, interaction,* or *chit-chat* had been chosen as less unpalatable substitutes for *interview* for internal promotion.

If the management could not have judged an officer's caliber and potential based on his performance over the years, how will a couple of executives be able to assess him in a matter of minutes of interaction?

An officer may be excellent in his present cadre. But, he need not necessarily fit the bill of a higher position. His communication skill, range of knowledge, leadership qualities, and so on, must be assessed before entrusting him with higher responsibilities. This can be done only through a personal interaction. And, more important, such a face-to-face interaction with a committee is helpful to the officer himself. If any element of bias had crept into his CRs, it can be dissolved.

This conflict had been negotiated over time with a compromise move, a win-win proposition: if you don't like the term *interview,* call it a *chit-chat.*

The interview, by whatever name it was called, would not deter Arvin. But, one thing was bothering him. Arvin's memory moved in reverse gear to the closing days of his overseas assignment. He was winding up his affairs. "When you return to Bombay," Puri told Arvin, "you expect to be promoted. Don't you? I know you are due for a promotion. Best of luck," Puri wished Arvin, with downcast eyes, giving a pause for effect. With a sadism-laden smile, Puri then poured out venom, "Let me see how you get your promotion. I'm sure you will be put on the dock. For your information, I have sent a negative report on you."

Bosses vary in their reporting practices.

Some will keep information as close to their chests as possible—their reports, good or bad—in fear of inducing complacency or fomenting confrontation. Some record good reports objectively and disclose them confidentially to the officer concerned to encourage him or to encourage more of his contribution. Some pen very bad, biased reports and lie to the officer voluntarily that he has given him an excellent report, just to hoodwink him.

But, Puri was unique. Having given an adverse report on Arvin, he wanted to please himself at the sight of Arvin's indignation. Even when sought to be ignited with indignation, Arvin would never lose his cool. To the surprise of the tormentor, Arvin calmly responded, "Thanks."

Puri's repeated attempts to repatriate Arvin midway through the assignment failed. He would suddenly, but without—as he thought—arousing Arvin's suspicion, collect, under some pretext, all important papers and files from Arvin to be retained in his own custody. He would ask for written notes on and endeavor to familiarize himself with the various financial concepts and calculations that Arvin taught the officers of PCB. A tap of reflection helped Arvin realize that it was just a preparatory move on the part of Puri to equip himself to carry on the job, at least for the time being, in the absence of Arvin. There were enough cursors pointing to Puri's motivated moves. He was clandestinely operating a lever behind Arvin's back to have him pulled back to Bombay. This he tried with all powers at his command at every opportune moment. He failed, however.

Puri failed miserably on many counts: to undermine Arvin's status; to deprive him of his due facilities; to dock his earnings at source; to vex him so much as to make him fall in line or pack up and return; to demotivate and demoralize him; to misguide the officials back at home; and to isolate him from the friends' circle. Puri's pent-up frustration reached a bursting point. As a last resort, he must have launched his deadly weapon of career destruction—his carefully crafted CR on Arvin. Not only did he intend to wreck Arvin's career prospects, but he wanted Arvin to know it too. It was a vicarious pleasure he did not want to deny himself.

Arvin was happy. He was now at least forewarned that he might be put on the dock.

50

• Listless Waiting

The forewarned "trial," the interview for promotion, had begun. After the usual preliminaries and chit-chat on a few current issues, discussions moved on to the offshore job experience.

Arvin's memory leaves flapped.

It was an overseas assignment calling for the contribution of professional expertise for institution building. The people at the host organization were simple, sincere, and receptive to suggestions. But, they could not be taken for granted. The gutsy management had proved in the past that the hands that seek aid could be dignified and firm enough to show any arrogant representative of a potential lender the door. The treatment meted out to the advisors was remarkably full of warmth mixed with reverence. A competent leader could have harnessed the full potential of the team, enhanced its contribution, set a milestone on the path of the institutional history, and rendered the experience memorable.

Arvin's services and contributions, in terms of on-the-job guidance, classroom lectures, and manuals dealing with principles and practices of project appraisals and monitoring were all well received by the client organization. A formal farewell at the office, personal courtesy visits to his residence—a rarity in that locale—and an emotional send-off at the airport were indeed touching testimony of the love and respect Arvin had earned.

Arvin's attention was clicked back to the present by the interview board.

"Mr. Arvin, will you please tell us about your experience in your recent overseas assignment? Be brief and specific."

Arvin described his role, narrated his own contributions, and added, "I have sent to headquarters a fairly detailed note on the subject, including copies of papers and manuals prepared for and submitted to the client organization. It also includes extracts of written feedback from the executives of PCB."

"Yes. We have seen them."

In hindsight, Arvin realized he had done the right thing: he had documented his contributions and furnished copies to his parent organization. Such a self-trumpeting is not normally necessary for anyone working under good leadership. If objective in his assessment and reporting, as an effective leader should be, the leader and his report would speak for his team member. But, when leadership itself is a missing element, it would be naïve to rely on a self-serving, sinister senior's sense of objectivity.

"Tell us about your personal experience. Was it pleasant?"

Stirred out of his introspection, Arvin responded to the leading question, 'So far as the job was concerned, it was to my liking. I relished it. I think I have acted well my part. It was a rewarding experience. I am glad that the client organization and its executives were exceedingly happy about our contributions. But for some interpersonal irritations within the team, the assignment would have been much more pleasant."

The panel did not pursue the matter further, for they knew it all. Probably, they wanted to provoke Arvin and see his reaction.

"Okay. Thank you, Arvin."

The discussion over, the panel members smilingly shook hands with Arvin. The smile could not be interpreted to mean anything more than a sign of courtesy.

As Arvin learned, the result would be announced in due course. *In due course* is a very handy term, generously employed to avoid rigid specificity and absolute indefiniteness as well. It normally took a few days, occasionally more, to finalize the list of successful candidates based on the ranking of the aggregate of marks obtained from the past three or five years of performance as reflected in CRs and those secured in the interviews. Almost equal weight was given to the CRs and interviews. For senior positions, the practice demanded the CEO's privileged informal concurrence to the list of promotees before its announcement. The numero uno was undeniably entitled to have the last word. The CEO, having a wider-angle perspective, might have to intervene as an arbiter if circumstances so warranted. Whether his intervention would be judicious or not would depend on his nature.

Three weeks passed. The selection list was not out. While Arvin kept his fingers crossed, some random thoughts crossing his mind, *Not all systems can be considered as absolutely external-intervention proof. Belated intervention can even happen at the time of finalization. Interpolation of a candidate may not be a serious issue. But, substitution due to constraint of vacancy is certainly an unfair act, for one will gain at the cost of another. However discreetly done, the matter may get smoked out sooner or later, causing heartburn. How an intervening call or chit, if any, is tackled depends on the Head's mettle and tact. The longer the interval between the interview and announcement of the results, the greater the possibility of any subjective intervention and the louder the rumors bred by gossipers, insiders, or mischief-makers. Such rumors, which do not speak well of an organization, can be stopped by top management through transparent policies and prompt announcement of results.*

The fingers remained crossed. Who knew what was lurking around the corner?

51

• Second Round

The awaited result was out, without undue delay, in just a month. Obviously, the WCD launched by Puri had failed. Arvin got congratulations from all around—well, almost all around. Except in rare cases, promotion is accompanied by a change of posting. If he had a choice, Arvin would have preferred the division that was the main focus of the institution. He did not, however, belong to the clique of choosers. Arvin, on promotion, was placed in a least-preferred division, which was believed, not without any basis, to be a breeding ground for negativism. Generally, people do not fancy any hospital atmosphere—a scene of suffering, writhing, bleeding, and dying; a place for medication, operation, and resurrection. What is required here is not any majestic munificence with pride but sympathetic, timely nursing with patience. One has to take responsibility to tend and mend even irresponsible procreations. People often fail to realize that a revived patient gratefully remembers the doctor concerned for his revival; none remembers the midwife who facilitated his or her birth.

For various causes, both internal and external, industrial units get afflicted by sickness. The contagion effect also plays its part. *Sickness* is a generic term. Even a cursory diagnosis discloses the nature and the intensity of sickness—congenital, incipient, seasonal, advanced, or terminal. Treatment needs to vary accordingly, and it must be entrusted to specialized hands.

The sickness ward was becoming more crowded than the maternity ward. More nurses than midwives were needed. Commensurate with the anticipated workload, staff positions were strengthened at various levels. Reporting structure got realignment. The newly revamped sick units division was responsible for drawing up appropriate restructuring or revival packages for sick or dying units. It grew into an important intermediary to play a crucial operating part in an emerging, powerful, quasi-judicial structure for industrial revival. The division became time bound and activity packed and gained importance. The SUD expanded.

When Arvin was posted in SUD, everyone warned that the underlying motive was sidelining. It was but a question of attitude and aptitude. Arvin believed in and acted on pragmatic advice, "Whatever you do, do it with involvement and dedication. Never lose your vigor."

Ignoring the warning, therefore, Arvin embarked on his new portfolio with enthusiasm. Soon, he became indispensable.

"May I come in, sir?" A familiar voice entered the office.

"Guru, what are you doing here?"

"I have joined this division today, transferred from Calcutta."

"Oh, I see. Welcome to Mumbai."

More than five years had elapsed.

"Yes, Guru, It appears you want to say something. Come on, tell me. Don't hesitate."

"Nothing, sir." In a shaking voice, he continued, "Please forgive me for whatever happened in the past. I have realized my mistakes. I swear I will not do any such things in the future."

"Okay. I'll be happy if you have really realized your mistakes.

Please have a positive attitude. Spend your energy in a constructive manner. It is up to you to choose your path. Crooked ways—take it from me—will never lead you to a desirable destination. Never lose the right way; you may get lost."

The next day, Doctor met Arvin. Neither an M.B.B.S, nor a Ph.D., he was called Doctor. The rationale for the cognomen was not known. He was a senior colleague.

"Arvin, Guru met me yesterday. He was upset, almost on the verge of tears."

"Why?"

"Guru is uncomfortable. In fact, he is scared. He thinks you have specifically asked for this posting in SUD to settle your score. I do not know what happened between both of you in the past. But, it appears Guru has realized his folly, whatever it is. He seems to repent. He says he has already suffered a lot in his personal life; he is not in good health; he has missed his promotion. He would now like to be posted in some other division. But, he is afraid you may not like to let go this chance of taking revenge on him. Tell me why he is so alarmed. Will you let him be moved to another division now?"

Arvin told Doctor everything that Guru did.

"Doctor, Guru's apprehension is justified. He knows that what he had done was so nasty that it should have normally evoked revenge. If he had been in my place, he surely would have been nastier in retaliation. He is not a mere flibbertigibbet, a criminal-minded crook. His proven villainy did cause righteous anger. Still, I gave him a balanced report, giving the devil due credit where it was deserved. He himself is responsible for his sufferings. It is not in my nature to go after anyone, including an enemy, to harm him. I only defend myself, with God's grace, against any offender, leaving it for the immutable laws of nature to deal with him appropriately. I have never asked for his posting, nor am I keen on retaining Guru in my division.

But, I will not seek his shifting. If he wants, he can approach the personnel department to move him out to any other division. I have absolutely no objection. I will not stand in his way; I assure you. Wherever he wants to go, let him go. But first, let his evil thoughts go out of his mind or else, wherever he goes, misery too will go with him."

"Arvin, you are really great. Better forgive and forget."

"I shall forgive him, Doctor."

"Misfortune is like history; it repeats itself; it revisits uninvited; it never comes alone."

Experienced people lament and rightly so. Arvin, it seemed, was now slated to taste such an experience. Realignment of portfolios placed a particular senior at the helm of SUD. As courtesy demanded, Arvin called on his new boss.

"Congratulations!"

"Thank you."

The new boss extended his hand for a handshake. Hands met for courtesy's sake. Eyes did not for one ocular pair was downcast.

"Arvin, I have a few months until I retire. I want my last days in the office to be peaceful. Let us be friends."

"A gentlemen's agreement?"

The boss, Puri, could not hide his blush. Hardly traceable in his face or tone was any reflection of his failed mission. There was a good swallow. It did not, however, look like a realization. More than repentance for misdeeds, his anxiety for a peaceful retirement longed for a frictionless relationship during the end of a career.

"Let us forget the past." Barely audible was the murmur.

"The past will not repeat itself, I presume."

Abruptly, the subject was changed to cut short the moment of awkwardness. A few more minutes lapsed on some dialogue on official matters. Arvin then returned to his office, mentally preparing himself to meet possible return of the bad old days of harassment.

The intercom buzzed.

"Yes, sir."

"Please come."

The intercom in any organization housed in a multistoried building should be meant for internal communication, for instant instructions or clarifications, and occasionally for seniors to give their juniors impersonal dressing downs. If required for a face-to-face discussion, a junior or peer could also be called through the intercom. Often, this convenient device was conveniently ignored by some senior executives. They imagined themselves to be too busy to waste their seconds to press the intercom numbers. Or, they assumed themselves to be too exalted to call even a senior colleague in an adjoining office, except through a peon. A momentary tingle was not preferred to a messenger's run up or, more likely, down in the lift or a flight of steps. Somehow, talk over intercom with a junior colleague was deemed beneath a higher-ups dignity. Instead, the executive preferred to press a buzzer, call a peon sitting or loitering outside the chamber, and tell him to go and call a particular colleague. The peon may take his own time to do so or his own decision not to do so. It didn't matter. In the process, the colleague must be made to feel small; that was important. On the other hand, a junior was not expected or encouraged to contact the senior through the intercom. It was considered nothing but daring indiscipline. But, this chairman was certainly different. He would not hesitate to contact even a junior officer over the intercom, nor would he mind even the reverse.

Arvin met the chairman.

"Arvin, be seated."

"Thank you, sir."

"Arvin, I am glad you are doing a good job. I am getting good feedback about you even from the outside. Keep it up."

"Thank you."

"By the way, I hope you have no problem with Puri."

"There's no problem as of now. There is some change I find in him—change for the better!"

Then, he told the chairman what transpired between Puri and himself.

"Okay. That is good." A smile flashed.

"Sir, I serve the institution, not any individual. I don't carry any ill will against anyone. I do my job professionally. On my part, I shall try to maintain good interpersonal relations."

"I appreciate your attitude. If you ever face any problem, tell me."

"Thank you, sir. Thank you."

No problem whatsoever surfaced. For one thing, Puri had failed in all his vindictive ventures. Arvin had established his credentials by his performance. For another, this was not a far-off locale beyond the vision of many in the organization who mattered. Puri himself was expecting, before his retirement, a promotion to a position—the highest below the board level, the acme of his ambition, the point which, in his opinion articulated in close circles, none of those next to or below him in line were competent enough ever to reach. Someone said that "mediocrity cannot recognize much less acknowledge talents." How true. While valuing others, he would not commit the same mistake as he did in his own case. While he overestimated himself, he undervalued others. Months later, relaxing in his rocking chair at home, Puri would learn to his discomfort that some of them, proving his valuation grossly wrong, had reached a point much higher than the range of his jaundiced vision.

The second round of association between Arvin and Puri passed without any skirmishes. And, Puri secured his aspired promotion and peaceful retirement.

52

• Board Room Trials

As part of his functional duties, a senior officer might be called upon to serve as a nominee director on the boards of one or more companies. It would be an inescapable obligation or a coveted job, depending on the company concerned. Arvin had, at different points of time, the opportunity or the obligation to be on the boards of companies sporting varied management styles and corporate governance standards.

Some were well-governed companies. Transparency and professionalism would mark their board meetings. Strategic plans, project proposals, capital and revenue budgets, performance, accounts, audit reports, statutory and regulatory compliance status, corporate social responsibility activities, or in short, all crucial matters would be presented before the board at appropriate time in reasonable details for objective deliberations and collective decisions. He had seen peaceful coexistence of ethics with economics. Even the directors not qualified to be counted as independent were indeed independent-minded and, more importantly, competent and fair-minded. These companies were earning tremendous respect from the public, besides of course, profit from business.

Some of the boardroom styles he had seen were, however,

discomforting. Some boardrooms were veritable family rooms. Minutes took hours for approval; chairmen read aloud, as prereadied minutes, scripts of imaginary dialogues. Board meetings turned rituals for sanctifying the decisions already made and like practices were all frustrating. There were instances of "trophies" adorning the board with their dignified presence, and discreet silence, and chairmen talking shop for an hour and suddenly closing the meeting as over. Some decorative boards were virtually darkrooms. It consumed a lot of his tact, firmness, and patience to usher in a semblance of good corporate governance in these cases.

He had also had witnessed bickering becoming a business. He had the unique experience of attending a stormy meeting of a fractious board of a company embroiled in management dissensions and court cases. The venue was secretly shifted, at the eleventh hour, to an entirely new location to bypass the board being beleaguered by a drum-beating, conch-blowing, sponsored crowd. The directors had been picked up from their residences or the airport and driven straight to the undisclosed venue to their utter surprise. It was a thoughtful, anticipatory management, indeed! This was at a time when such mass protests by noncorporate organizations were unheard of even at the venue of the meetings of multilateral institutions. With the drum din audibly nearing, a few directors, unaccustomed to such an atmosphere, looked too scared to sit comfortably through the meeting. The meeting over, the board swiftly dispersed before imminent seizure.

One particular board meeting attended by Arvin was a typical example of the perverted standard of corporate governance: The board meeting had just begun, in a "homey" atmosphere. The nominee director was flipping through the papers on the table. Those included annual accounts for approval. These had not been sent in advance to the nominee director on confidentiality grounds. One of the notes to the accounts revealed a nonprovision of interest, accrued and due on term loans. The disclosure was discreet—in the fine print. The amount of liability was, however, undisclosed. It ran into millions of rupees. The auditors' "true-and-fair view" certification had been subjected to the note. The qualification had satisfied, at once, the demands of professional obligation and personal loyalty. The nominee was reading the accounts and the chairman the nominee's face.

The nominee, Arvin looked up and pointed out the accounting omission and the auditors' qualification. The shrewd chairman said, "The accounts have been audited. Let us not waste our time, at this stage, in fiddling with figures."

"I am sorry; I can't allow the accounts to be passed as presented. The accounts need to be redrawn. Please call the auditors in. We may discuss the matter with them," Arvin suggested.

An awkward silence descended. The chairman went out of the boardroom and phoned someone. Resuming the chair, he said firmly, "The auditors are out of the station. There is no need to amend the accounts; there is a time constraint to hold the annual general meeting. I would not like to violate the law."

The "law-abiding" chairman warned the nominee director not to induce the company to commit such a violation. The chairman's phone call did not seem to be to the auditors, as it was intended to be and so believed. Anyway, the call proved to be futile. The nonchalant nominee nagged, "The accounts are neither true to the company's state of affairs nor fair to the lenders. I cannot be a party to passing such accounts. Let my dissent be recorded."

The meeting was adjourned. The accounts were duly recast and then passed at the next meeting.

Such varied exposure had seasoned Arvin enough. Consequently, he was nominated on a troublesome board. Arvin was deliberately chosen by his institution, in fact, by its Head, for the purpose. Age, seniority, experience, exposure, and attitude were all among the factors taken into consideration for the choice. Nomination on the boards of borrowing companies was a potential favor-dispensation vehicle. But, for a company like this, there were no demands, external or internal.

"Sir, we do not nominate any officer normally on more than three boards. He is already on three."

"I know. I want him to be on this board. He can handle it."

The confidence the head of the institution had in the capability of the officer overruled the department's clerical observation. That was how Arvin happened to be on this particular company's board. Arvin was wondering as to why this was considered a difficult board. He would cease to wonder soon.

Arvin attended the first board meeting of the company after his nomination. The company chairman, Adhav, moved an important proposal to be acted upon immediately and sought the board's nod. All other directors were keeping mum, either inattentively or deliberately. The silent promoter directors were a spectacle of sparkling innocence. Arvin was the solitary member who asked some questions, which were rather inconvenient. The points raised by the nominee director were so relevant that they could not be easily brushed aside, especially when he was representing a prime lender. Adhav was more irked as the questioning director was once his junior.

Arvin had high regards for the aged and experienced chairman. But, he was also conscious of his position of responsibility, "A director is entitled to hold and express his opinion on the agenda items; he is accountable. He has to be faithful to the institution he represents. Above all, he has the responsibility to discharge. Of course, an independent director must not prove to be a nuisance by striving to stall whatever the management proposes. But, where warranted, he should not hesitate to intervene."

Arvin knew it all well and was aware of the obligations cast upon him. He would not like to be a nominal director, just to come, attend, greet, grin, shake hands, talk shop, nod his head, sip tea, pocket the fee, and take leave.

It was not that Adhav was an unprofessional entrepreneur to be oblivious or regardless of good boardroom practices. What made him flip his lid was not clear.

"Is this what I taught you?"

His anger burst out in words. His face was contorted into a form of frown. His words were scornful. The rhetoric was intended for the rest of the board to know his humbling skill as well.

"No, Chairman."

What the unruffled member meant was, *This is not what I learned!*

"Then?" The chairman was still glowering at the questioning colleague. He was intolerant of the independence of the member of the board. The dialog continued for a few more minutes. Others were quietly relishing the verbal clash.

"We have wasted enough time. The company does not need the property. The company spends tons of rupees for its maintenance. The promoters are prepared to take it. What is wrong? Let us proceed. Okay?"

The frustrated chairman, looking around the table for endorsement, but without waiting for it, proceeded to declare, "Okay, with your consent, the board resolves that the company's properties mentioned in the agenda paper be sold to the promoters at book value; the consideration will be paid over a period of two years. I shall now take up the next item in the agenda."

The chairman tried to force his decision down the throat of the board.

This is despotic molestation of the board. There is no point in being gentle anymore, felt Arvin. With honest thought as his armor, he was prepared to tell the simple truth.

"Excuse me, Mr. Chairman. I do not agree with the proposal. I would not like to be a party to a decision, which in my opinion, is unfair. The market value of the property must be far higher. I am sorry; please pardon me for saying this, Chairman, the proposal may be construed as a fraudulent transfer."

The pebble of this remark caused a ripple of comments around the table. While a few members now wanted the proposal to be dropped, a few others still egged on the chairman to go ahead. The chairman was not prepared to give up; he changed his track. He used what he thought was a potent silencer to disarm the disagreeing member, "I have spoken to your chairman. He has no objection."

A hoax? Arvin had discussed the issue with his boss and secured his concurrence before leaving for the board meeting. He could not, therefore, be hoodwinked. He listened to his own conscience, *Be objective. Never lose your independence.*

"Chairman! As a member of the board, I have expressed my views. Let me repeat: The proposal is not in the interest of the company or its secured lenders or its public shareholders. I have already explained why. If the majority of the board, in its wisdom, is still in its favor, you may go ahead with the proposal but after recording my dissenting views."

His voice carried enough emphasis without emotion.

"Is it your personal view or your organization's?"

"Both."

There was a sound. A pin had dropped.

"Gentlemen, let us defer the item."

Adhav knew well of the repercussions of carrying the proposal disregarding the expressed dissent of a nominee director, particularly when the objection was indisputably sensible. He had a choice: to drop the proposal altogether or defer it for the present. He preferred the latter.

The meeting over, the chairman came around the long, oval-shaped table toward the member, who was sitting opposite him. Arvin stood up as a gesture of normal courtesy. Adhav extended his hands for a handshake—smilingly. All his anger seemed to have disappeared.

"I am sorry if I upset you."

"I am sorry if I had offended you, sir."

Both shook hands.

No sooner had he reached his office that Arvin promptly apprised his boss, the head of his organization, of what transpired at the board meeting.

"I hope there was no bitterness."

"No, sir."

He told him what happened after the meeting as well.

"Good!"

A week later, two of the company's board members called on the head of the organization to which Arvin belonged. It was stated to be a courtesy call. *Courtesy* often means nothing but business. Plainly speaking, all directors are but nominees of one set of stakeholders or another—promoters, collaborators, lenders, investors, shareholders, employees, or management. Yet, some are deemed independent in the absence of any direct or indirect relationship—kindred, pecuniary, or contractual—or very long association with the company or its promoters, or substantial shareholding. Whether any such directors could honestly boast of independence of mind is a moot point. Independence of mind is independent of education, position, or relation. It is a function of inherent character. Independence is nothing but dependence on objectivity. Many who join as independent are gradually rendered dependent on sponsors. Independence wilts in a climate polluted by environmental, ethical impurity. Anyway, the duo was classifiable as independent.

The duo emerged out of the closed-door meeting beaming with happiness, with one whispering to another, "We have accomplished our mission, I think. Adhav will be happy to hear." On their way out, in the corridor, they met Arvin unexpectedly.

"Hello, Arvin. How are you? Just now, we met your boss. To some context, your name figured in the discussion. We told him how useful you are on our board with your constructive suggestions. He was very happy."

"Thanks."

"By the way, our next meeting will be on the fifteenth of next month. We understand you may not be able to attend."

"Why?"

"We learn you'll be on tour."

"No, who told you so? I'll be in station; I'll try to attend."

"Okay, sir." They hurriedly left with broad smiles.

What transpired in the closed-door meeting oozed out through an unidentified leak: after some goody-goody chat and discussion on some pending issues relating to the company, the visitors slowly, tactfully crawled toward the point—the disguised purpose of their courtesy.

"Sir, the company is in a critical stage, at a crossroads. This is the time—you will agree—that it needs the proper directional guidance. The board needs to be strengthened."

With this cryptic preamble, they continued, "Sir, we know it is your prerogative, as a major lender, to nominate a person of your choice on the company's board. We cannot intervene in the matter. We should not. Still, we take the liberty to make a suggestion. Kindly consider appointing a more senior, mature representative to the board, who could contribute to the deliberations. We should not be misunderstood; we have nothing—absolutely nothing—against your present nominee. But, sir, kindly keep it to yourself."

The motivated message presented in a casket of polished politeness, however, was crystal clear, *The incumbent nominee is junior, immature and incapable of any contribution.*

"I see."

The Head was very attentively listening to the visitors with a smile on his face masking his surprise. The two delegates had been carefully chosen by Adhav to deal with the delicate matter very discretely. They were professionals, had held high positions in their prime, and had been on the board a long time. They apparently had no conflicting interests of any nature. Their words should carry weight. They carried out their given task admirably well. While taking leave, they did not forget to remind the Head to consider their request seriously.

"Please, sir, do the needful soon. The board is scheduled to meet on the fifteenth of next month."

"I understand your problem; let me see . . ."

Probably, Adhav has succeeded in his plan, Arvin surmised when he learned what transpired in the closed-door meeting. Weeks passed, with Arvin expecting every passing day the withdrawal of his nomination.

The Head, Arvin's boss, was skillful and, more importantly, tactful. Once, a VPP (very powerful person) met him in connection with the affairs of his family business. Arvin, being the dealing official, was summoned to be present during the discussion. The boss was at the receiving end for nonsanction of the demanded facilities. Much blame was laid on Arvin.

"This chap has been raising all sorts of irrelevant queries repeatedly. Why don't you transfer him to some other division?"

Normally, any borrower–client, mostly shrewd businessmen, will be as gentle and discreet as possible while complaining against any senior official of a lending institution. But, the VPP, being more powerful, could afford to be crude and arrogant. He could have been much worse, really.

The boss knew very well that Arvin had been raising only relevant, albeit inconvenient, questions in the VPP company's case and had to repeatedly ask them in the absence of proper responses.

The boss told the VPP politely, "Whatever possible will certainly be done, sir. Please ask your people to furnish the particulars."

The VPP, obviously unsatisfied, rose to leave. He was seen off with all due courtesy at the elevator lobby.

After returning to the office, the boss told Arvin, "Don't get upset. He is behaving out of desperation. Do your duty. The rest, I will take care of."

The Head was indeed a pressure absorber. It was, therefore, not surprising that he could now quickly sense the motive behind the duo's suggestion: removal of the impediment-causing director.

However, as his wont, he would not offend anyone with an immediate "no." No, never—he was a characteristic combination of calm, charm, and calculation.

The mission of the delegation failed miserably. Arvin continued to be on the board of the company even after Adhav left.

53

“I Will Kill . . .”

Those days, bankers were not subjected to regulatory command of KYC (know your customer). Bankers, however, knew their customers too well. Today, only computers recognize them. Then, there were entrepreneurs who would, on their own, gather market intelligence reports for KYB (know your banker) purposes.

A visitor entered Arvin’s office following his business card.

“Yes, please come in.”

“Good morning, sir.”

“Good morning. I just remembered you. Please be seated.”

“Thank you, sir.”

“Sir, what happened to my application for a project loan?”

“I am sorry. Based on a detailed appraisal, we find the project as unviable. We sincerely feel you should reconsider your plan. If you go ahead with the project, you’re bound to fail.”

“No sir, I have seen the projections our consultants have made. The project will be viable.”

“You know, projections are only as good as the underlying assumptions. All the assumptions are absolutely unrealistic. The market is overcrowded; the technology out dated, the machinery all secondhand.”

"I am an entrepreneur. No venture is risk free. I am prepared to take the risk."

"Fine. You may like to risk your own money. Even then, prudence will demand taking a calculated risk, not gambling."

Arvin was aware that some would merrily gamble with borrowed money by venturing into riskier, larger projects for the thrill of action, for one-upmanship, or as a status booster.

Is it due to some inexplicable brain chemistry of the borrowers or conducive systemic conditions? Arvin used to wonder.

If the project turned unviable, the borrower would embark on capacity expansion or product diversification. The project implementation would go on and on in a seemingly eternal search of viability. If loans were not serviced, only the loans would be branded as bad. Once loan defaults grew endemic, then they would morph into the banker's problem, a systemic risk, a regulator's concern, and not necessarily the borrower's anxiety.

"Sir, sir, I am emotionally attached to the project."

"Please do not mix up emotion with business. It will be a toxic cocktail."

"The main objective of your organization is financing projects. Is it not?"

"Of course, it is. It is our business too. But, projects should be bankable."

"Mr. Arvin, don't think that I am a beggar. For your information, there are many lenders very keen to finance this project."

"Are there? Please go ahead; take loans from them. Good luck. Anyway, never lose your cool."

"But, they will come in only if you sanction at least a small part."

"I know. I also have learned there are really no takers for this project."

"You are not development oriented. You're negative, unhelpful."

"Please don't get upset. We do support even somewhat risky, long-gestation projects, provided long-term viability is not in doubt. But, yours is not one such. You know it very well."

"If you want, I am prepared to give you my personal guarantee."

"Personal guarantee cannot be a substitute for project viability. It is the project that should pay back the investment."

"After all, it is not your personal money you are lending."

Unmistakably, the tenor of the tone was changing.

"I am afraid you are mistaken. It is precisely because the money is not personally ours that we have to be all the more careful, diligent, and prudent."

"As a citizen, I have every right to demand the loan."

"My dear friend, you are wrong; none can demand a loan."

The dialog between the banker and the loan applicant continued in the same vein for a while.

"Sir, you are so intelligent, so dynamic. I admire you. Please, please help me." The rapidity and versatility of his tone change was stunning. He tried to wheedle Arvin.

"Thanks for your kind compliments. I am sorry; I cannot help."

"Please help me, sir; please support my project. I shall ever remember you, sir."

Once a loan was drawn, *prosopagnosia* could afflict many a borrower. It was not an unusual phenomenon, as any banker knew.

"We will be happy if you remember to repay the loan. But, I am afraid, we cannot make you happy now. If you come back with some other viable project. We will definitely support you."

"I know how to get the loan."

Perhaps, he will walk out in a huff in search of some remote pressure buttons. This is what the banker thought.

But, what the visitor did was the least expected. He rose from his seat, raised his voice, and threatened, "If you do not sanction, I will kill . . ."

For a chilling moment, the banker was frozen in disbelief. He had heard of the killer instincts of competitive corporate achievers. But, it seemed, this chap might turn out to be a real killer. The banker's eyes were focused on the movements of the visitor's hands. *Maybe, he is carrying some deadly weapon. Who knows?* It was years before 9/11. There were no metal detectors or frisking guards at the entrance. If determined to carry out his murderous attack, the visitor, a six-footer with the frame of a wrestler, would need no weapons. The banker certainly would not be able to escape from the hazard or overpower him. Even his help-seeking shouts would be of no use in that soundproof, opaque, wooden-paneled office. The momentarily paralyzed banker, however, remained calm, steadily looking into the eyes of the menacing guy.

"I will kill myself. I will jump out from this floor through the window outside your office in front of everyone."

Arvin heaved a subdued sigh of relief. *An empty threat? Emotional blackmail? Whatever it is, better play it cool.* Such pressure tactics were not new to the banker.

"My dear friend, please sit down, please calm down. If you want to end your life, it is your call. I cannot poke my nose in. You would not want me to stand in the way either. But, but . . . think it over. By ending your life, you cannot achieve anything. Your family will suffer. The nation may perhaps lose a potential captain of industry. Who knows? You may be destined to survive. It is possible. This is unlucky thirteenth floor. If you jump from here, you will fall, surely. But, you may probably survive but crippled. You will suffer the consequences of an attempted suicide and blackmailing of a banker. In fact—yeah, I have forgotten—you cannot jump from here. All are toughened-glass windows; they are all sealed. You cannot open them to jump out. If you are prepared to heed my sincere, friendly advice, please do not jump . . . into such a rash conclusion. Never lose your zest for life. It is more precious. This is not the end of life. Please come back with some other bankable project. We will certainly support it."

The visitor left crestfallen.

Both were destined to live longer.

54

A Blocker

"Arvin, how are you?"

"Fine, sir. Thank you."

"How long have you been in your present position?"

"Six years."

"You have been performing well. I think you deserve a promotion."

"Thank you, sir."

"Why are you keeping quiet?" A patronizing smile adorned his face.

"Sir, I know there is a vacancy. But, I am not given to bragging and nagging."

"I do appreciate that. Talk to MD."

The chairman has all the powers. He could have taken the board into confidence and instructed HR dept to do the needful. Or, he could have constituted a selection committee to recommend a name based on the scrutiny of CRs of those in the zone of consideration for promotion. After all, the process was well established. If the chairman had any reservation in elevating me, he would not have broached the subject on his own. His body language did not suggest any sadistic teasing. His face and voice reflected his genuine concern. Has the chairman been rendered helpless by organizational bureaucracy? Maybe—otherwise, why did he ask me to talk to the second in command?

Arvin was puzzled. Almost on daily basis, he had been in touch with MD in the course of his official work. It never occurred to him that he should specifically ask for his promotion. Right or wrong, he had never done it.

Positional elevation should not be based on demand or ingratiation with the bosses. It should be performance based and policy driven. This was Arvin's perception.

Those days were different. Job hopping was yet to start in a significant way. Self-trumpeting of performance, actual or assumed, or flaunting of offers of better positions from elsewhere, genuine or managed, were unfamiliar tactics. The chairman's casual observation was screwing with Arvin's mind.

"There must be some reason for his hint."

Arvin met MD Seveen in his sprawling office. A showpiece, obliquely placed, adorned his oval table without blocking the view of the MD. Standing on one side, an IT chap was booting the desktop to open e-mails for the MD's perusal. Arvin waited for the mail opener to leave and then tactfully mentioned his patient wait for his promotion. Seveen pricked up his ears. After taking a deep breath, he responded, "Yes. I know. You deserve it. But, unfortunately . . ."

After a minute, he continued as if he were talking to himself, "That chap is not moving out."

Arvin understood.

"That chap" was no stranger; he was a colleague, an immediate senior, a "friend," a soft speaker face-to-face, and a subtle mischief-maker behind the back. This was the second occasion of his being a speed breaker on Arvin's promotional path. Earlier, to be fair, it was not entirely his fault. Then, both were promoted, but with a solitary vacancy at that center, that chap was transferred to another place of his preference, and Arvin's promotion was to take effect only from the date of that chap's being relieved from duty. It was as per HR policy. Arvin was not so privileged as to be accommodated in a supernumerary position for the time being. He had to wait for a few weeks.

Now, merit-wise, that chap had fallen out of reckoning for promotion. He was given informally an honorable option: to quit voluntarily from the ignominy of being superseded. He, however, chose to ignore it, biding time until his due date of retirement. He probably thought, *Why should I leave, giving an early chance to Arvin? There are a few months for me to retire. Anything could happen in the meantime. The age of superannuation may be revised up. The top management may change its mind. I may succeed in bringing pressures. Or, something may happen to Arvin. Who knows? I may not get the promotion; it doesn't matter. I will not let Arvin get it earlier.*

He had lost his credibility but not his hope. His faction of friends was scrambling to preempt the ignominy.

An undeserving chap gets unmerited sympathy. A deserving one is denied his due. Why? Is it because Arvin did not belong to the region of favor?

There was a meek prick in the conscience of the organization. It went unheard. The blocker stayed unmoved. Nearly a year quietly moved.

At last, that chap retired on his due date, unblocking the way for Arvin's elevation. The MD called Arvin and informed him of his elevation, "Congrats. You are promoted."

"Thank you, sir," Arvin's response was robotic. The undue delay had robbed Arvin of all the cheer a positional elevation would have normally given anyone.

"Sir, promotion is also like justice."

"I know what you mean. Delayed, delayed for over a year but, not denied, denied forever. Such things do happen. We are helpless."

What would have happened if that chap had been in my place? A hypothetical question nibbled Arvin's mind. *Possibly, merit would have been given its legitimate right of passage to supersede sympathy.*

Soon, there was a change in placement. Job responsibility is as important as positional elevation. Arvin was asked to head a new division formed to carry on a new business. It was a new field. A challenging job it would be. Arvin took up the challenge not because he had no other option; he had no hesitation whatsoever.

"Do you know why you have been placed at the head of the new division?"

"Why?"

"To accommodate Pramuk in your place and to make you flounder in new waters."

Arvin ignored the whispers. "A threat? It may turn out to be an opportunity. Who knows?" He plunged into uncharted waters ungrudgingly and swam, against currents, to the shore of success. The division became a profit center. Establishment of credible systems, procedures, and control measures and their consistent application fetched ISO certification. This caused a flurry of activities in a competing organization to follow suit. Within, there were a few mischievous elements to conspire to do whatever possible to trivialize all the contributions and achievements of Arvin. Among the elements were a few rare specimens of weasels. Individually, they would compete with and conspire against one another, and together, they worked against others. By networking, they would work their way up. Boss gripping was their masterly art of progression. They knew and did what exactly would please their bosses. More important, the bosses seemed really pleased with them. For, these were the chaps who would readily come forward with solutions to emerging problems. But, the bosses would never ever come to know that they themselves were the behind-the-scenes problem originators.

Systematically, they could ensure that their competing seniors were shunted out and potent juniors undermined. Masked masters of mischief-making, they had an illusion that theirs would be fail-proof means for lifetime, joyful success. Anyway, they could not fully succeed in their attempts to undermine Arvin. But, Arvin had to face many challenging moments.

55

• Challenging Developments

At an elite gathering, Arvin was delivering a keynote address on "Challenges in the New Millennium" with particular reference to his own organization.

"This institution is a historic creation, playing its defined role on prudent lines. Without limiting its role to mere intermediation between savings and investment or mere lending for asset creation or capital formation, it has acted as an instrumentality for translation of plans and policies into projects and accomplishments. Outperforming even its elder siblings, it has emerged a leader and has grown into a banyan organization giving birth to multiple, self-rooting institutions."

Many heads in the audience were seen nodding in acknowledgement.

"Even spinning off some of its business activities has not stunted its growth. It has been a good profit earner and a decent dividend payer. A nursery bed of talents, it has been a supplier of executives to many organizations of strategic importance."

A few of these executives present were seen smiling.

"A repository of domain knowledge and expertise and an institution of international repute, it has come to be ranked high in the pecking order of domestic protocol and significance. It can legitimately claim significant credit for the success of many of today's globally recognized corporate houses and their prime owners, first-generation entrepreneurs, and the resurrected sick units. In fact, credit for the broad-banded development and spread of entrepreneurial culture in the country should go, in no small measure, to this great institution. It has survived many environmental and reformative challenges—industrial downturn, disintermediation, interest deregulation, Basle prescriptions, and whatnot. The grand vision of its founding fathers, I feel, has been substantially realized. And, I am sure their souls would have been gratified to find the institution flourishing for over a quarter of a century."

The echo of the applause that erupted would have been heard by departed souls. Arvin continued, "The strategies adopted in the initial years may not hold for all time to come. They have to be revised, reshaped, or redrawn in line with the changing landscape of development. Many comparable institutions in the world have transformed themselves. The past should not lull us into complacency. The future has formidable challenges in store."

He then elaborated on the changing paradigms in the industrial and financial sectors. He also hinted at the emerging opportunities. In conclusion, he observed, "While the pace and degree of institutional transformation will be dictated by regulatory directions and commercial considerations, harmonization of conflicting views and interests and smoothening of transitions will be a challenging bump to cross over to seize the opportunities in the new millennium. I am confident we will meet the challenges."

"Thank you."

An elderly gentleman sprang up from the audience and ran toward Arvin. Many heads turned to see what he was up to. It was only for a handshake.

"After hearing your speech, I am relieved. My money is in safer hands. I hope you become the head of the organization."

He happened to be an investor in the bonds issued to the public by the organization.

The institution, with which Arvin grew over decades, had prided itself for its enormous economic contributions. Not spared by the fast-spreading reform wind, it had to face a Hobson's choice: Run as a mere bank or fall into obscurity!

Amid widespread discussions and debates, ideological confusion was prancing around. Whether the institution would run or fall depended on its emerging leadership.

The ship was riding on high tide. The brewing storm was yet out of sight. The vice-captain was elevated to captaincy. Seveen was now perched at the helm. A meeting was organized to facilitate him. Among others, Arvin spoke, "Sir, you have assumed this responsibility when our organization is at a crucial stage, crying for a decisive direction and visionary leadership. We cannot be blind to the wind of change that is sweeping over the financial sector. We cannot stand still to be swept aside into obscurity. We have to run steadily with courage and conviction and, yet, with caution and circumspection.

"The task before you—the task of change management and risk management—is indeed formidable. But, look at the army of skilled, energetic, and dedicated professionals you have at your disposal, and the burden will look much lighter. Given appropriate motivational engineering, these resources can be harnessed and galvanized to achieve the task. For accomplishing the task, let me assure you, we are all behind you. We shall join our hands, lend our shoulders, share our ideas, and lighten your burden."

Years passed. The tailwind was favorable. The ship was sailing majestically under the stewardship of Seveen.

A further elevation became due for Arvin. This time, the elevation was crucial. It would take him to the second rung from the top or in the vicinity of his lifelong ambition. The next step would be the top. He had everything required—qualifications, experience, performance, and seniority. Still, elevation was elusive. There was no stumbling block now. The current captain had no such flimsy, if-only-that-chap-moves-out kind of reason.

Doing the rounds, however, was another whisper, "Arvin, the delay is purposeful to meet two ends. One, with long delay, your residual service will fall short of the minimum required for the top position. Two, the chum, currently out, is waiting for simultaneous elevation. Though junior, if now placed at par, he can also stake his claim for the top later."

Truth, at times, is only whispers.

Despite frantic efforts, the chum's return could not be advanced. Arvin's elevation, too, could not be held up beyond a point. He got it, with accustomed delay.

Arvin was not averse to a proper leadership development process being adopted.

"Development of a suitable successor is also the responsibility of the leadership. Executives with leadership potential should be identified quickly through transparent processes. They must be steadily groomed by means of proper placement and timely movement upward on career paths. That would really be a highly motivating factor, facilitating succession planning."

This is what Arvin as a professional thought and management institutes also preached. But, theory and practice often differ.

56

• SIM Card

A career development course for young bankers and budding executives was in progress. There ensued a group discussion on a case study. The theme was *leadership.* The hypothetical organization was a government-sponsored organization engaged in financial field. As a faculty member, Arvin was moderating the discussion. The interaction with the participants was stimulating.

"Sir, every organization aims at growth. But, managements do not adopt identical methods. Can you explain why?"

"Yes you're right. Direction and destination of an organization will largely depend on its CEO. Essentially, there are two routes a management may take."

Arvin took a pen and listed the routes on the drawing sheet.

I	II
i. Grow at breakneck speed	Grow steadily
ii. Consider cost as investment	Cut unnecessary cost
iii. Never mind changing times	Adapt for changing
iv. Make minimal provisions	Make prudent provisions
v. Show high profit	Book fair profit
vi. Declare maximum dividends	Declare decent dividends
vii. Get thundering applause	Hear subdued clapping

"Which route will you follow?" Arvin asked the participants.

Many hands went up.

"The first one."

"The second one."

"The first."

"The second."

"First."

"First."

"First."

The opinion was divided.

"You are all almost of the same cadre, caliber and capability. But, you see, you differ in your approaches and attitudes. Similarly, there are CEOs and CEOs. They differ in their aims, attitudes, and styles. By the way, I have not completed my chart. Let me complete it."

Arvin completed the chart.

I	II
viii. Forget the future	viii. Secure the future

"The channel choice largely depends on the attitude, outlook, and vision of the CEO. A CEO with myopic self-interest will take the first route, aiming at a quick semblance of success to be applauded instantly. A CEO with a selfless, long-term-vision will follow the other route to ensure sustainable growth and stable success for the enterprise. He may not be immediately applauded but will surely be honored before long for his solid contribution. But, it is rare to come across such a CEO these days."

The participants squirmed uncomfortably. They were exchanging glances.

"Sir, it is said that growth often contains seeds of decay. Is it so?"

"It all depends on how the growth is engineered or how it is managed. In a hypercompetitive environment, growth becomes an obsession; it happened in the case we studied today. Numerical growth gains prominence. Health implications are ignored. Competition compels. Personal ambition propels. Short-term expediency succeeds; long-term prudence loses. Impressive statistics help in self-trumpeting for longer chair retention or for a possible future berth. As the head turns, so does the body. Cutthroat competition gets whipped up even internally. Targets are constantly chased. Caution is contemptuously shooed away. Credit grabbing and colleague ditching sneak in. Hugging close to the honcho matters more than performing efficiently. Boss pleasing succeeds. Credit goes awry. Accountability gets unbalanced. Visibly, these are symptoms of myopic, mediocre leadership. Such a leader's action results in the creeping corrosion of the health of the organization. Invariably, his sins will visit upon his successors."

"In this case study, sir, the organization adopted different criteria for selecting its CEO at different points of time. Was it also responsible for its slip from the pedestal? What, do you think, is the proper criterion for leadership selection?"

"I am glad you have raised that pertinent issue. There are some myths about the choices of leadership: seniority versus selectivity, insider versus outsider, and technical versus financial.

"Debates on the appropriateness of choices are sparked off from time to time, depending on emerging circumstances. One or other of these criteria gets flagged to back up a prepicked candidate. All arguments for the criteria that suit the candidate are advanced and get orchestrated. None care for any empirical evidence. In fact, we tend to forget there can be effective as well as ineffective leaders in any category. It all depends on the individual concerned. Normally, the leader should emerge from the ranks of the organization through a fair process. You have to look outside only when no insider is fit enough. Another contentious issue concerns tenure. A reasonably long period, no doubt, enables a CEO to work out and put through a suitable strategic plan for sustainable growth. But, what is a reasonably long period? One year? Two years? Five years? Again, it depends on the circumstances and the person. An effective leader can accomplish in one year much more than what an ineffective one may be expected to do in five years. Likewise, a tenure of three months is enough for an unfit leader to do irreparable damage to an organization. The longer the period, the greater are the chances of problems. Incidentally, a CEO need not necessarily be a maverick or act over smart, claiming all unbranded cattle as his, so that others may incur the cost of branding theirs. Sooner or later, he will lose his assets. Besides basic qualifications and relevant experience, all that an effective CEO should possess are excellent leadership qualities and a SIM card—sincerity, integrity, and maturity."

"As time changes, I think the leadership qualities required must also change. Do you agree, sir?"

"I fully agree. Time and tide do not stand still. Both move; both also change. The change pattern also changes. This is also true of corporate environments. With the changing circumstances, a suitable change in the leadership caliber and style will also be called for. Often, mismatches occur. When the organization needs bold, innovative, dynamic leadership, it may get one with exactly the opposite attributes. Consultants, advisors, committees, groups, conferences, discussions, brainstorming sessions, reports, reviews, and the like are indeed potent instruments for hammering out pathbreaking initiatives. But, these may also be deftly employed to ensure caution. The organization, however, may run mechanically. A systematized organization is like a cockroach. Even beheaded, it can run, though unsteadily, for quite some time. Leadership then becomes a decorative head presiding over the proceedings. In this case, this is what happens. A titan gets virtually dwarfed for want of right leadership at the right time."

Arvin was dreaming for a day to translate his ideas into action and to lead his organization further up the pyramid of success. Now, on his last lap, he could glimpse the winning post. For gaining the post, however, he must succeed in managing one major risk—the risk of stumbling upon a hurdle.

57

• Risks Named

What is in a name? One can't just pooh-pooh the issue. Dispensation with the caste-suffix might have helped in avoiding an instant push forward or toss backward. But, not only the name proper but even its length could spell a problem. Computer-formatting stereotypes names into first name, middle name, and last name. In some places, the given name will be the first. Sequencing may also differ in some countries. This creates confusion in the name of a South Indian like Arvin, with the initials expanded. Arvin had fixed it by filling in his full name, disregarding the part-wise classification. A few letters of his name had to be printed outside the given boxes.

"I am sorry, mister. I can't permit your entry."

"May I know why?"

"Your name. Your name is the problem. It is too long to be swallowed by the format in the computer. Sorry, you may have to go back."

"What?"

"Yes. Your name has not been fully captured in the system."

"Is my 'distinguished' name an entry barrier?"

Arvin never imagined that his schoolteacher's contribution to his name would land him in such a predicament in a foreign land. *Is the computer a tool meant for enhancing human efficiency or deleting human discretion?* Arvin wondered.

"I've come here on an official invitation to attend the fund bank meetings. My stay here will be only for three days. It'll be a pity if I have to go back just because your computer program format doesn't fully accommodate a long name."

Disregarding Arvin's observation, the officer disappeared into another enclosure. Arvin had been to many countries, in the East and the West, for official purposes in the past. Nowhere had his longish name been an obstruction. A few minutes passed. The immigration official came back and returned the passport without uttering a word. And, he beckoned the next person patiently waiting at the yellow line. Arvin moved out and anxiously opened and flipped through the pages of the passport. A stamp in the passport brought a smile to Arvin's face. He had permission to stay in the country for six months.

All major hotels in Washington were full of bankers, bureaucrats, and ministers from across the globe. As usual, the delegates and visitors were rubbing shoulders and exchanging views with the honchos in the financial world. Organized protests by some NGOs against globalization were barricaded at a safe distance. Investment bankers, better dressed than some billionaires, could strike many business deals for millions of dollars in hotel suites, lobbies, corridors, and coffee shops. Seminars, symposiums, discussions, PowerPoint presentations, and Q&A sessions were all interesting and informative. This time, the jamboree was dominated by discussions on universal banking and corporate governance. There were breakfast meetings, luncheon sessions, and cocktail dinners galore. The closing ceremony was equally grandiose as the opening, with colorful cultural programs. After wading through some of the events on a hectic schedule for three days, Arvin flew out over the Pacific.

The cab was speeding on the Rainbow Bridge.

What a change since my last visit! Am I in new New York?

Arvin reached the conference venue in time. With the address slip clearly written in the local language at the reception desk of the Hyatt, the cab driver had no problem in reaching the destination. Arvin was received courteously, with head bows and handshakes, at the entrance and was swiftly conducted to the hall. His talk on "Risk Management in Banking" was scheduled to begin at 2:35 p.m. The delegates had reassembled after the lunch break. All were in pinstripe suits. Pin-drop silence prevailed.

At 2:31 p.m., the session started. What precision in time management!

At 2:32 p.m., Arvin was introduced in fine English.

At 2:35 p.m., Arvin took the mike.

"Ladies and gentlemen, I deem it my privilege to share, at this forum, a few of my thoughts on risk management in the banking business. I am aware of the risk I am running by venturing to speak on a subject like this at a post-lunch session—the risk of slipping you into slumber. Let me manage the risk."

There were smiles with undiluted solemnity.

Arvin continued, "As the banking business is getting increasingly globalized, the marketplace has turned into a competitive field. In a multilocation and multiproduct operating environment, which is progressively being deregulated, risk management has become crucial for success and even for survival."

Enumerating what risk management for a banking institution would involve, he said, "As the sector emerges from the cocoon of patronage and protection to face the world of market discipline, it needs to strengthen its wings by upgrading its risk management techniques; only then can it come out with flying colors."

Then, he covered various risks inherent in banking in a globalized business environment, sprinkling in some interesting, relevant stories.

He also touched upon his Indian experience and went on further saying, "The market-driven environment, deregulation-led volatility in interest rates, intensifying competition, deteriorating portfolio quality, dwindling patronage funding, and demanding investors have all made the regulators and banking institutions realize the imperatives of a refined risk management system."

Touching upon the pillars and principles of the Basle Accord, Arvin continued, "Risk management is gradually turning from intuitive to systemic; still, it remains largely a defensive measure to minimize risk. It should emerge as a coherent process to optimize risk and return."

Finally, he stressed the need for further strengthening information systems and database and also upgrading risk management skills. "More importantly," he observed in conclusion, "top managements themselves should be in a position to understand and appreciate these sophisticated risk management techniques. And, all said and done, we should also bear in mind that a lack of common sense will be highly risky."

At 3;00 p.m., Arvin resumed his seat.

Arvin had managed his risk well; the audience remained awake. Amid ovation, Arvin was given a plaque in appreciation of his talk.

Arvin's second visit to Japan turned out to be equally pleasant and purposeful. But, he missed one great soul. The unforgettable Good Samaritan, the noodle-like, soft old man whom he had met in his last visit, he learned, was no more.

Sayonara.

Completing the circle clockwise, Arvin returned to Mumbai. A beckoning call was waiting for him.

58

• "You Deserve This Chair."

Ring . . . ring . . . ring . . .

It was the premobile era. Arvin lifted the receiver.

"Hello, Mr. T. S. Aravendan?"

"Yes, speaking."

"Sir, I have been trying to contact you for the last ten days. I was told you were traveling. Can I talk to you now for a few minutes?" It was an unfamiliar but honey-soaked voice!

"I am afraid I do not know you. May I know whom I am talking to?"

"I'll tell you, sir. We have your CV."

"Will you please come to the point? I have a meeting to attend."

"Okay. We are headhunters."

"Not literally, I hope."

"Ha-ha. We are an executive search agency."

"Oh, I see. Now, tell me. What can I do for you?"

"Sir, we are looking for an executive for an MNC. The compensation package will not be an issue. Would you be interested?"

"May I know the name of the organization?"

"Sorry, sir. We cannot disclose the identity of our client at this stage."

"Sir, if you say you're interested, we will then advise our client to get in touch with you."

Of late, Arvin had been receiving such feelers, personal and indirect. This was the first occasion of a telephonic contact by a placement agency. It seemed the agency had already done its due diligence exercise. Decades back, he would not have hesitated to grab such a chance; he had then been frustrated with a tantalizing transfer. But now, he was nearing his acme of ambition. A fat purse cannot compensate for the soul satisfaction of serving a larger cause.

"Thanks for your inquiry. I am not interested."

Disbelief echoed in the silence for a few seconds. "Okay, sir. In case you change your mind, please contact us at this number."

"Sure, thanks."

Surya succeeded Seveen, who had retired with thunderous applause. He entered the same sprawling office, the same showpiece, and the same e-mail opener. With no effort to learn how to use them, on the part of top executives, the desktops remained a mere status symbol. The programs were not user friendly, nor were the IT chaps. They were zealous guardians of their own indispensability. Executive ignorance was a conducive operating environment for computerization to progress at the speed of a snail. The organization was floating, drifting. Surya had to navigate through troublous troughs. He kept his eyes and ears closed. A storm was brewing ahead. Floundering of the ship was feared. A few opportunistic rats started leaving. The steward was unconcerned. His term would end soon anyway.

Arvin had plenty of ideas bubbling in his mind to take his institution to greater heights. He could not, however, translate all of them into action. He was constrained. Protocol barricaded. Without a hankering for any personal credit, he shared his ideas with the captain. The captain did not care.

Arvin articulated his views at every opportunity, at every internal forum. Periodically, there used to be jamborees, when all divisional heads would meet for performance evaluation and free exchange of strategic ideas. Arvin rarely missed such opportunities to air his views, share his ideas, and post his messages.

On one such occasion, he spoke candidly and forcefully. He quoted the story from *Who Moved My Cheese?* and then added, "The environment has changed; regulatory framework has changed; corporate performance has changed; the market condition has changed; portfolio quality has changed; profit margin has changed.

"So, we have to change; our policy should change; our strategy must change; our practices have to change; our attitudes must change; and our approach has to change. As Darwin said, it is not the strongest or the most intelligent species but one that is the most responsive to change that survives. To survive, we must change and change fast."

The parabolic story did not amuse the presiding boss. In a seemingly eternal search for new vision and mission, innovation and dynamism were missed. Talent exodus was trivialized. Evaporation of team spirit went unnoticed. The status quo was adopted as a safer bet.

Arvin painted a picture of the prevailing environment in another important internal conference and conveyed a clear message to the line functionaries, "With the pragmatic exercise of embedded options, high-cost borrowings stand reduced. Exuberance for fresh borrowings has been contained. Treasury yield has improved.

"A reversal of the downturn is visible. Even the sectors that were rusty or cracked are now showing sure signs of recovery and consolidation. Recovery of overdues should receive our focused attention. In deserving cases, do restructuring. In other cases, remind, request, coax, cajole, demand, dare—do whatever you can, within the domain of a decent creditor, and recover. Litigation is an available tool; use it judiciously. Do not get bogged down in the quicksand of legalism.

"Fresh asset creation shall be made on highly prudential lines.

Work environments need improvement. Leadership, at all levels, should inspire confidence. We should move forward swiftly in terms of innovation and technology."

Most of the messages missed the target.

For day-to-day running of the organization, Surya relied on Arvin most as his Man Friday. In fact, Arvin was Man Saturday and Man Sunday, too. Yes. Surya would summon as many executives as available to the office on weekends and holidays, presumably to prove the vibrancy of the organization and his own dynamism. Spot-running may be a health booster for an individual but not for an organization. Surya knew it. Still, he chose the strategy, probably as a risk-free exercise.

Invariably, Arvin would accompany Surya as a privileged coparticipant in all high-level meetings. For one such external meeting, Surya ignored an egoistic participant's suggestion not to have Arvin tag along. The participant, who had organized the meeting, was no stranger to Arvin. That he was now heading an organization had gone to his head. Position brings power; power, arrogance; and arrogance, downfall—downfall from power and position. From one end, the other end may not be visible through the mist of ego. The organizer saw to it that Arvin would have no chair to sit in. He was to be tossed into a chair tucked in a corner far away from the oval table. Surya was visibly embarrassed but remained helplessly quiet. Arvin understood the colleague's silly intention and was amused by his childlike behavior. He did not mind it. But, the presiding personality, a seasoned, senior bureaucrat, did.

"Sorry, Arvin, please wait for a minute."

The chairman of the forum was looking for someone who could be asked to bring a chair. Sensing it, with a smile masking his discomfort, the egoist himself dragged a chair in for Arvin. Even in such situations, Arvin would not lose his dignified quietude.

Surya was more a transmitter than an absorber of pressures. Noncompliance with his compulsive hints would make him shiver with agitation, like a mobile set in vibration mode. Otherwise, he was the embodiment of ego-free simplicity. Except for occasional frictions, Surya and Arvin had a smooth official relationship. In relaxed moments, Surya would point to his seat and would say, in a sincerity-soaked tone, “Arvin, you deserve this chair.”

59

• Tripped Up!

Arvin kept his hands stretched. The pendulous branch bearing the fruit of labor of three decades, he hoped, would be swung, by a whiff of fair wind, down to his grasp anytime.

One day, Prasad, a friendly guy, stormed into Arvin's office with a vexed mood, "Arvin, why is he spitting so much venom against you?"

"Who?"

"You should know whom I am referring to."

"Honestly, I don't. Tell me, Prasad."

"Shekar!"

"Oh, I see."

"He says you are his number one enemy."

"Really? How many does he have? Anyway, Prasad, I have never considered him as my enemy."

Arvin never imagined that Rupak Kumar Shekar would have so much enmity brewed in his broad bosom. Usually, those who snatched unmerited positions behaved with rancor and arrogance. He was no exception. He was the embodiment of envy. His inimical feelings against Arvin were internally simmering. These were fanned, by his cronies, to flare up. He was spewing vitriolic vituperations.

Why? Envy? Insecurity? Prejudice? Chemistry? Or, enmity, carried forward from an earlier birth? No rational explanations were available.

Pending completion of the process of selection and placement of a fit and proper person at the helm of affairs, Shekar had been made a *pro tem* caretaker for a few weeks. He did not want to let this God-sent chance go a waste. Not a day would pass without his attempting to humiliate Arvin by all silly means. Arvin ignored them all. His philosophic patience frustrated the persecutor and astonished others. *This too will pass,* Arvin knew.

The stint over, Shekar, who on retirement might need Arvin's cooperation, came over to Arvin's office and hugged him, saying, "Let's be friends!"

Arvin smiled. He looked around for a pinch of salt.

"Thanks, Shekar."

A week passed. Prasad came in with a blooming face. "Congrats, Arvin. You're going to be elevated. You'll now sit on the board. Next, I am sure, you'll chair it. This is unstoppable."

"Thanks. How do you know?"

"I know the papers are moving."

Arvin had some premonition: a stray dog may jump in the manger.

Another week passed. Prasad again met Arvin.

"Arvin, Shekar has retired."

"Yes, Prasad."

"But, he is still working against you. He is leaving no stone unturned and nobody unused to stop your elevation."

"I know."

"Why? Why should he do this? He doesn't stand to gain or lose."

"Prasad, in this world, there are a few who derive more pleasure at others' pain and feel more pain at others' pleasure. Shekar is one. Like Sambu. Remember the story I told you some time back. It is his nature. He is always animated with an uncontrollable sense of animosity. I think his envy is eating into his vitals. I really pity him."

"I thought at least, after retirement, he would have a change of heart."

"No, Prasad. Even a heart transplant would not change him. The new one would be instantly infected."

"Arvin, congrats! I'm outside the country at the moment. Will be back next week. I understand you have been elevated to a board position. I knew you would get it. You deserve it. I am so glad you got it. My best wishes." The congratulatory message was from an outsider privy to the inside story.

"Thanks."

"Have you got the order?"

"Yes, I got it."

"Arvin, come again. Have you really got it?"

A shock reverberated in his voice. "Yes. Why?"

"Mm, nothing."

The caller was confused; the call ended.

Arvin could very well surmise it was the caller who had probably been instrumental in blocking his elevation. Having learned that the process of elevation had been successfully stalled, the caller had tried to hoax or tease Arvin for vicarious pleasure. Arvin knew it. He, therefore, bluffed to call the caller's bluff.

Arvin's hunch proved right. A disgruntled colleague appeared claiming seniority over Arvin. He had not been considered fit for the earlier promotion to Arvin's level. After around three years, he was elevated on sympathetic grounds. Linking this with the calibrated delays of earlier promotions and abrupt placement changes, some suspected it as a strategic move to checkmate Arvin.

In a government-sponsored organization, a mere A4 size representation could jeopardize someone's chance of promotion. Whether the representation was merited or not, justice demanded its consideration. Ultimately, the representation may be turned down as utterly baseless. So, what? The real purpose would be achieved. Someone's elevation would be unnecessarily delayed if not altogether stopped. Here was an instance of justice done meaning justice denied. The process of justice was such there was no remedy for such a travesty.

On examination in the light of past records, the challenge was found unsustainable and turned down. In the process, Arvin's elevation was delayed by a few months. Unjust? Yes. Yet, Arvin had to grin and bear. The only solace was that it did not drag on for long.

At last, Arvin reached the top row. He would now sit on the board of the institution he had joined as an officer three decades back.

60

• The Flight of Imagination

The top position, 1A, the Chair, was still dodging Tantalus. Like a mirage, it was continuously receding out of his reach. As he advanced toward the receding winning post, he was losing his stamina, the length of his residual service. He did encounter fresh hurdles hurled on the runway. The environmental impurities alongside the runway were nauseating. Unsolicited guidance and uncalled-for suggestions poured in. Interestingly, a commercially successful astro-numerologist, obviously well informed, proffered advice, ostensibly *gratis*, to Arvin to add one more letter to his already longish name and gain magical powers to clear the path of his ascendancy. It was a unique experience for Arvin.

The race for the Chair was gaining velocity. Among the contenders were, besides Arvin, a few of his juniors including the "chum." Remember the whisper?

"Like life, career is also a journey. Rather, it is a race, a combative game. Too many and too varied are the playmates. Their differing dexterity, disparate dispositions, and desperate aims can be challenging.

Not all the players may be sporting enough to stick to their own tracks or roles or disciplined enough to abide by the rules of the game. Booing and cheering, cheating and beating, passing and chasing, pushing and pulling, bumping and jumping, tipping and trampling, and many such things may occur in the arena. Why, even accidents may happen or can be caused. It is all part of the game. In the process, one may or may not reach, or may not be let to reach, the targeted destination or the winning post or the set score. The medal or trophy may be elusive.

"If you win, do not lose your head;
If you lose, do not lose your heart.
In any case, never lose the spirit."

These philosophical words he had uttered in a talk years ago were constantly reverberating in his memory.

Arvin had an important official appointment in Delhi. He took the early-morning flight, executive class. Preferred 1A had been kept vacant. Any VVIP might turn up any time.

Arvin handed over his coat to the air hostess, occupied the allotted seat 2A, and fastened his seat belt. When the flight was airborne, the seat belt sign was turned off.

"What would you like to have for breakfast—veg or nonveg?"

"Only coffee please."

After coffee, Arvin leafed through an in-flight magazine. A funny story caught his attention.

On your march:

Some aspiring household rodents lined up. One or two from the neighborhood had also been inducted.

Get set:

All were in readiness, bent upon sprinting.

Go:

The race started.

A shrill whistle:

Stop!

The sprinters were stopped on the track. They had to retrace their steps to the baseline. Some were blinking, some fuming, and some smirking.

An announcement:

The rules have just been amended; the number one is ineligible.

The ineligible was pulled aside by its tail. The others were happy, a potential winner was out. Even some spectators were as happy as the achievers.

Go:

The race now resumed. It went on and on . . .

Arvin closed his eyes, the magazine slipping from his grasp.

"Congrats, sir."

"Thanks."

The pretty girl was looking forward to some sound bites, with a smile hanging on her lips, a scribbling pad lying on her lap, and a ballpoint pen held between her pointed, polished nails. "Now that you are heading the organization, what will be your perspective plan?"

"Please wait. My dream will unfold in the months to come."

"Sir, sir, please give me some indications now."

"Okay. Broadly, my strategic plan will include upgrade technology, revitalize human resources, and reinforce the core strength of project appraisal and funding—"

"Sorry for the interruption, sir. Don't you think project appraisal is losing its relevance?"

"No. Project appraisal and funding will continue to be relevant for many years to come. It is too premature to trivialize it. A lot more remains to be done for infrastructure in the country—power, roads, bridges, airports, housing. I do not subscribe to the idea of abandoning what you have just to create something new. Consolidation should be preferred to proliferation."

I shall try forging a lifetime public-private partnership with another monolithic organization for serving the cause of the development of the nation. Why only a public-private partnership? Partnerships between GSOs may also be tried for public good and public profit.

"We shall go retail with newer products, nurture all subsidiaries, giving them proper leadership and controlled freedom for faster, healthier growth and harmonious relationships."

I shall merge synergetic ones with the parent, despite possible motivated resistance, and unlock the values of others at appropriate stages.

"We may aim at inorganic growth too."

I have already identified a large-sized bank, based on a comparative study. I will start my courting with its owner and manager and marry, with parental and regulatory blessings.

"In short, if given adequate freedom of action, I shall do whatever is necessary to render the future of the organization more glorious than its past; prove that size surely matters; show that an elephant also can dance elegantly and make the nation proud of it."

Arvin briefed the press reporter, revealing only a part of his dream and reserving, in his mind, certain strategic details.

"Great. Best wishes. Thank you, sir."

Some noise jerked Arvin out of his nap dream.

Where is the pretty press reporter?

The aircraft was spinning in the air. From the window, the ground was invisible. The seat belt signs were on. The engine roar and the bumpy ride had stirred the passengers out of their naps.

"Due to dense fog and zero visibility, we are unable to land. Please fasten your seat belts, relax, and wait for an update of our position."

It seemed the pilot was struggling to land in spite of guidance from the instrumental landing system. The turbulence was becoming more and more severe minute by minute. The aircraft was wobbling, petrifying the passengers. Some regretted having chosen this flight and some not having written their wills.

"This is your captain again. Weather conditions are getting worse. We are returning to Mumbai. Sorry for the inconvenience."

This soothed the nerves of the scared passengers. Many, however, started complaining about their missed meetings.

"The captain has switched on the seat belt signs. Please return to your seats, fold back your tables, and fasten your seat belts. We will be landing in a few minutes."

The landing was smooth.

"Welcome to Mumbai Chatrapathi Shivaji International Airport. The outside temperature is 22 degrees Centigrade . . ."

Unbuckling his seat belt, Arvin, with disappointment writ on his face, got up, took his coat returned by the air hostess, and readied himself to step down.

II

• Swan Song

The guest of the evening, Arvin recovered from his long reverie. He found himself on a dais. Seated by his side was the woman behind his success, watching the proceedings.

One after another, his colleagues spoke eloquently about his caliber, characteristics, and contributions. "A man of few words," "a patient listener," "a committed executive," "a thinker of ideas," "a gifted writer," "an advocate of change," "a balanced person," "an ideal boss," "an independent professional"—these were the epithets generously sprinkled on him by the speakers.

A mix of emotions—joy and pride—flashed on her face. This was the first time she had heard, in an open forum, accolades being showered on her husband. As for him, he knew, but for her efficient home management and congenial companionship, he could not have succeeded in his career.

Amused, he wondered, *Why should people wait until the parting time to express their appreciation of the qualities of the head and heart of a colleague? Is it pure and simple hypocritical courtesy to say pleasant things only on the eve of departure?*

His thought process continued, *Is superannuation the end of working life? Does the age of superannuation mean the stage of superfluity? Is there no life postretirement? If the life still has miles to run, will it be on a different track?*

To be fair, one must exit at some stage to yield a place to another younger and move onto some other space. But, to which space? A quiet corner to hibernate until final shutdown? Or, to a standby reclining chair, pending a move to another very different environ to do whatever still he can?

Immediately, tomorrow will be the first day after retirement. Will it be a day of grief or a day of relief?

It will, no doubt, be a day of unbundled leisure: no pestering visitors, no bulky files, no prickly calls, no stormy meetings, no heated discussions, no external pressures, and no mental tensions. It's a moment yearned for. But, with the hangover of the decades of a workaholic life, can I suddenly breathe comfortably the fresh air of leisure?

While his mental browsing for answers went on, farewell speeches were winding up. The last speaker was at the podium. Quickly closing his mental search, he organized his thoughts for an appropriate response. Now, invited to say "a few words," Arvin spoke, "My dear colleagues, let me, at the outset, thank you for your bouquets of flowers and garlands of compliments. I am really touched. I wish I deserved them all.

"I feel proud of my momentous association for over three decades with this magnificent organization. Nowhere could I have derived so much job satisfaction. Nothing will be more material than the inner satisfaction I gained.

"I have remained wedded to the organization, through thick and thin, despite alluring attractions from outside. Along with the institution, I, too, have grown. My upward mobility has been one of a steady climb. The climb, however, has ended just short of the peak due to a twist in the rope. I take it as an accident of life, not because of fatalistic quietism. It is, in fact, my experiential realism.

"The process of change in the organizational thrust and direction is already on, as dictated by the changing paradigm. However, it will be necessary, in the words of Tom Peters, to 'move beyond change and embrace nothing less than the literal abandonment of the conventions that brought us to this point.' I am sure, the organization will, on revitalization, resume its growth and continue its contribution to the nation building.

"Friends,

The time has struck for me to part;
I take your leave with heavy heart.
A sigh of relief, you may heave!
But forget me not, so I believe.

"During my long, official journey, I had the company of many, many cotravelers, preponderantly memorable. Throughout the journey, I had the benefit of excellent learning, enormous exposure, and extensive experience. I have enjoyed, all these years, your support, cooperation, love, and affection. I thank you all.

"As an olive leaf falls when it is ripe,
Blessing the branch that bare it and
Giving thanks to the tree that gave it life,

"I leave the institution with grateful thanks. May God bless this institution! May God bless you all!

"Thank you. Good-bye."

Amid prolonged applause, Arvin resumed his seat, wiping his specs.

A memento was given.

The clapping died down.

Arvin stepped down.

Everyone present shook hands with Arvin.

"We will keep in touch."

"Sure."

Some eyes glisten.

The swan song was over.

The curtain fell.

III

Afterword

One humid evening, the door bell chimed.

"What a surprise! Please come in."

"Hey, how're you?"

"Fine. Thank you. Be seated. Tea or coffee?"

"Coffee. I came to know that you're settled here. Happened to pass by this side. Thought I would drop in."

"So kind of you. Welcome."

"Hey, you're in fine fettle. Knock on wood. You don't look like retired. I see some betraying hair. But, no baldness, no wrinkles . . ."

"Really? Anyway, I don't let wrinkles encroach my heart."

"Ha ha, well said! You appear very relaxed."

The visitor was an old friend, senior in age, sincere in friendship, rich in experience, jovial in manners, kind at heart and, truly a well-wisher. A rapid talker and an animated conversationalist, he could turn even a taciturn person talkative. Free from the fetters of self-imposed reticence and reservations, the host too warmed up and regaled his experiences.

The visitor interrupted, "I know you missed what you deserved. Such incredible things do happen. But, tell me why the guys were so much against you."

"It was not that all these chaps were against me as a person or a colleague. Envy, greed, or malice had set them against me. And, in the matter of a choice between two persons for any purpose, there are so many overriding considerations that dictate the choice. If someone is a favored choice for any position, whoever happens to be his competitor is sought to be undermined by all means, fair or foul. In this part of the world, merit doesn't merit primary consideration. You know it all very well."

"I know, I know. Don't worry. May be it's a blessing in disguise. You'll never lose what you're destined to get. Something better, something bigger may be waiting for you. Who knows? My best wishes."

"Let's hope so. Thank you."

The friendly visitor enjoyed the chat, sipping strong, aromatic coffee.

"It is almost ages since we had a long chat like this. I enjoyed it. You must share your experiences and thoughts with others as well. Let me take leave."

"Wait a minute."

Arvin hurried into his study room and returned in a minute, unbundling a parcel. "Here is my book for you"

"Wow, you've done it. What a surprise! Thank you."

Flipping through a few pages, he said, "I will finish reading the book in a week's time but will never lose it."

"Thanks."

About the Author

T. M. Nagarajan, born in India in 1942, a first-class master in commerce and a university rank holder, is a former DMD of the Industrial Development Bank of India and full-time member of Securities and Exchange Board of India. He has been an advisor to an African bank under a World Bank-sponsored international consultancy program, director or chairman of a number of Indian companies in diverse fields, and a faculty member in various training programs. Widely traveled, the author is an avid reader, a good speaker, and an adept writer. He lives in Chennai (India) and is accessible at:

011 91 44 24402411

tmnrajan2011@gmail.com

CPSIA information can be obtained at www.ICGtesting.com
Printed in the USA
BVOW080836110413

317926BV00001B/9/P

9 781618 974778